R E M A K E

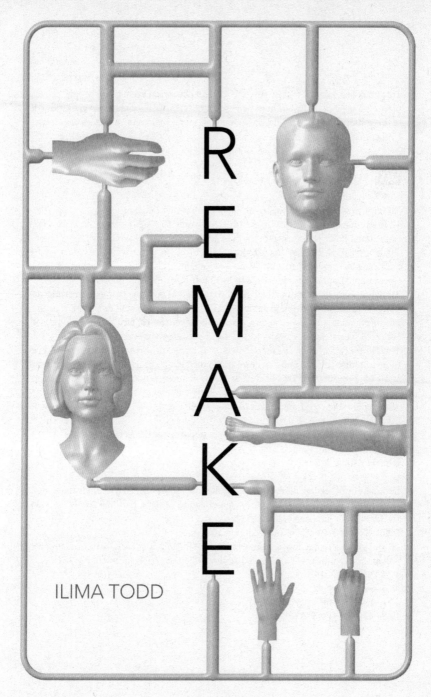

REMAKE

ILIMA TODD

Simon Pulse

New York   London   Toronto   Sydney   New Delhi

SIMON PULSE
An imprint of Simon & Schuster Children's Publishing Division
1230 Avenue of the Americas, New York, New York 10020
First Simon Pulse paperback edition July 2016
Text copyright © 2014 by Ilima Todd
Published by arrangement with Shadow Mountain.
Cover photographs copyright © 2016 by Oliver Burston/Getty Images
All rights reserved, including the right of reproduction in whole or in part in any form.
SIMON PULSE and colophon are registered trademarks of Simon & Schuster, Inc.
For information about special discounts for bulk purchases, please contact Simon & Schuster Special Sales at 1-866-506-1949 or business@simonandschuster.com.
The Simon & Schuster Speakers Bureau can bring authors to your live event. For more information or to book an event contact the Simon & Schuster Speakers Bureau at 1-866-248-3049 or visit our website at www.simonspeakers.com.
The text of this book was set in Berkeley Oldstyle Book.
Manufactured in the United States of America
10 9 8 7 6 5 4 3 2 1
The Library of Congress has cataloged the hardcover edition as follows:
Todd, Ilima, author.
Remake / Ilima Todd.
pages cm
Summary: In Freedom Prime, young adults can choose their name, their trade, and their gender, but the one thing they cannot choose is to be part of a family, because the family unit has been eradicated.
ISBN 978-1-60907-924-6 (hardbound : alk. paper)
[1. Individuality—Fiction 2. Self-acceptance—Fiction 3. Identity—Fiction. 4. Free will and determinism—Fiction. 5. Families—Fiction. 6. Science fiction.] I. Title.
PZ7.T5665Re 2014
[Fic]—dc23
2014019074
ISBN 978-1-4814-5762-0 (pbk)

For Daniel

Adoring husband, loving father, epitome of perfection.
Basically the greatest man on the planet . . . happy now?

REMAKE

To: All Seekers and Security Force <staff@freedomone.gov>
From: Prime Maker, Freedom One <corehq@freedomone.gov>
Subject: The Rising Threat

This message has been marked High Importance

The attached document was found on the grounds of Freedom One. As you know, the information presented in this piece of propaganda is nothing but traitorous lies.

I call upon you, as loyal citizens of Freedom One, to be on the lookout for any hint of the Rise in your area. If such treasonous activity is uncovered, I authorize you to take swift and necessary action to put down this rebellion. Destroy all of these flyers immediately.

Eridian
Prime Maker

<u>View attachment</u>

You are a prisoner.

They shackle your wrists with chains of fear.

They cut you to your knees with blades of oppression.

The noose they bind around your throat silences your voice. And you hang lifeless. Useless.

Yet you boast religion, peace, and freedom. Freedom?

You are not free.

You are no more free than their own citizens. Those people think they are equal—choosing their names, their bodies, their consequence-free lives.

But they are bound just as you are.

We must make them realize their lives are not real ones. We must introduce them to a new world where words like family and love and real freedom abound.

Only it's not a new world—it's an old one. One that's been forgotten by some, yet remembered by many.

Because you cannot kill truth.

They have forgotten. But you know the truth. You remember.

Make them remember too.

There is a time to run. A time to hide. A time to keep silent in an effort to protect all that is precious. That time has passed.

Now is the time to fight back.

We are no longer safe. We are no longer content to stand aside and feign ignorance.

We are the Rise, and we will be silent no longer.

Join us.

PART ONE

Chapter One

*M*ale or female?

My finger hesitates over the touch screen. How can I decide which to be for the rest of my life? It's so . . . permanent.

Theron puts his hand on the small of my back in encouragement. I glance at his blue eyes beneath long lashes. They're longer than the hair on his head. I smile, knowing what little hair is left will be shaved off in a few minutes.

He returns my smile and rubs my own shaved head. Our lack of hair keeps those in our Batch equal—both the boys like Theron and the girls like me. Except the stubble that grows from my head is red, while everyone else's is dark brown. The Maker that designed me must've had an odd sense of humor.

Theron tilts his head toward the computer, reminding me why I'm here. I push my shoulders back and focus on the screen again.

Male or female?

My finger connects with the third option.

Undecided.

"You know, Nine," Theron says. "In three days, you won't have that option anymore."

"I know," I say. "I'll be ready."

In three days we will turn seventeen and travel to the Remake facility. Through advanced cosmetic modification, we'll be Made into whomever we choose. Blond or brunette. Tall or short. Full lips, broad shoulders, slender thighs, dark skin, tiny waist—whatever we wish. Though we can make our choices at any time, our last chance to choose will be just before the shuttle flight to our Remake. I sigh, wishing I could decide on the one thing that has haunted me the most: male or female? Why is this particular question so hard?

My finger slides across the transparent screen, logging me off the system. When the display goes blank, Theron leads me through the automatic doors and out of the computer room. We walk down a brightly lit corridor that makes me feel like I'm on display. I instinctively clutch my elbows and try to cover as many freckles as I can, even though it's just Theron with me, and he doesn't care. I wish my hands were bigger—supernova big. Then maybe they could hide the evidence of another Maker mistake, one that singles me out like a target. No one else in our Batch of ten males and ten females has anything but flawless, light skin.

We come to the back of the line at the next station. My bare feet are cold against the perforated metal floor. I never wear shoes when we stay inside all day, but I wish I'd at least worn socks.

"Nine?" Theron's comment reminds me I will need to choose a name as well. I'm the only one of my Batch that still goes by my given Maker number.

"Yes?" I ask.

"Check out the Healer," he says, pointing ahead. Several kids from our Batch stand in front of us. Wearing matching white tank tops and gray sweats, they're all the same height as Theron and I, so I have to step out of line to get a better look.

The Healer is small and blond. Female. Her eyes are a sunset: swirling shades of gold, red, and orange. I look at Theron to see him grinning, and I wonder if he thinks she's beautiful. Turning back, I see what he wants me to. She opens her mouth to speak, though I cannot hear her words. Her teeth are the color of deep ocean.

I scrunch my face at Theron, and he snickers, satisfied with my reaction. But inside, my heart races so fast my chest aches. Making a bad choice on the day we are Remade has permanent consequences. We cannot change back—ever.

In three days I must also decide what Trade I will study. After a month of recovery at the Remake facility, we'll all begin our nine-month placement training in our Trade. I glance back at the Healer. That's what Theron has chosen to be. I shudder to think he'll be around needles all the time.

The line moves quickly, and it's Theron's turn. I don't think he fears anything, needles least of all. As if to prove my point, he strides to the Healer with his chin up. After a quick backward grimace at me, he tilts his head, exposing his neck to the woman. She taps a long needle to release any air, then presses the hormone suppressant into his neck.

I squeeze my eyes shut. After a lifetime of blockers, I still can't stomach seeing the long needle pushed deep into flesh, even when it's not mine.

And then Theron's done. I remind myself it will be over quickly and walk to the Healer. She smiles a blue smile, and I press my lips together to hide my nervous grin. I tilt my head and tense as the needle breaks through my skin. The cold liquid spreads through my neck and down to my shoulders and limbs. A familiar tingling enfolds me for a moment, and then it's gone.

This is the last dose of hormone suppression I'll receive. If I choose to remain female, my natural hormones will surface within a month, and my body will respond accordingly. My breasts will develop; my hips will widen. If I choose to be male, testosterone pill treatment will begin and a permanent female-hormone block will be installed in my shoulder. I'll likely gain height and muscle mass, and my voice will deepen. I don't fully understand the emotional changes that will take place either way, though. I hate how much that scares me.

I rub my neck as I follow Theron to the shearing station. Does he ever worry what his gender choice will mean? I lean against a wall and watch him get his hair shaved off by a wide man with several tattoos and body piercings. The man laughs at something Theron says. I crave Theron's confidence. He's already chosen to be male. He plans to keep his blue eyes and dark hair, though he wants to grow it out for a while.

REMAKE

"No more monthly shearings for me," he said last month at this very spot.

I try to picture him with longer hair, but I can't erase the image I've always had of my best friend: bald, blue-eyed, and smiling since we were small children.

"You're up, Nine." Theron waves me over and sits in the chair beside me. He looks at my reflection in the broad mirror in front of us, then asks the tattooed man, "So why would one choose to be a Shearer? For the glamour?"

The man chuckles and brings a razor to my scalp. "I'm not a Shearer," he says. "I'm a Hair Artist." The studs in his bottom lip shift as he speaks. I nibble on my lower lip and wonder what piercings would feel like. But that would mean more needles. *No thanks.*

"Hair Artist?" Theron asks.

"As lovely as you kids are," the man says with a smirk, "this is just a small part of what I do. Mostly, I style hair in a small shop on Freedom's Main Street. I can cut hair to any specification, or form it into a special shape for a wild evening in the nightspots." He shrugs his shoulders as though it isn't a big deal, but I can tell by the glint in his eye he loves his Trade.

"In that case," says Theron, rising to stand behind me, "let's take a little off the top and curl the sides a bit." He motions across my bristly head and winks at me in the mirror. "We're getting Remade in a few days and want to look our best."

Theron knows how to get me to relax. I reward him with a wide, freckled smile as the Hair Artist shaves my head. Small bits of red hair fall to the floor among the otherwise dark brown pieces. I look at my reflection and try to convince myself I'm not as hopeless as I think. Although I haven't decided on a gender, name, or Trade, at least I know I'll be getting rid of these freckles and my blazing hair.

"All done," says the Hair Artist.

His lips remind me of another choice: I won't be pierced. No freckles, no red hair, and no piercings. I sigh—what a sorry model of resolve. It's a tiny list of things I don't want. What about the things I do want? I would exchange all three decisions for the courage to make the hardest one.

I often wish we were all the same gender. Or better yet—neither. Why bother with gender at all? The Makers' job would be easier without having to decide who is Made into what, and our Remake would be simpler without gender changes since there would be no gender *to* change. Most of all, I wouldn't lie awake at night worrying what my life would be like as male or female.

I walk with Theron to the eatery for dinner. We quickly grab individual square metal dishes containing tonight's meal—some kind of colorless mashed starchy vegetable, pale meat patties that smell like our protein supplements, and hard rolls. As always, I force myself to eat as much of the bland food as I can and let Theron pick at my leftovers. I hope the food we eat outside the Batch tower after our Remake will provide more variety for my taste buds. I stir what's left of the mashed veggie and realize I'll only have to endure this food for a few more days.

"Sometimes I want to hurry and get this over with," I say. "Close my eyes and let the time melt away before our Remake."

"Are you anxious to change, Nine?" Theron stuffs a piece of

bread into his mouth. "I'll sneak you into the Remake facility tonight." His face lights up, and I think he actually would if I asked him to, if the facility wasn't an ocean away.

He knows it's not what I mean, but I play along and nod. I *am* ready to be who I'm going to be. I'm just not sure who that is yet.

I glance around the room. It's filled with the familiar faces of my Batch. The same faces I've seen my entire life. Our Batch does everything together. Thanks to the hormone suppressants, we are all the same height and build, with the same immature bodies. In almost every sense, we really are equal.

The thought makes me glance at my freckled arms. I rub at the skin there, trying to wipe off small bits of hair left over from my head shaving. I should have showered before dinner.

"Doesn't matter how hard you try, *Spots*." Cree's familiar voice pricks me like a needle. "You can't rub them off."

Sora and Bristol snicker beside her, the three of them pausing in front of our table. Bristol narrows his eyes at me while Sora sticks her tongue out like a child. I choose to ignore the loathsome crew; their taunting is a normal part of my routine. Theron, unfortunately, does not.

"Take it back," he says, shoving his chair back and standing to face them, his eyes focused on Cree's.

I stand and move behind Theron, touching his elbow in an effort to calm him. He'll stop at nothing to protect me. These three know that better than anyone, which is why they usually stay away when Theron is near.

Cree hesitates and steals a quick glance at me. I can see the resolve in her eyes. She can't resist a final chance to goad me before our Remake. With a look of disgust, she turns back to Theron and steps closer until they are almost touching. "No."

"I said, take it back." Theron speaks through clenched teeth, and his hands ball up at his sides. His shoulders shake from the tension. He's going to snap. Maybe this time is just one too many.

I open my mouth to say something, then bite my lip, not sure which of the two I should warn.

"That's right, *Freak*." Cree reaches to me and shoves my shoulder. "No one wants to hear what you—"

Before I can blink, Theron dives into Cree. The two of them fall to the ground and tumble across the floor to the side wall. Cree shrieks and the noise attracts a crowd; Batchers gather around the fight. Theron is on top of Cree, punching her face like it's a practice bag from our training room. She tries to shove him off, but Theron swipes her hands away and she can't find a grip.

"Theron!" I yell. "She's had enough."

Theron doesn't think it's enough until three punches later. He stands and spits on Cree. Her nose is bleeding, probably broken. Blood spills onto the floor. Bristol swears and glares at me, as though I was the one who beat up Cree. He and Sora pull her to her feet and lug her out the room.

"You should thank me," Theron calls after them. "I've given the Remakers a head start with improving your dog face."

Theron turns to me and frowns—his way of apologizing.

I say nothing—my way of telling him it's all right.

Blood drips from Theron's hand, and he removes his tank top to wrap around his knuckles. I follow him to a utility sink in the kitchen area so he can rinse his hand clean. I take a long look at him. Both of our shoulders are slender, our chests are flat, and our hips are narrow. The only real difference in our anatomy is hidden beneath gray sweats.

We are taught the organs that distinguish us male or female are nothing more than superficial features. They are trivial, insignificant parts of us. But sometimes I wonder if there's something more. Something greater. Because I can't find anything else about Theron that would support his fearless nature. Nothing that's different from the rest of us, anyway.

I wonder, not for the first time, if the gender I choose will affect more than the way I look. If it will affect who I am inside. Though my body will be Remade, what will happen to the rest of me? My weakness and cowardice? Will they still exist?

We abandon our food trays and head for the showers. I press the start button on the panel in front of me, the cycle beginning with hot water on my bare skin. It comes from above and the side. When the water changes from clear to soapy, I squeeze my eyes shut, imagining my fear and uncertainty slipping away into the drain below, wishing there was a *courage* option on that computer screen.

When we go to our sleeping quarters, Cree is not there. She must still be at the Healer station. Bristol and Sora are missing too. The rest of the Batch is there, though, climbing into bed. We are a sea of white tank tops and gray sweats.

I slide under my sheets while Theron settles to the ground next to my bed, his chin on my mattress. His bed is a few feet away from mine, as it's been since I can remember. Just knowing he's close makes me feel safe.

13

"Are you okay?" he asks.

I nod. "I'm glad you hit her." And I am. Cree deserved it. I just wish I had been the one to do it. "Theron?"

"Hmm?"

"What do *you* think I should choose?" I try to look at the wall behind him, not sure I want to see his reaction. But it's hard to focus on anything other than his blue eyes right in front of me.

"You know it doesn't matter. Whether you're fat, green, or floppy-eared, you'll always be Nine to me." Theron smiles. "Okay, maybe you shouldn't go with floppy-eared. But other than that, you're good."

I know it's not fair to ask him. It's my burden, not his. But . . . "Theron?"

His hand squeezes my shoulder. "Nine, you're my best friend. You will *always* be my best friend, whether you're a male or a female. I'm not going to disappear either way. You don't need to worry."

His touch is a comfort. I wonder if this closeness will feel different when I'm Remade. If *he* will feel different.

"I'm not worried," I say. Not about Theron leaving me. Theron at my side is the one thing I'm certain of. I just thought maybe he saw something in me that I couldn't.

"You're the only thing I've got too, you know." His fingers poke at my arm. "You and your skin spots . . . all mine."

"Oh, please don't mention the freckles. I've had enough freckle talk today."

"Don't mock the spots. I love the spots. They are flecks of

paint on the canvas of your skin. A living masterpiece. My very own magnum opus."

I pinch my lips together to keep from laughing.

"I'm serious," he says, biting back a smile. "Imagine the sky void of stars. Without them, there would be no reason to look up."

"Nice," I say. "Aren't there, like, three visible stars in the sky?"

"Not outside of the province. If you get far enough from the lights, you can see hundreds of them. Thousands, even."

"Thousands?" I raise an eyebrow. Neither of us has ever left Freedom, so I know it's impossible for him to know this. But I smile and let him continue.

"Yes," he says. "Every one of them unique and special."

I roll my eyes. "Just like me?"

"No. Just like your spots."

"Shut up."

"No, you shut up." Theron leans forward and kisses my forehead. "Seriously, shut up and go to sleep."

I watch him climb into his bed. He drifts to sleep and falls into his familiar pattern of snore-breathe-whistle that I'd recognize anywhere. And just like that my somber mood is chased away. It's magic what Theron can do sometimes. He is strength and comfort and surety and humor and love.

Why couldn't I have been Made like that?

It's dark, but I've lived in this building my entire life so I feel my way easily through the halls. Theron and I have had plenty of night adventures sneaking into the kitchen for the chocolate stashed behind the dish machines. I've never roamed at night by myself before though, so this is a little unnerving.

I find the room and am grateful the automatic doors don't shut off at night. When I walk in I nearly knock over the metal stand holding the flat computer screen. It wobbles for a second then settles back into place. I glide my finger over the display and it comes to life, recognizing my print immediately. The screen temporarily blinds me, and I blink several times as my eyes adjust to the sudden brightness. There, exactly as they were earlier in the day, are the words that continue to haunt me.

Male or female?

I sigh and quickly scan through the questions until I find the one with an answer I do know.

Trade?

My list of Trade choices is longer than some Batchers because of my high academic scores. Healer, Farmer, Teacher, Seeker, Techie . . . the list goes on and on. But there's only one thing I want to do for the rest of my life. Without hesitating, I select what I want to become.

Maker.

If there's any Trade that will give me a clue as to why I am the way I am—and the power to not let it happen again—this is it.

Chapter Two

For the first time in a long while, I wake with a smile. Theron is asleep, his face inches from mine. The little scab must've snuck into my bed early this morning. My foot catches on twisted sheets as I try to roll away from him.

Theron moans in his sleep, draping his arm over my shoulder, trapping me.

"Theron, I have to pee."

"No, I don't." His voice is groggy, but his lips give him away. He can't hide his playful grin.

"Let me go, you idiot."

"C'mon, Nine. You're not an idiot." He's clearly awake now, though he keeps his eyes squeezed shut. "Five more minutes."

"I'm serious," I say. "I'll pee all over you."

"Go ahead. It's all good."

"I'm warning you."

"Warning me?" Theron's eyes open. "What will you do?" His arms are vise-like, and I can't move.

I narrow my eyes at him. "Fine," I say. "Five minutes."

His grip loosens slightly, and I slide my hand up his spine, stopping between his shoulder blades. I find just the right spot and apply pressure with my fingers.

"Aaah! That tickles." Theron flails backward and off the bed.

I'm still tangled in the sheets and fall with him. "I tried to warn you," I say, scrambling off.

His laughter fills the room. I can't help but beam as I run to the toilets, but my face falls when I get there. Cree and Bristol are at the washbasins. Cree removes a bandage from her swollen nose and tosses it in the refuse. They both glare at me through the mirrors. I lower my head and hurry into a toilet stall. I really, really do have to pee.

When I come out, they're still there. I clean my hands and face, then turn to them head on, digging deep for any bravado I can muster. "Lookin' good, Cree," I say, hoping my words mask the slight tremor in my voice. "You get a new haircut or something?"

Cree sneers and steps forward.

I stand firm. I can't back down now.

Theron walks in and spreads his arms. "Hey, it's like a Batch reunion in here. My best friend, my worst enemy, and the dog we'll eat for breakfast."

After a glare in my direction, Bristol and Cree walk out, not waiting for another confrontation with Theron.

I give a half smile before smoothing my expression. "Theron?"

"Hmm?" he asks from behind a stall door.

"I made another choice on the computer last night."

"What'd you choose?"

"My Trade." I bite my lip, suddenly nervous about telling him, though I'm not sure why. It's not like things will be different between us because of it. It won't affect how we are together. But I value his opinion over every other, even my own, and I want to make sure he's okay with it.

He exits and washes at the basin, then turns to me, his face serious and warm. "Well?"

I'm bold and say it plainly. "Maker."

He raises an eyebrow, waiting for me to explain.

"I want to make sure this doesn't happen again." I look down at my freckled arms and tug on my tank top. "They can't possibly know what something like this . . . can do to a person." My lips tremble, and I turn away, crossing and uncrossing my arms.

He reaches for my hand and holds it, studying it for a minute. Sliding his fingers into mine, he turns my hand back and forth as though memorizing every part of it. His silence makes me nervous.

Say something.

Theron brings my hand to his lips and keeps it there. He finally looks up. "You're not a mistake." He touches my face, the tips of his fingers lingering on my spots. "Sometimes I think you're the most deliberate thing I've ever seen. The rest of us are just shadows of what could be."

He pulls me close, and I nod against him. He's told me the

same thing a thousand different ways. It doesn't change what others think or say, though.

Theron sighs against my ear. "A Maker, huh? I don't think I've ever met a Maker before." He pulls back to look at my face but still holds me close. "I think it's a great idea, Nine." He smiles and taps his fingers on my shoulder. "While you're at it, maybe you can figure out a way to program Cree's mouth shut."

I smile. A Trade chosen. It's something.

The Teacher grunts as Theron and I walk in, and I know we're late. She doesn't look familiar. It's not that unusual since Teachers rotate daily, but I don't know if she'll give us a hard time about it. I silently slide into my usual workstation opposite Theron and swipe my finger across the computer screen that doubles as a desk surface. Words appear in the far left corner. *Batch #1372. Member #9. Provincial History.*

I sneak a glance at the Teacher, but she just yawns and looks at her transmitter device as though checking the time. Our tardiness is forgotten. Searching the rest of the room, I notice smiles are wider and talk is louder than is usual for my Batch. There's a buzz of excitement in the air, and I can't help but grin too. The next hour will be the last academic module we'll ever have to attend. It makes me that more anxious to finally be Remade, even though I still don't know what gender I want to be.

I slide in my earpiece and catch a familiar high-pitched female voice mid-sentence. " . . . Made and equal stay / Beyond our given Remake day."

REMAKE

Theron makes faces at me as he mouths the rest of the familiar refrain since we can all hear it at the same time. "Free to choose and free to live / Our lives to Freedom we will give." He pretends to flip his nonexistent long hair behind his shoulder and waves his hand in a way that I know is meant to be feminine, matching the voice we just heard.

A couple of Batchers laugh in reaction, but my smile falls slightly. What is it that makes something feminine? Or masculine? If gender is just an accessory, why do people—including Theron—act as if there's more to it? I glance at the Teacher and wonder what she thinks, but I won't ask. Because her answer will be the same as every other Remade adult I've questioned in the past: There is no difference. Which is just another way of saying they don't know either.

Theron curses and slams his palm against his computer screen repeatedly. This time I join in with the others laughing at him. His computer stalled. *Again.* The Teacher rolls her eyes and flicks her finger toward me. Theron grins and jumps on the desk-screens, sliding to my side without bothering to walk around. He bumps me over so we're sharing my chair and plugs his own earpiece into my computer.

I elbow him in the side. "I think you break your computer on purpose."

He gives me an innocent look. "Why would I ever do that?"

"Um . . . because you like cheating off my answers, you scab."

"We don't even have questions to answer today," he says, his hands up in defense. "It's just a listen-and-recite history module. And a boring one too."

21

"Force of habit, then." I elbow him again but smile so he knows I don't mind.

"Don't distract me with your pretty face." He narrows his eyes at me, all serious, and taps the screen. "We've got important things to learn . . . like how to achieve world peace and unity."

I nod and try to focus on our lesson, but I'm anxious to get out of here like everyone else. This module's just the same old information about how overpopulation nearly destroyed the Earth and how Batches are the only way to control the population now. Theron pretends to fall asleep, and I'm almost tempted to do it for real.

Halfway through the lesson, a man in a dark gray suit appears in the doorway. By his clothes and the way his head tilts up, I know he must be a cabinet member—one of the leaders that work directly under the Prime Maker, head of our province. This man walks into the room followed by a small girl. Or woman, I guess, since she has a full head of straight black hair. Her eyes are wide and nervous and her frame so slight, I'd have guessed she was younger than me if she wasn't obviously Remade.

After speaking with the Teacher, the man glances around the room before his eyes settle on me and pause. His nostrils widen slightly, almost threatening. I look away and try to focus on the history module, but the man and small woman stop in front of Theron's broken computer, making it hard to ignore them. He speaks to her in short, clipped phrases as he points to the desk and gives her instructions on fixing the computer. I catch bits of her quiet response, something about how the terminals will keep breaking and how they never give her the right tools for the job. He grabs her arm and whispers something in her ear. She nods obediently without saying anything more. They finally leave, but not before the man gives me another scathing look.

I'm not sure how one becomes a member of the Prime Maker's cabinet. I don't remember seeing it as a Trade option on the computer last night when I selected Maker, but I could be wrong. Of the eight cabinet members of our province, six are male. Are males more prone to leadership positions than females? Our Prime Maker is female, so I don't think that's necessarily true. And I've never noticed an imbalance of males versus females in any other Trade. Maybe there isn't a deeper meaning to gender beyond the physical.

When the lesson is over, I nudge Theron's shoulder to silence his pretend snores and yank my earpiece out. The Teacher excuses us, and our Batch erupts into cheers, thrilled to be one step closer to our Remake. As we leave the room, I see the small woman standing outside alone. She holds a container of tools in one hand and seems to be waiting for all of us to leave so she can enter. Her Trade obviously involves fixing computers, though I don't know why she had to be escorted by a cabinet member or why he gave me such strange looks.

I shake it off, deciding he must have been surprised to see a freckled girl among the Batch, that's all. It just surprised him. I'm used to being singled out as *other;* I don't know why I let it bother me this time.

As we walk past the woman, her eyes brighten and the corners of her lips twitch as though she wants to smile at the sight of me. Not a cruel or nasty smile, but the kind that brightens your whole face. Like seeing me changed her day from miserable to hopeful. But I must be imagining it. How could the way I look make anyone happy?

I wrap my arm around Theron's waist. "I have a surprise for you," I say.

"For me?" He feigns shock as we walk back to our sleeping quarters.

I slip my hand under my mattress and pull out two blue laminated cards. A picture of each of our faces is on one side. A red five-pointed star inside a white circle—the symbol of our Freedom province—is on the other.

"Passes to Freedom Central?" Theron grabs the cards from my hand and holds them up to the light, as though verifying they're real. "How did you get these?"

"I have my ways," I say, snatching them back. My ways may or may not involve flirting with the eatery manager and working extra dish cleaning hours for a month. "I'm not completely helpless, you know."

"I knew there was a reason I loved you." He pinches my chin and smiles at me.

"And here I thought I was just a warm body to snuggle with on sleepless mornings." I wave the passes in front of him with a grin. "They're only good for today, though."

"Then what are we still doing here?" Theron grabs my hand, and we fly out of the room.

Chapter Three

Main and Center Streets are usually off-limits to Batch members, and except for a few unfounded rumors of rogue Batch kids getting beyond the gates a time or two, I don't know anyone who's been there. I wish we had something else to wear besides our tanks and sweats, but the eatery manager assured me no one would care, as long as we had our passes.

As we reach the gates, I can't contain my excitement and squeeze Theron's hand while humming under my breath. The nightspots in central Freedom are supposed to be nuclear, and the people wilder than ever.

The line is long but it moves quickly. Still, the man in front of me complains to the guard, wondering why there's only one on duty today instead of three. The guard just shrugs her shoulders like it's no big deal, and then it's my turn.

"Party time," Theron whispers to me as I hand the guard my pass.

I scan my fingertip across a portable identifier screen and wait while the female guard looks back and forth between me and the picture on the pass. She finally returns it with a smirk and says, "Have fun."

"Thanks." I slip past the metal gate and wait for Theron on the other side.

"Can you feel it?" he asks when he's beside me again.

"Feel what?"

"Freedom."

I'm not sure if he means the name of our province or our lack of restrictions for the day. "And what is freedom supposed to feel like?"

He presses a fist against my chest. *Thump, thump, thump*— he applies pressure to match my heartbeat. "It's like your heart is about to explode right out of your chest. And if you can jump high enough, you'll just keep going higher and higher. The Earth can't hold you down 'cause you're on such a high."

"I love that about you, Theron, that underneath all this"—I mock punch him on the arm—"you're just a hopeless, sentimental poet."

"I'm just perceptive," he says. "I can't help my cleverness."

"What's first on the agenda, oh wise and wonderful sage?" It's strange having the rest of the day to ourselves with no Trade visits or academic modules to attend anymore. Just a two-day countdown until our Remake. I slide my fingers into Theron's and turn toward Freedom Central.

The street is filled with adults of all ages. Some look no

older than me. Others don't—like the man standing in front of an antique bookshop window; he stoops with age, and gray hair falls to his shoulders. He wears a silky robe with shimmering red and purple threads. Another man walks past us with sharpened teeth. The woman he holds hands with has bright blue hair sticking straight into the air, converging in a single point. Everyone I see is colorful . . . their skin, their clothes, their hair. It's beautiful, especially compared to the dull gray and white of my everyday life.

"Let's eat," Theron says. "I'm starving."

The smell of fresh bread reaches my nose, and my stomach grumbles. "This way," I say, leading him to an eatery nearby. We each have fifty points on our Freedom passes, more than enough to pay for a day full of mischief. We order fresh bread and honey, a large bowl of some creamy soup, and a giant piece of chocolate cake. Theron lets me finish off his frosting. The florescent green drinks they bring us give my head a slight buzz. After a few sips, I push it to the side. "It's a little too early to start losing my wits," I say.

We decide to walk it off and roam Main Street. A tattoo parlor advertises glow-in-the-dark ink and gambling machines. Music booms in the streets from a dance club. Too early for that, too, I think. Simulation centers are on every corner, boasting any craving one can imagine. We stop in front of a cinema building with a giant billboard of two sparsely dressed women holding firearms.

"What do you think?" I ask, spreading my feet apart, bending my knee down one way and twisting my torso the other, trying to mimic one of the women. I hold my head and chest up but I can't quite get my arm around my waist like the actress on the billboard.

Theron laughs and taps my shoulder.

I pretend to fall over from being so off balance. "It's anatomically impossible to make that pose," I say. "Who are they kidding?"

"Well, look at the other woman," he says. "Are anyone's legs that long?"

"After being Remade? Maybe."

We both tilt our heads to the left to follow the impractical way one of her legs folds over the other.

Theron makes a face. "That can't feel very good."

I laugh and pull him down the street. The variety of people around us is astounding and makes me think everyone is anything but equal. But that's the beauty of it. Theron and I are equal with our other Batchers now, and we all have an equal chance to choose who we want to be when we're Remade. Apparently the choices are endless.

A man steps toward us from the side of the road and looks me up and down. He is tall and thin with long black hair pulled back into a simple braid. His beard is a shaved design of swirls and sharp turns that almost looks like a tattoo. I wonder if a Hair Artist works with facial hair too. I rub my chin, imagining what a beard would feel like.

I look behind him to what is obviously a brothel. Women with too much makeup and not enough clothing loiter out front. The man nods at us. "Batchlings," he says. The scent of jasmine and tobacco drifts to my nose.

His voice feels like sand scraping across my skin. But I

don't think it's him. It's the whole idea of the place. A Prostitute is supposed to be a respectable Trade. Why does the thought make me want to run and hide in my Batch tower?

"Let's go," Theron whispers in my ear. He must sense my apprehension.

We turn and walk right into the Hair Artist who had sheared us the day before. His wide frame, added to his piercings and tattoos, is even more intimidating in the bright sunlight.

He glances behind us at the bearded man. "A little early in the day for getting into *that* kind of trouble, don't you think?" He grins and motions for us to follow him. "I'm Dagan," he says. "And what are you two Batchers doing outside of your tower, hmm?"

"One last hurrah before our Remake," Theron says.

Dagan nods and leads us into a shop with mirrors for walls. "This is my place," he says. "I'd offer to do your hair, but . . ." He laughs and points to the wall behind him. "You can try on the wigs if you want."

Wigs? The wall behind him is filled with plastic heads wearing a rainbow of hairstyles. Theron puts on a set of purple curls, while I try a length of thin brown braids that falls to my waist. We make faces at each other in the mirror and laugh as we try on several more sets. I try to guess whether I look more like a boy or a girl with each one. Every sample is heavy and warm and makes me wonder if real hair feels this way too.

I sit Theron down in one of the rotating chairs and pick up a long, thin tube filled with black ink and a short bristled brush on one end. I hold it up to Dagan with an eyebrow raised.

He works on a woman with pink hair. She is having it

straightened into spikes that stick out in every direction. "It's for temporary tattoos," Dagan says.

"In that case, Mr. Theron," I say. "What will it be today? A shooting star or a fire-breathing dragon?"

"Surprise me," he says, grinning from ear to ear.

I push his head forward and bring the ink to the back of his neck.

"It's warm," he says. "And it tickles."

I roll my eyes. "Everything tickles you." I keep my hand as steady as I can, but it's still not as clean as I would have liked. The word *Nine* sprawls across the base of his neck in curving letters.

I hand him a small mirror, and he examines my work. "That's great," he says with a bemused smile. "How am I supposed to attract the ladies now, with your name claiming me as your property?" He jumps up from his seat and beams. "Your turn."

"But—"

"Ha! Don't think you're getting off that easy. Sit."

I sit and wonder how long this temporary ink will stay. With two days until we're Remade, I guess it doesn't matter.

"Close your eyes," Theron says.

I sigh and obey, hoping he isn't feeling vengeful. The ink is surprisingly hot, despite Theron's warning. I feel the brush curve this way and that across my bare skull, down my neck and even toward my face. It's soothing, and my shoulders relax. I could stay here awhile.

"Okay, open."

I open my eyes and inspect Theron's masterpiece. Thin and

thick black lines swirl across my head and neck, each ending in decisive points. They weave a pattern that complements the curves and bends of my head. It's beautiful—and decidedly feminine.

"I love it," I say, trying to determine what makes it feminine and wondering what it means that I really do like it.

Theron's eyes sparkle. "At least now I don't mind being your property, if you're looking like that."

I stand and pinch him on the arm. "Thanks, Dagan," I say as we walk out.

"Anytime," he says. "And go get yourselves something else to wear before you attract unwanted attention."

"Will do."

I hop on Theron's back and wrap my legs around his waist while we search for a suitable clothing shop. We pass a couple of Seekers in black jumpsuits with large firearms. They stare at us like we're a couple of free-breakers about to disturb the peace. As long as we're not infringing on anyone else's free will, we should be safe. Maybe they're out looking for someone lost in Freedom Central.

I rest my head on Theron's *Nine* tattoo and finger his tracker, a small sphere sitting just in the fold of his right ear. It's fused to his skull through a thin layer of skin. You can't see it unless you know where to look, and even then it's barely noticeable.

"I'm not lost, am I?" he asks, making a joke about his tracker, the device Seekers use to find people.

"Not yet," I mouth into his neck.

"How about you, Nine? Are you lost?"

I touch the metal stub just behind my ear. "No." With

Theron at my side—making me feel like I belong to something, someone, no matter where I am—I'll never be lost.

Hurrying past the suspicious stares of the Seekers, Theron takes us into a clothing shop. We spend ten points each for some new clothes. I go for a pair of sleek black pants and a long-sleeved, red cropped top lined with metal studs. Theron wears a leather vest and white slacks that rest low on his hips. It's the first time we've worn anything but our gray and white issue, and though he looks like a completely different person, it is still so Theron.

After feasting on sizzling meat sticks from a roadside vendor, we stop behind a throng of shouting people. A cage with walls of metal links rises twenty feet into the air. Two females are inside, kicking and punching and pushing and slamming. It's a cage fight. I see the crowd waving their Freedom passes, making their wagers. Theron pulls me through the gathering to get a closer look. We emerge in front of the mass, just ahead of the enclosure. Theron's eyes widen with excitement, following every move and motion. I watch too, trying to memorize their movements and follow their speed.

One girl throws the other over her head onto the matted ground, and her opponent doesn't get up. The crowd goes wild. Cards swipe across portable scanners. The cage opens, and the girl is dragged away, leaving the winning female bouncing on her toes. She calls out for another challenger and waits while no one bites.

"C'mon," she shouts. "Surely one of you out there is daring enough to fight." She's tiny and can't weigh more than a hundred pounds, far from intimidating. I wonder how she became so confident. Her stringy green hair bounces as she does. "Cowards," she says with a hiss.

Volunteering to get pummeled in a cage would be foolish. Reckless. Bold. The exact opposite of what I am. Before I can think too long about it, I climb the steps. "I'll do it."

"Nine!" Theron is behind me in an instant. "What are you doing?"

The woman laughs. "Don't waste my time, Batchling."

"I'm no Batchling," I say. "I'm here to fight."

"Don't be an idiot, Nine. Let's go." Theron pulls me hard, but I yank my arm away.

"I want to do this." I want to be brave, for once.

Theron grips me so hard my arm throbs. "I won't let you."

"All right," the woman shouts. "The Batchling it is. Place your bets." She waves me into the cage, but before I take another step, Theron yanks me away and pushes me down the steps. When I land at the bottom, I look up to see him closing the gate behind him as he takes my place in the cage.

I run up and rattle the metal links. "This is my fight, Theron."

"Don't be so cracked."

I slam my palm into the cage in frustration. How will I ever find my courage when Theron's all too eager to protect me?

"Let's do this," the woman says.

Theron immediately lands a kick across her face that sends her to the floor, then another into her side while she's down. She jumps up and jabs into his ribs, but his arms are up, protecting his torso. Her foot connects with his groin, but he doesn't flinch. He pushes her against a metal wall, holding her there as she flails against him for any hit she can land. With a hard jab to his stomach Theron doubles over, and the woman brings her knee up into his face. He flies backward and onto the ground. Before he can get up, she jumps on him with a fist to his face, sending blood flying in my direction. He's out.

The woman stands and bets are settled as Theron is dragged out of the ring by a pair of identical-looking men with short curly hair and piercings running the length of their eyebrows.

I follow the men to a small room in the back corner of the arena, where they lay Theron on a low table. I am gifted with a bucket of ice before they walk out again to wait for the next victim.

Theron wakes and tries to sit up. "What happened?"

"Hold on," I say, pushing him down and placing a handful of ice on his already swelling cheek.

"I lost?" he asks, genuinely surprised.

"Yes, you lost. You're such an idiot. What on earth was that?" I slap his forehead lightly with the back of my hand, and he rewards me with a painful groan.

Theron's bloodied lips curl into a smile. "That was me stopping you from getting killed, you idiot."

"I could've taken her," I say. Though looking at the reality in front of me, I doubt I would've lasted ten seconds. I smile despite my brave words. "I guess we'll never know now."

Theron sits up and moans.

"What is it?" I ask, reaching for more ice. "Is it your head?"

"No, my pants."

I look down to see a splatter of blood across his new white

34

slacks. I laugh out loud. "You know, Theron, for someone bent on being a Healer, you sure risk getting hurt a lot."

"Side effect of being property of number Nine, I guess."

I wipe the blood off his face. "I'm sorry," I say. It was crazy for me to want to fight, and now Theron's suffering for it.

He touches his hand to my face. "I didn't want this to get messed up." His fingers brush my cheek, and he slides off the table. "I think I'm ready for some of those mind-numbing drinks now."

I smile and slide my arm into his. "To the nightspots it is."

It's getting dark out. The sun has almost set by the time we reach the dance club closest to the gates. I feel the music thumping from outside, but it's nothing compared to what's just inside the heavy doors when we enter. I cover my ears with my hands to minimize the noise, but it only takes a few seconds to adjust, and I lower them again. A scented smoke fills the air, blurring my vision and numbing my senses. Theron's lips move, but I can't hear what he says. I shrug my shoulders, and he has to press his mouth against my ear.

"Don't let go," he yells, holding up our knotted hands.

I nod and let him lead me through the crowd. The room is so congested it's impossible to avoid bumping into people. It's dark, but light flashes from the floor, the walls, and the orbs suspended from the ceiling, letting me see Theron in front of me in brief flashes.

I wonder how many of these people have someone to care for. To love. Someone who loves them back. How many of them live alone, their only contact with others in nightspots like this one? Because I don't know how to live without Theron. If he wasn't in my Batch, my life would be a hollow eggshell—something that once had the potential to hold existence but is now an empty fragile thing that could break with the slightest pressure. He fills the inside of me and makes me stronger.

Theron hands me a drink from a counter, then grabs himself another. It's the same fluorescent green from earlier in the day, and I swallow it in one long drink. The lights seem to flash faster, and the pounding bass of the music hypnotizes me.

I drag him to the middle of a dancing crowd. There are so many bodies, we're like a giant being with a thousand limbs moving in a wild rhythm. I raise my arms high above me and jump and twist to the repetitive beat. The thunderous booming of synthesizers drowns out my thoughts.

Closing my eyes, I get lost in the rhythm, not thinking—just feeling. The *thump, thump, thump* of my heart feels like it will explode out of my chest, and I know this is what Theron means. This is freedom. I jump higher and higher, willing the Earth to release me. To reach such a high that it can't hold me down any longer. It's almost enough to make me forget who I am and who, in just two more days, I will have *used to be*.

Almost.

Chapter Four

A loud and steady beeping throbs inside my head. I groan. I don't want to wake up yet, but my head is on fire. After a late night of loud music, wild dancing, and endless buzz drinks, I'm paying for it now.

"Get up, Nine!" a voice shouts from across the room. A pillow lands with a thud on my head. "And turn off your transmitter."

Moans from a few other sleepy Batch members join in complaint.

So it's not just in my head. The beeping is to inform me I have a message waiting.

I open my eyes and hiss at the hurt the light brings to the already throbbing ache in my head. Sitting up slowly, I groan again as I reach for my transmitter device on the shelf above me. I slide my finger across the screen, and after blinking my eyes a few times to adjust to the light, I try to read the glowing message.

Batch member Nine to meet with Prime Maker at 09:00 hours in the Core building, Room 001.

I glance at the current time on my transmitter: 08:53. I wonder how long the beeping has been going on. I crawl to the bed next to mine and shake the boy lying there. "Wake up, Theron." His snoring doesn't break its pattern. He's as good as dead. *Grr.*

I stumble to the toilets and cringe at my reflection. Running the water at the washbasins, I try to rub the black ink off my head, with no luck. I've never met the Prime Maker before. *No one* has met the Prime Maker before. And she wants to see me. *Me?* The day before I'm Remade. I hope I'm not in trouble for the Freedom passes. I frown at myself in the mirror—I'm still wearing the studded red top and black pants from the night before. With no time to change, I sprint out of our Batch tower toward the Core building, eight blocks north.

I'm late. Really late. I'm certain of it as I run into the reception area on the ground floor, out of breath. I smile at the man behind the metal desk, who scowls at me. I'm late and hungover with a tattoo on my head. I look down and try to smooth the wrinkles on my shirt, only to realize one side of my pants is torn up to my thigh. I sigh and give up.

"I received a transmission this morning," I say. "I'm here to see the Prime Maker."

"She's waiting for you," he says flatly. "Go on in." He points to a door behind him that reads: ERIDIAN, PRIME MAKER.

I take a deep breath, lift my head, and let myself in the room.

A tall woman in a sleek gray pantsuit greets me. "Nine?" She holds her hand out, and I shake it, shocked at how cold her touch is. "My goodness, it really is you." Her voice is high and clear, and I realize it's the one I've heard so often through my earpiece during my academic modules.

"Have we met before, er . . ." I don't know what to call her. Eridian? Prime Maker? Freedom sovereign?

"Eridian," she says. "But please, call me Eri." Her smile reveals brilliant white teeth. She smooths her hair back, a familiar blazing red that's pulled into a tight knot behind her head. I rub my scalp, feeling the barely-there hair growth, wondering why anyone would actually *choose* that awful color.

"And, no, we haven't met," she continues. "Although I remember the day you were Made." Her eyes wander down my body, brows puckering as she takes in my nonstandard clothing and adorned skull. She steps forward and runs a finger along my cheekbone. "Your freckles hadn't come in yet."

I flinch at her icy touch, and my hands ball up at my sides at the reminder of why I've chosen to be a Maker—though I don't dare ask why I was Made this way. I'm uncomfortable speaking to the leader of our province. So I just stand there and wait for her to continue.

"Have a seat, Nine." Eri motions to a chair in front of a glossy black desk. She walks to the other side, her heeled shoes clicking as she goes, and slides her fingers back and forth across a clear computer screen. I cross and uncross my legs, looking around while I wait for her to find whatever it is she's searching for.

Her office is large, the ceiling ridiculously high. The walls are covered in panels that rotate through painted images of landscapes. Beaches, deserts, mountains, and forests phase in and out of display. Behind Eri, on the wall beyond her desk, is a quote from one of our most ancient texts. It's a passage all Batchers have to memorize as small children:

> *And the Maker formed man of the dust of the ground*
> *And breathed into his nostrils the breath of life;*
> *And man became a living soul.*
> *The Maker created man in his own image.*
> *In the image of the Maker created he him;*
> *Male and female created he them.*
> *And they were both made equal before the Maker.*
> *And the Maker blessed them, and said unto them,*
> *Be ye free, choosing for thyself, for it is given unto thee.*

It references the first male and female ever Made, though their names have been lost through time. The words are beautiful, and though my initial reason for wanting to become a Maker is somewhat self-serving, the inscription is inspiring. The first Trade ever recorded was that of a Maker. It'll be humbling and thrilling to carry on in a duty set forth from the beginning of mankind.

"Nine." Eri looks up at me from behind her screen. "Is there a reason you haven't chosen a name yet?"

"No, ma'am."

"Please just call me Eri."

"Okay . . . Eri. I haven't thought much about it." My fingers tap the fabric armrest of my chair; I resist the urge to pull at a thread that has come loose.

"And why is that?"

"Um . . . I guess I've been so concerned about other questions, I haven't given much thought to that one."

"Yes," she says. "I see that." She scrolls through the file on the screen. "You still haven't decided on a gender either. Is that right?"

"Yes." I don't understand what all these questions are for. I'm supposed to have until tomorrow to choose. "Is that a problem?"

"No." Eri slides her finger to shut down her screen and walks around to my side. She leans against the desk just in front of me. "Your gender choice will not be a problem, but your Trade choice is."

I raise my eyebrows, confused. "I thought everyone is free to choose whichever Trade they want."

One side of her mouth turns up briefly before dropping again. "Unfortunately, becoming a Maker requires preapproval."

"Approval from whom?"

"Approval from the Prime Maker," she says curtly.

I can't believe she woke me early and made me race down here just to tell me *she* did not approve of me. Being rejected is not exactly new to me, but with just a day left until my Remake, it's kind of annoying.

"And why is it I'm not approved?" I ask with gritted teeth.

"For one, Makers must be willing to sever all social ties with those they know in their Batch. And from what I read in your file, I doubt you'll agree to that term without protest."

41

I think of leaving Theron for any length of time, and it makes my stomach churn. *Sever all ties.* Maybe that's why we've never met any Makers before. "Do Makers live outside of Freedom?"

Eri crosses her arms and smiles. "Actually, most live here in the Core building, just two stories down. But their work is extremely demanding and leaves little time for mingling with anyone except other Makers."

The mere suggestion of being separated from Theron is enough to dissuade me from the Trade, but I have this burning need to defend myself. "So if I agree to social isolation, then I could become a Maker?"

"Second," she says, ignoring my question, "Makers are not allowed to request a gender change in their Remake."

"But I haven't chosen a gender yet. You don't know that I won't remain female."

"You're right. I don't know that." She studies me for a minute, thinking something through.

"What does that have to do with anything anyway?" I ask, my frustration building. "There's no difference between males and females; why does it matter which gender I choose?" Maybe the Prime Maker herself will give me a straight answer this time.

Eri sighs. "Even if you didn't change, I still wouldn't approve you. Your . . . difference in appearance will not be accepted readily by the other Makers."

My jaw drops. I should remind her I won't look this way after I'm Remade, but my anger takes over. "You mean my freckles aren't even allowed?"

Eri presses her lips together at my outburst.

"This is exactly why I chose to be a Maker in the first place," I say. "Because you people have no idea what these spots have made my life like. And I don't want anyone else to have to go through what I have." I stand and rush to the door, done with this conversation.

"Nine." Eri's voice is soft and warm.

The comforting sound is such a surprise, I turn around and wait for her to continue, my hands in fists.

"You're not a mistake."

I stop, unable to answer. Yeah, that's what Theron says. And guess what? It doesn't sound convincing coming from his lips either.

A part of me wonders if I choose no Trade at all, would anyone notice? How big a difference will I make to our province anyway? I'm just a random number in a random Batch. Freedom has been producing ordinary Batchers like myself for years. I'm nothing special.

Eri tilts her head in my direction. "You're an experiment."

"What?" My jaw drops for the second time in the same minute.

She comes to stand beside me. "You're an experiment, the results of which are not yet conclusive."

Being rejected isn't new to me. But *this*? I'm not prepared for this. I'm a freak on purpose? I suddenly feel like a caged animal being prodded by a group of cruel handlers, just waiting to see how I'll respond, when all I really want is to be set free. Have they been spying on me my whole life, logging in data on their experiment every time I move, every time I breathe? I touch the tracker behind my ear and wonder if it's used for more than just finding me if I'm lost.

"You should feel honored, Nine."

Honored. Not exactly how I would describe the feeling of knots in my chest.

Eri leads me back to my chair. I follow numbly, still in shock.

"You're a pioneer. First in what may be countless to follow." Eri pats my shoulder. "I'm going to let you in on a secret," she says. "World map. Freeze."

Her words confuse me until I see the wall panel to my right. A large map appears, familiar landmasses and oceans filling the screen.

"Here we are," she says, pointing to the southeast edge of the smallest continent on the map. The words FREEDOM ONE label the spot. Eri drags her finger across a large ocean to a continent in the north. "Here's the Remake province," she says. Almost as an afterthought, she adds, "It's where everyone in the world goes to be Remade, no matter what province they originate from."

Our shuttle will transport us there tomorrow. The map does nothing to comfort me. That's one big ocean, especially for someone who can't swim and is afraid of the water like myself. I sigh. What am I still doing here?

"And?" I ask, shifting in my chair.

"If you want to be a Remaker, Nine, *that* I can approve. Though you'll need to live there . . . permanently." She gives me a pitying smile. She knows I won't leave Theron. Why is she doing this to me?

REMAKE

"How about Refuse Collector?" I mutter flippantly, though loud enough I know she hears me. "Or Sewer Specialist? Would you approve me for those Trades?" I've no idea who would want to perform those duties, but someone must choose them, right?

Her eyes widen briefly, and she folds her arms, struggling to remain composed. Something I said upset her. She lifts her chin and continues, as though pretending she didn't hear me.

"There are Makers in every province on every continent in the world." As she speaks, labels appear on the map. Freedom Two, Freedom Three, all the way to Freedom Twenty-Six. "The entire world is watching us, here in Freedom One." She clenches her hands and releases them twice before continuing. "They wait to see what will happen with you, Nine. And if all goes well, you'll be the first."

The first what? All this information is overwhelming and makes me dizzy. As if being an outcast in my Batch of twenty wasn't hard enough, now I've got the whole world following me. There are twenty-six Freedom provinces on Earth. Looking at the wall, I realize there's a lot of land *not* labeled, emphasized by the sheer size of the map. I wonder, briefly, who lives in those far-off places, if anyone. Are they watching me too?

"What do you want from me?" I ask, resisting the urge to bite my nails. "What result is it you're hoping for?"

"Now if I told you that, it wouldn't be much of an experiment, would it?" Eri crouches down next to me. "I've already said too much, but it breaks my heart to see how disappointed you are about not becoming a Maker. At least now you realize you're far more important than some simple Trade."

"Now what?" I don't know what to do with all of this. And freaky experiment aside, I'm back to not having a Trade chosen.

"Your Remake can proceed without a name or Trade selected," Eri says, anticipating my concern. "I've made a note in your file that you'll be allowed to choose those after your Remake recovery." She pauses. "Of course, you'll still need to choose a gender before you get on the shuttle."

I nod and head for the door, anxious to get out of there.

"Good luck with your Remake," Eri says, her warm voice betrayed by the cold of her touch on my back as I leave.

Just outside the Core building, my composure breaks, and my legs begin to shake. A part of me wants to run to Theron. I want to get lost in his arms and his words. I want to forget how much more like an outcast I feel. Another part of me is disgusted with my dependence on him, and I end up stumbling to a metal door just around the corner of the building. It's unlocked. I slip in and close it behind me, sliding to the ground in complete darkness.

I cover my ears and close my eyes, blocking out the whole world. How could things have possibly gotten worse? This isn't fair. It wasn't my choice to be this way. Where was the standard of equality on the day I was Made? No one asked me if this was what I wanted—to be the lone oddity in a throng of equals. I don't care what the cracked Makers hope for me to accomplish to make their experiment a success. After tomorrow the playing field will be level, I'll be like everyone else.

After a while my hands fall, and my eyes crack open, slowly

adjusting to the darkness. I'm sitting on a cement slab against the cold metal door. To my right, a set of stairs rises, and to my left they descend. I'm in a stairwell. I stand and compose myself, turning to the door behind me, ready to face the world again. But as my hand turns the handle, I hear something. It's a faint wailing sound. And though I can't place it, I know it comes from below. I hesitate—and there it is again. A dim howl from the stairwell beneath me.

I lean over the rail but see only a weak green light. Keeping my hands on the metal railing, I descend two sets of concrete stairs. A door on my left reads CORE BUILDING, SUB LEVEL ONE in faint glowing green letters. I'm still in the Core building. What was it Eridian had said? The Makers live two stories down. I walk down another two sets of stairs and find a similar green sign: CORE BUILDING, SUB LEVEL TWO. I try the handle. The door is unlocked. I slip inside and hear the noise again, louder this time. It sounds like the echo of a scream from far, far away.

I walk through a dimly lit hallway filled with dust and a flickering, buzzing sound. Cobwebs and rat feces spread along the ground. It looks as though no human has been here for years. The sound grows louder and is joined by shouts from several people. I peek my head around a corner and see a large door at the end of another hall. As I step closer, I notice this door has a small glass window in it at eye level.

When I'm just outside the door, the screaming is loud and distinct. I still can't tell if it's male or female, but whoever is making the sound must be in a lot of pain. The glass window has a film of dust over it, and I can't see through. I pull my red sleeve over my hand and rub at the dirt. Peering in, I see a white, brightly lit room. It's clean and spotless, a stark contrast to the abandoned hallway I'm standing in. On the far side of the room is a row of individual, white tents. They are roughly the length and width of a bed, but the plastic is opaque. I can't see inside of them. Strange wires and tubes are attached to the tents. Are there people inside those tents? I don't understand what it could mean.

I see one woman in the room. She is laying on a bed, screaming; the veins in her head and neck protrude in her distress. And there's blood, loads of blood, on her clothes and staining the bed beneath her. A sharp, metallic smell sifts under the door, edged with an odor that reminds me of scorched earth. She screams again as a man stands in front of her, blocking my view.

My heart races. I have no idea what's happening, but everything about this is wrong. This can't possibly be the Maker level. There should be a lab or computers, shouldn't there, used for programming or harvesting those being Made? I can't think why someone would be isolated or tortured for any reason. This is Freedom, after all.

A few others gather around her bed, moving with purpose as though excited for something that is about to happen. I fear for a second they're hurting her, or worse . . . but they keep their distance. They don't even touch her. Wherever the pain is coming from, it's not from them. It doesn't make sense.

I reach for the door handle and jiggle it, but it's locked. One of the individuals across the room turns his head toward the door. Toward me.

REMAKE

I duck my head in an instant and crouch as low as I can beneath the door's window. My hands press against my sour stomach, beads of sweat forming on the back of my neck. I force myself to wait, suffering through the sounds of more screams—a symphony of horror. As soon as I'm sure I haven't been seen, and no one will be looking for me, I run back down the hall, turn, and race to the stairwell. I run up the two flights of stairs, skipping steps and tripping once as I hurry.

When I break free into the light of day, I don't stop. I head straight for my Batch tower, feeling as though every Seeker I pass stares suspiciously at me. Once in the tower, I decide I'm not ready to see anyone, not even Theron. I strip and stand in the showers through three entire cycles, then I dress in a fresh tank top and pair of sweats and climb into bed. Theron is still asleep, though it's almost midday. My eyes close, and I try to fall asleep and forget everything that has happened this morning—with Eridian and Sub level Two. It's a futile wish, though. I know I'll never forget the spine-chilling sound of that woman's scream.

Chapter Five

"Come with me," Theron says, leading me out of the eatery after dinner. We enter our building's stairwell, and I freeze just inside the doorway, the memory of this morning still fresh in my mind.

"What's wrong?" Theron asks.

I straighten and shake my head. "Nothing." I don't know what I saw on the Maker level today, but I do know I'm not ready to talk about it yet. Not even with Theron.

I follow him up the stairs until we reach the final door at the top. Walking out onto the roof of our building, I gasp in surprise. Layers of bright-colored blankets sprawl along the ground. Portable hologram screens on low tables surround the clearing, casting a glow in the already dark sky of Freedom. Each screen projects a moving image, floating in the air above it: a bird flying through the air, snow falling on a mountain ridge, clouds drifting across a full moon. The images are beautiful. Magical.

"Where did you get all this stuff?" I ask, grateful for the distraction.

Theron grins. "I have my ways," he says. "I'm not completely helpless, you know."

I laugh, wondering whom he had to flirt with to acquire such things. It's as good as a pair of Freedom passes. I jump into his arms and give him a giant hug. "It's wonderful."

"One more thing," he says, sitting me down on the pile of blankets. He reaches into a metal box on the ground and pulls out a plastic jar filled with firm, glossy squares of something edible. As he unscrews the lid, the sweet scent of cocoa drifts to my nose.

"Chocolate!"

Theron's laughter fills the night. After stuffing our faces with as many pieces as we can, we lean into each other and watch the lights of the province do their thing. Blues, reds, greens, and yellows weave a path through the streets and buildings as far south and west as we can see. But near to us in the east is the black mass of ocean. The lights of Freedom and dark water meet in the far north, converging on a giant building used for music concerts. It sits at the edge of the water, next to a harbor, glowing like giant fingers fueled by light.

"They are shells at the edge of Freedom," Theron says, looking at the building. "Caught in the earth just out of reach of the water."

I shake my head. "They are sails of an ancient ship, heading out to sea."

"Yes." Theron sighs and grins. "Can you imagine sailing a boat across the seas like the explorers did a millennia ago?" He looks out at the water. "I bet the stars are never-ending when you see them from the middle of the ocean."

"There are no boats anymore," I say. "Isn't it scary to know we'll be flying over the ocean for hours in a shuttle? I won't be able to relax until we've landed on the Remake continent."

"Not scary," he says. "Free. Heart-thumping, high-jumping kind of free."

"You're crazy."

"Are you really afraid, Nine?" He wraps an arm around my shoulder and pulls me closer to him.

I don't answer. Of course I'm afraid. The ocean is a dangerous place, full of monsters with sharp teeth and disease and death. It doesn't help that I can't swim—no one in my Batch can. I watch the white water where it meets the sand near the lighted building. It sloshes and splashes, like a dance that alludes to chaos, yet if you watch long enough, falls into a pattern that soothes at the same time.

"The water *is* gorgeous," I say.

"Too bad we can't get closer."

My eyes find the glint of barbed wire topping a thirty-foot high fence along the edge of the beach. I surprise myself by wishing the same thing.

"Why do you think they trap us in?" Theron asks. "What's so terrible about getting out?"

"I don't think it's so much about keeping us in, as making sure other things stay out." Most in my Batch have a fear of the ocean, though I wonder if they'd change their minds seeing it from up here. We learned as children of the dangers the ocean poses. Creatures that swallow men whole or tear off limbs, piece by piece. I've heard rumors of people escaping, but I doubt any of them are true.

And then there's the Virus. The one said to have originated from the ocean itself, killing millions of humans centuries ago, when we didn't fully understand what implications a crowded Earth would have on the sea. It fought back, in its own way, killing that which was killing it. With small Batches to control the population now, I don't think the Virus will ever be a problem again. It doesn't make the water any less fearsome, though.

I lean my head against Theron's neck and watch the movement of the white-water edge. I can almost hear the lapping of water against the shore. Taste the cool and salty air. Would I choose to sail away from Freedom like a ship on the ocean, or stay, wedged in place like a shell in the sand? I glimpse Theron's face, the holograms casting a flickering glow across his skin. Which would Theron choose? Safety or adventure? I know the answer, and I know it'd be the opposite of what I'd choose. I wonder whether my choice would be different after being Remade. Or if maybe it's a *male* thing.

Theron grabs my hands and presses my palms against the top of his head. I massage his scalp. His head is still smooth after the two-days-ago shearing. He sighs and closes his eyes.

"I went to see the Prime Maker today." I say it like it's not a big deal, making it a pretty big deal.

"What?" Theron pushes me, and I fall backward onto the pile of blankets. "When? Why didn't you tell me?" He falls next to me, and I prop my head up by my elbow, turning to face him.

"This morning, while you were passed out."

"And . . . ?"

"And what?" I bite my lip to keep from laughing. It's amusing to watch Theron grow red in the face with anticipation. He's made me forget my distressing morning on the Maker level, and I love him for it.

"You little scab," he says, sitting up again. He grabs both my arms and shakes them, as though that'll get me to talk. "Tell me." I bet he doesn't even notice my efforts to fight back.

"Or what?"

"Or I'll tickle you to death."

"You don't have any hands free." Bubbling laughter escapes my mouth. "And you're the ticklish one, remember? Not me."

"Well, there's that one spot." He tries to pull one of his hands away, but my free arm pushes his chest, and he changes his mind. He holds both my arms again.

"Ha!" I say. "Good luck with that."

With a knowing grin, Theron carefully grips both arms with one hand.

"Oh no."

He digs his fingers into the side of my belly. I scream in bursts and try desperately to roll away from him, to no avail. I'm breathless, and it takes a minute for Theron to hear my pleas among his own loud laughter.

"Okay," I squeal between short, quick breaths. "I give up. I'll tell you. Please . . . stop."

He releases my arms and stops tickling, then lays his head

on my stomach and turns to face me. "I'm staying close," he says. "Just in case."

Propping a bundled blanket beneath my head, I grin and breathe out a relief-filled, "Fine."

He pulls my hands back to his head to massage some more.

"I got a transmission," I say, still out of breath, "to go see her this morning. I was late and still wearing my cracked Freedom clothes—and this." I point to my adorned head.

Theron nods with a lopsided grin, and his eyes sparkle, like the story is just getting to the good part. "What did she look like?"

"Like a silver needle with blood beading at the tip. She has red hair, like me." I make a face. "And she told me to call her 'Eri.'"

"Scary Eri . . ."

"She was nice enough, but she called me all the way to her office just to tell me I couldn't be a Maker."

"Why not?"

I shrug my shoulders. I don't want to tell Theron I'm an experiment. He wouldn't treat me any different, but saying it out loud would admit he was right—I *am* deliberate, though not in the special way he thinks. I don't want to ruin that idea he has of me. "She said I could choose a Trade and name after I'm Remade, since there's not really any time left."

"Hmm. Maybe you could be a Tattoo Artist. You did a fine job on me."

"Shut up." Tattoo Artist would mean needles. Again, no thanks.

"Or a Seeker," Theron says. "That Trade's pretty high-status.

And I'd never be able to get rid of you—since you could find me anywhere." His hand brushes my weak tickle spot, and I smack his bald head in warning.

I touch the tracker behind Theron's right ear. Seekers work in the Core building too, when they aren't in the field on searches or detaining free-breakers. I remember a Batch trip we made to the Core as children. I was in awe of the amount of computers they used and the screen the size of a three-story building. Blinking lights moved slowly across a giant map of Freedom, giving the location of every citizen in the province. Remembering what Eridian had said about why I was Made, I wonder if Seekers have anything to do with keeping track of me—the experiment.

"How about a Techie?" Theron asks. "I hear they sit around and gamble all day."

"Yeah, what do Techies even do?"

"They detect technology. So I guess they're like Seekers, only they hunt for electrical energy instead of humans."

"But why?" I ask.

"In case Eri loses her message transmitter. Duh." Theron rolls his eyes as though it's the most logical thing in the world. "The province will crumble if its Prime Maker can't summon Batchers at a moment's notice while they suffer from a hangover."

"Yes," I say. "Such a demanding Trade. Hence the gambling."

"I wonder if it's too late to switch my Trade choice."

"You can't change," I say. "If I become a Techie, who's gonna support my gambling habit? I need the high points your Healer status will bring in."

Theron slides up next to me and shares my makeshift pillow. "We're sharing an apartment. So if I'm bringing home the points, what are you providing?"

"Something nice to look at?" I suggest.

Theron shakes his head and smiles. "Not good enough. What else?"

"I can cook," I say, although we both laugh at that suggestion. Theron knows what terrible food I've attempted to make in the past. As with most things, between the two of us, he's the expert.

I sigh. "I have no idea what I should choose."

I wish we had someone to talk to about all this. Someone who's been through it before and could tell us what it's like and what our choices really mean. Because stumbling into our lives by accident doesn't seem like the wisest thing in the world. But what else can we do? At least with Theron beside me, I won't stumble alone.

I shrug. "Maybe I'll know better what Trade I'll want after I'm Remade."

"Maybe."

"Theron?"

He raises his eyebrows. His blue eyes stare into mine, waiting for me to continue.

"Do you think they'll keep us separated?" I voice a concern I've had for a while. "During our recovery, I mean?"

"I don't know." He pauses as though thinking about it. "Your Remake might be more involved than mine."

I nod, knowing if I decide to become male, my Remake will

be more complicated. "It's just . . . I can't remember a night I've ever spent without you near me."

"I know." Theron wraps his arm around me and pulls me tight against him.

My body relaxes. My best friend. This is home.

"I can promise you I'll be there with you as soon as I can," he says. "And a month is not so long compared to the rest of our lives. We'll be back in Freedom in no time, together and never apart again."

"You promise?"

Theron pinches the tip of my nose. "I promise. I'll never leave you, Nine. I love you."

"I love you too." I can't imagine us closer than we already are. Should I remain female? It makes sense, doesn't it, Theron and me together? But as a friend or something more, I'm not sure.

A familiar buzzing comes from Theron's pocket. He pulls out his transmitter, squints at the screen and grins. He turns it toward me, and I see the time: 00:00. It's midnight.

"Happy Maker Day," he says.

We're seventeen today. Ready for our Remake. Officially adults and citizens of the Freedom province.

"Happy Maker Day, Theron." I frown, realizing this may be our last stolen moment together for a long time. I try to memorize the feel of his arms around me, the smell of his skin, hoping it will carry me through lonely nights after my Remake. And hoping that after all of our changes, this same feeling will welcome me—welcome both of us—after we are Remade.

Chapter Six

The metal platform feels cold against my naked skin and makes me flinch. I want to hurry and get through this station so I can join Theron in the commuter taking us to the Core building. There we'll make the final selections for our Remake then head for the shuttle port. Not that I've made a decision on my gender choice yet, but being near Theron relaxes me, and I'm definitely not feeling relaxed right now.

"Don't move." The female Healer's voice is quiet, distant. "You need to lie still for the scanner."

I start to nod but stop myself. "Okay," I say instead, though my voice is so soft I wonder if she hears me from outside my medical cocoon. An electronic voice from the body-scanning machine tells me to hold my breath, so I do. Blinding light shines into my eyes and makes me shut my eyelids. I hope it's okay to close my eyes. The light is warm, and I feel the heat travel down my body, an arc of illumination scanning every part of me.

The light comes back toward my head and shuts off. I open my eyes. It's dark as night now. There's no voice to tell me I can breathe again, but I can't hold my breath any longer. I gasp for air and shut my eyes again, starting to feel claustrophobic. Just as I'm about to say something to the Healer, who I hope is still outside the scanner, the platform slides out of the machine into the medical room, and I gratefully breathe in the expansive air.

I start to sit up, but the Healer shakes her head at me. My head hits the metal under me with a loud *thunk* as I try to remain still. She holds a portable computer and slides her fingers across the screen.

"Any numbness in your fingers or toes?" she asks.

"No."

"Blurry vision?"

"No."

"Do you ever feel short of breath or overly anxious?"

Only when I'm in a medical coffin. I shake my head and wonder why she asks me these questions. Doesn't the full-body scanner give her everything she needs to know about me? A cold air current comes from a high corner in the room, and I shiver.

The Healer puts her computer on a table and picks up a length of cloth that has been sitting in a bucket filled with pale blue liquid. She brings it to my scalp and wipes away my tattoo. The cloth tingles my skin and smells of peppermint. Evidence of my Freedom excursion is gone in under a minute, ink staining the formerly spotless fabric. She drops it back into the bucket, wipes her hands on her medic pants, and leaves the room.

I'm still naked and cold, and after a few minutes I sit up, not knowing what else I should do. A man with shoulder-length navy blue hair walks in. He wears a black jumpsuit with a red star in a white circle on each of his shoulders. He holds what looks like a miniature firearm in his hands. He's a Seeker, and unlike the Healer who had just been with me, he gives me a wide, warm smile.

"Last thing on the list today, kid," he says. "I just need to test your tracker and make sure it's working."

"With that?" I ask, pointing to the weapon, hoping against hope there's no needle involved in testing my tracker.

He holds it up in front of him. "It's not so bad." A trigger and handle connects to a long tube made of clear plastic. "I push this end"—he points to the nozzle—"against your tracking device and pull. If there's a green light, here, at my thumb, you're good to go. If it's red, we'll do a quick replacement."

"Replacement?"

"Sure. You don't want to be walking around with a faulty tracker, do you?"

Another tracker installation? Oh, please no. I still remember the day it was installed when I was four years old, my first memory. It had taken three adults to hold me down while they inserted the oversized needle into my skull. I screamed and still recall the loud *whack* echoing in my head for the rest of the day. Not fun. I'm no fourth-year anymore, but I still make a silent plea for the cracked light to turn green.

He must sense my panic because he brings the gun closer

so I can get a better look. "The diodes, here at the end of the tube, signal the tracker to release from your brain tissue. Try to get it out any other way, and . . ." He makes a slicing motion with the gun across his neck.

Yeah, that doesn't make me feel better.

"You'll need to lie on your stomach," he says.

I obey and flinch again as the cold metal touches my bare skin. The Seeker turns my head so I'm looking to my right. I gasp when the nozzle snaps over the tracker, like two magnets suddenly sticking to each other. A shock rattles my head and makes me gasp again.

"Green," he says. "You're good."

I sigh with relief and sit up again.

"There's a fresh set of clothes on the chair, there." The Seeker points to a spot behind me. "And don't worry. It'll be the last pair of gray and white you'll ever have to wear. Promise." He winks and walks to the door. "Good luck with your Remake."

I smile and get dressed, anxious to leave the Healer building. The woman Healer returns and leads me to a commuter parked just outside the building. I climb aboard and see Theron sitting in the back, his head leaning against a window, gazing outside. I bounce from foot to foot, making my way to him while ignoring glares from Cree and Sora as I pass them.

Theron looks up and smiles at me. "I guess you didn't need a new tracker, then, with that smirk on your face."

I collapse into him, and he winces. "Oh, Theron," I say, seeing the bandage behind his ear. "I'm so sorry."

"You are not."

"I am. It must've been awful. Terrible. Brutal."

"Wipe that cracked grin off, then, if you feel that bad about it."

I kiss his ear with a giggle. "I really am sorry for you."

"Yeah, sure." He pulls me onto his lap and wipes the commuter window with his hand. "Check it out. It's raining."

"Whoa." Sure enough the roads are wet, and I can almost see drops falling from the sky. It hardly ever rains in Freedom. "Maybe it's an omen. A bad one."

"Nah. It's a good sign. Freedom is sending us off with a bang."

Just as he says the words, a beam of light flashes in the distance, followed a few seconds later by the sound of thunder.

"A bang, huh?"

Theron turns to me and slides his hand across my tattoo-free head with a frown. "My masterpiece is gone."

"I know." I feel him trace the lines of a pattern no longer there. "I'll miss it too."

"At least you can't tell me what to do anymore." Theron pulls down his tank at the back of his neck. "I'm no longer your property." Sure enough, the tattoo scrawl of my name is gone.

I scowl. "First thing when we return to Freedom, you're getting a tattoo of my name, permanent this time, on the back of your neck. I'm not releasing my hold over you that easily."

"Ooh," Theron says, scrunching his shoulders. "I'm so scared."

Another boom of thunder fills our ears. I give him a wicked smile. "You should be."

* * *

My light mood disappears as we pull in across the street from the Core building. The rain has stopped, but the darkening sky is a promise of more to come, I think. I linger in back as each member of our Batch exits the commuter, then finally follow Theron off and glance to the building. I can't help but look to the side of it . . . where a heavy door leads to a stairwell, and the stairwell leads to an abandoned hallway, and that hallway leads to—

"Hey, are you okay?" Theron turns me toward him and looks back and forth between my eyes, as though they'll tell him what he needs to know.

Only now do I notice my shallow breathing and shaking hands. I don't want to go in there. Not when I've seen what happens two stories down. Not when I've heard those awful sounds of terror. Of course I don't exactly know *what* I saw, but I know it isn't good.

"Nine, you're going to be fine." He lifts my chin and gives me a lopsided smile. "Don't think about it too hard. Because whatever you decide, you'll still be *you*. That's all that matters."

He thinks I'm nervous because of my Remake questions. I nod, knowing the sooner I choose, the sooner we'll leave and be on our way to the Remake continent. And I won't have to worry about Sub level Two for a long time.

Theron tilts his head toward the Core building across the street. "I'll race you there."

A smile grows on my face, and my apprehension melts away. A memory surfaces of a day long ago, when we were young Batchers, maybe fifth- or sixth-years.

Our Batch had been playing in an indoor recreation

room with climbing equipment and an open space for running around. Everyone was playing Seeker Track, a game that involved chasing one another and tagging players on their right ear, like Seekers catching you by your tracker. The kids refused to let me join in, and I ended up in a corner, huddled against myself with my head down.

Theron came and settled next to me. He started plucking at my arms and face.

I swatted him away. "What are you doing?" I asked, annoyed.

"Trying to get some of your spots," he said.

I frowned and narrowed my eyes at him. "They don't come off," I whispered.

His face fell. "That's too bad. I wanted some for myself."

I perked my head up. "You want my freckles? Why?"

"Because they make you run fast. Duh." He threw his hands up in the air as if it were obvious. "Why do you think cheetahs have them? They're the fastest animals in the world."

I shook my head at him, convinced he was making fun of me. "If I'm so fast, why won't they let me play?" I motioned to the kids running around, their laughter echoing in the large room.

"Because you're *too* fast. It wouldn't be fair for the rest of them."

I extended my arms to get a good look at them. I had a lot of freckles. I wondered if that meant I was even faster than a cheetah. "You think so?" I asked.

Theron huffed. "I know so. I'll prove it to you." He stood and pulled me up next to him. "I'll race you around the edge of the rec room. Start and finish right here. Ready?" He leaned forward at an angle with his lips pursed together in concentration.

I raised my arms like his, fisting my hands, ready to pump them into action.

"Set," he said, peeking at me out of the corner of his eye. "Go!"

I took off and ran as fast as my feet could move, rounding each corner of the room with a new burst of speed. I imagined myself a cheetah, lengthening my stride and not slowing down until I reached our starting point just ahead of Theron.

He doubled over and took exaggerated breaths. "See?" he said between his panting. "Way too fast."

I forgot about the other Batchers and their game, challenging Theron to several more races. Of course I realized years later he probably let me win, but it didn't matter. Because I had decided that day, if there was one person I could share my freckles with, it'd be Theron. My best friend.

"Well?" Theron elbows me in the side, bringing me back to the present. "Wanna race?"

I glance across the street and shrug my shoulders, feigning indifference. As soon as I see his stance relax, I yell, "Go!" and take off before he realizes what's happening.

"Cheater!" he calls from behind me, laughing through the street.

I reach the doors just before he does and join in his laughter, my fear forgotten. How does he do that? How does he make me feel safe and loved and just plain happy in an instant? I smile at him with a look of appreciation. Theron is everything I wish I were. Everything I wish I could become. And as we enter the building, it's as though something inside of me sparks like the electric lights along the walls. I've always wanted to be like Theron, and I think I know how I can be.

When it's my turn at the computer station, I slide my finger on the screen and watch as those haunting words appear.

Male or female?

Theron stands beside me, his presence giving me the courage to ignore the doubt that sticks in my throat like an unpleasant taste. I force myself to swallow it and bury it down.

Where's the spark I felt just seconds ago?

Theron leans against me, reminding me I don't have to do this alone. This choice, this journey, this life—he'll be at my side through it all.

This time I don't hesitate, and my finger connects with the rest of my life.

Male.

I turn to the boy at my side, his eyes wide and surprised for a fraction of a second before warmth invades his expression.

"You know what this means, don't you?" he asks with a serious face.

I shake my head and hold my breath.

"It means I'll have to teach you how to pee standing up."

A burst of laughter erupts from my mouth, and Theron wraps his arm around my neck and kisses the top of my head, making me feel like I made the right decision.

Even though, somehow, I still can't find that spark.

Chapter Seven

The interior of the shuttle is way smaller than the outside makes it look. But there are still ten times as many seats than our Batch of twenty needs. Theron and I hijack an entire row, push up the armrests, and sprawl along the seats.

"Maybe I can sleep the whole way there," I say.

"Hurtful." Theron yanks off my shoes and tosses them to the floor. "These are our last moments together before our Remake, and you're gonna sleep them away?"

I hold my hands in front of me, palms up, replicating a balance scale. Lowering each, one at a time, I pretend to debate the matter. "Hmm. Sleep through a terrifying flight over miles of deadly ocean . . . or . . . listen to jokes that make me want to shoot my ears off." I tap a finger on my chin. "That's a hard one."

"After a lifetime of providing comic relief to our sad and simple lives, this is how you repay me?"

"Don't worry," I say, snuggling up to him. "I promise to laugh at every word until I'm out. It'll be a win-win."

With an exaggerated sigh, Theron says, "Fine. But if your snoring interrupts my creative thinking, I'm stuffing you in the lavatory."

"Deal," I say, tucking my head under his chin.

"So three Makers enter a bar—"

"Nine, wake up." Theron is shaking me.

But I want to sleep.

"Wake up."

I open my eyes. We're still in the shuttle. "Are we there?" I ask. "How long have we been flying?"

"Not long." He shoves me away from him into one of the seats. "Put your safety belt on." His words are rushed, and his hands fumble with the straps at my waist. I thought I'd seen every expression Theron could possibly make, his face the most familiar sight of my existence. But I've never seen this one. What is it? Panic? Desperation?

"What—" I notice the beeping sound. My hand automatically goes to my pocket for my transmitter, until I remember they took those from us back at the Healer building. I rub my eyes and look around the dim interior. A few Batch members are walking to the front of the shuttle. Others are whispering to each other, some with the same panicked expression I see on Theron.

"I'm sure it's nothing." His words are barely audible. "Put your shoes on, Nine."

I ignore him and look out the tiny passenger window to my far left. Lightning streaks the sky, and the rain against the glass blocks any clear view of the outside. I can't even tell what time of day it is in the dark gray of the storm.

A sudden banging at the front of the shuttle rattles me. My stomach flutters twice as the shuttle drops suddenly before leveling out again. It's like I'm on one of those thrill rides at the Freedom exposition. My mouth goes dry as I clench my fingers around my safety belt. This is a ride I want to get off. Right now.

"I said put your shoes on." Theron yanks my leg toward him and shoves one of my shoes on, his fingers shaking as he ties the laces into a mess of knots I know I'll never get out. I don't have the heart to tell him it's the wrong foot.

"Th . . . Theron?" My voice is shrill, and I nervously glance behind us, not knowing what I'm searching for.

"It's fine," he says. "I'm sorry. We're gonna be fine." He finishes with the second shoe and pulls me as close as our straps will allow.

There are shouts in the cabin, and crying. I have just enough time to wonder if we're crashing before large sparks erupt in the front of the shuttle and everything goes dark. The beeping has stopped, but there's screaming now. A lot of screaming. And I have enough sense to realize some of it is mine.

Theron pushes his mouth to my ear. "Stay with me!" He grabs both of my hands in his. "No matter what happens. Don't let go. You stay with me! Do you understand?"

I nod vigorously as his nails dig into my palm.

My stomach lurches, and I hear a groaning sound, metal sliding against metal, that must come from the shuttle itself. It's thunderous. I can't see a thing, but I know we are falling. The safety belt presses hard into my lap, the only thing keeping me from flying out of my seat. I squeeze Theron's hands so hard I could burst.

As the shuttle hits the water, my body is thrown back, and I lose my grip. A jolt of pain flows through me. The sound of rushing water fills the cabin.

"Theron!" I move my arms frantically in the dark, scrambling for the familiar feel of his skin.

A hand grasps my arm. "I'm here. I'm right here." I feel him unlatch my safety belt. "We're sinking. We need to get out. Stay with me."

Where else does he think I'm going to go? I don't know how he can see anything, but I follow him with no intention of ever letting go. We stumble through the aisle to the back of the shuttle. It feels like we're heading up a steep hill, the front of the shuttle sinking behind us. A door to the outside hangs partly open at the end of the aisle. With one swift kick, Theron knocks it off, and I watch it fall to the water that's about thirty feet below us, but coming up fast. It's night out, but lights on the outside of the shuttle are still working, blinking, revealing the reflection of the water with every terrifying flash.

I look back into the cabin of the shuttle.

Where is everyone?

Theron grabs my shoulders. "We're gonna jump." His eyes briefly glance over my body with his eyebrows drawn together. He knows neither of us can swim. He should just leave me now. Save himself. He'll have a better chance of surviving with one body to worry about instead of two. But I'm not brave enough to suggest it.

He grabs the cushion off one of the seats and squeezes my hand. "Together," he says. "And don't let go." He holds our gripped hands in front of my face.

"I'm not gonna let go, you scab!"

He nods with a grin and pulls me with him. Down, down. I expect to hear a splash, but there's only silence as my body slaps the water, sinking immediately. Water rushes over me and drags me down. I kick and flail and try to breathe but it's water, not air, that enters my lungs. Cold, freezing water. Something tugs on my hand, and my head breaks the surface. I cough out saltwater as Theron drags me to the chair cushion still in his other hand.

"Hold on," he yells. I can't hear him, but I read his lips through the flashing lights. I nod and throw my arms across the square pad. Behind me, Theron puts a hand on either side of me and kicks us away from the shuttle that's still sinking fast.

All at once, sound seems to find my ears again, and I wish it had stayed away. I hear bending metal, like a giant beast moaning from deep water. The crackle of sparks from the shuttle makes me flinch. Worst of all is the screaming. Screaming from other Batchers I cannot see.

Debris crowds the surface of the water, and we don't have time to skirt around everything. Theron plows forward and away from the crash as fast as he can. An otherworldly shriek screeches at an impossible pitch, and I realize it's from the shuttle, not a person.

"Theron!" I try to warn him, but he cannot see where we're

going, and we collide with a body that floats face up in the water.

With a shaking arm, I push the body aside so we can get through. It's Cree. Fresh blood streaks from her nose; it probably started bleeding again during our quick descent. Theron tells me to close my eyes, but that would be trading one terror for another, dark for dark in a horrible ocean that threatens to swallow us at any moment.

When Theron thinks we've gone far enough, he moves across from me to the other side of the floating cushion. "We're okay. We're gonna be okay."

We both look at the shuttle in the water, a broken piece of machinery that will eventually sink and spend the rest of time at the bottom of the ocean. We don't speak, just watch as it submerges. The lights finally go out on its sides and wings, then it disappears as though it had never been.

The air smells of fire, and it's very cold. Screams die down to sobs and moans, and I realize we're not the only survivors. The moon is full and, as the smoke begins to settle, casts a surprisingly bright light on the water. Debris bobs up and down, and I am sane enough to be grateful I'm alive, thanks to Theron.

"Theron." My voice is hoarse.

He pulls my hand to his lips and holds it there.

"I love you," I say.

"Don't do that." His words are harsh, his eyes warm. "Don't you start saying your good-byes."

His image blurs, and I can't tell if the salt on my tongue comes from my tears or the ocean water.

He wipes a hand across my face. "We're going to make it,"

he says, his voice solid, as though by saying the words he wills them to be true. "They tested our trackers, remember? They'll be here any minute because they know exactly where we are."

I nod and look at his right ear. His bandage is gone, and blood flows from behind his earlobe. I don't say what we both suspect—that trackers don't work outside of Freedom, least of all in the ocean. I open my mouth to ask if his ear stings, when I notice something coming at us fast.

"Help . . ." It's Bristol, and his voice sounds burbly. He flings himself onto our cushion, but the weight is too much, and the pad starts to sink beneath us. I swallow water as I go down with it, but I refuse to let go. Arguing voices flow in and out of my ear, becoming distorted as I sink below the surface. I am not letting go. I scream for Theron but end up swallowing more water, so I squeeze my eyes shut and start counting.

One, two, three . . .

A swift kick connects with my stomach, and I curl my body in pain. But I don't let go.

Seven, eight . . .

I feel the cold night air on my face and know I have breached the surface again.

Twelve, thirteen, fourteen . . .

I keep my eyes shut and cough out too much water. Buckets worth of water.

Nineteen, twenty . . .

Something grabs my hand, and I scream, opening my eyes in an instant. It's Theron, and I reach for his other hand. "Where's Bristol?"

"Gone. He's . . . gone." Theron looks straight at me with

those blue eyes I know so well. "I had to save you, Nine. I couldn't save him too." His hands are shaking, and I squeeze them tight.

I feel something rub against my leg that is definitely not Theron. "What is that?" I ask, thinking Bristol had somehow returned.

"What is what?" Theron's eyes go wide as something large and slippery slides against our bodies. "Holy—"

And then Theron's gone, pulled under the water faster than I can blink.

I scream louder than I ever thought possible. So loud it feels like my lungs will burst. "Theron!" I cannot see him.

He's under the water, and I can't see him.

And then he's up, twenty feet away from me. He struggles to keep himself afloat with flailing arms.

"Theron!" I reach for him. Start kicking toward him. But he shakes his head in desperation at me.

"Swim, Nine! Swim!"

"I'm coming," I try to say, but I have no voice. My words scratch against my throat, dying before they can leave my lips.

"No!" Theron manages to keep above the surface, but I know he's in pain by the twisted look on his face. "Swim away, Nine. You kick hard and don't stop."

I freeze and stare at him, trying to make sense of his words.

"Swim away from here, and don't stop kicking. Don't stop kicking, do you understand?"

I nod, but I'm still in shock, not moving.

And then the head of a beast with a thousand teeth breaches the surface and sinks below the water again.

"Go," Theron yells. *"Now!"* He turns away from me and moves the opposite way, toward where the shuttle went down. Toward the mass of debris.

The beast is gone, lost under the water somewhere.

I turn away and kick. Kick and kick and kick. Crying and sobbing and screaming from a raw throat. I kick until my legs feel like they will fall off. I kick after I can't feel them anymore. The water turns so cold I can't feel my arms or my hands gripping the cushion. But still I kick, at least I think I do.

I. Can't. Feel. Anything.

My lips stop trembling.

Kick. Kick. Kick.

The sun rises on the horizon and blinds me. I don't like the bright, so I close my eyes to keep it dark. In the dark, I can pretend I'm not alone.

Kick. Kick.

I think of Cree and Bristol. Their bodies lost in the depths of the ocean.

Kick.

I think of Theron. No. *No.*

And then, in the midst of my kicking—or nonkicking—I think of nothing. It's a blissful thing, to have no thoughts. I welcome it and let it seep through me. I grasp it and command it to not let go. *Please don't let go! Don't leave me,* I tell the nothing. *Don't ever leave me.*

PART
TWO

Chapter Eight

In the nothingness, I hear a voice. Smooth and soothing, strong and confident. It is Theron's voice, telling me to kick and never stop. So I do, I kick my legs but go nowhere. No—I go in circles. It's the same as going nowhere, I think. Why does he want me to go nowhere?

A body floats in front of me. *Close your eyes*, the soothing voice tells me. But I'm afraid. And the body is in my way, so I push it aside, expecting to see a bloodied nose. But instead, it's an ear that bleeds from this dead body. His empty blue eyes are open, staring at me, pleading with me. *Help*. A thousand teeth emerge from the water and grab him, pull him under in an instant. I cannot see him. He is under the water, and I can't see him. He's gone, disappeared, as though he had never been.

I'm kicking again, though not at the water. Instead, I kick and hit and punch and pull at the nothingness. Don't leave.

Please. Come back. I don't want to remember, I don't want to *know.*

And then I hear a voice. But this voice isn't smooth or soothing. It's not Theron's voice.

"Help me turn her over." The voice is low and deep. Male. The way he speaks, his *R*'s blend with other words or get lost all together: *Help me tun hurovah.*

"I'm not touching that thing," says another male voice, sounding mature but younger than the first. "And how do you know it's a girl?" Every sentence he speaks rises in pitch at the end.

I feel hands on my shoulders, pushing me onto my back.

"I don't," says the first male. "You volunteering to investigate, Kai?"

The younger one—Kai—erupts into coughs. "No. Way. It can be a girl for now."

Something pries my fingers from the floating cushion. I hold on tight, refusing to let go. But the something else wins, and my hands are empty. I hear the cushion land beside me.

"Dad, we should just leave it . . . um . . . her," Kai says. "She's one of *them.*"

A pair of rough, large hands grip my throat, and I think I am being strangled. *Bristol is back,* I think in a panic. But in a moment the hands pull away, and I am still here, aware.

"She's alive," Dad, the older voice, says. "Her pulse is weak, though. We need to get her to your mother."

I don't know what a mother is, but I'm not going anywhere. I try to open my eyes, but the light from the sun is still blinding, so I keep them closed.

"Help me sit her up," Dad says.

Kai grunts. "I told you, I'm not touching it. Remember what we saw on the west—"

"Quit being an idiot, Kai," Dad says, his voice loud and commanding. "You're eighteen, not a snot-nosed pip anymore. She's just a child. And she's alone. Man up, and take her on that side."

I feel two pairs of hands slide under my back, but instead of allowing myself to be lifted, I roll to the side and throw up seawater and anything else still lingering in my stomach.

"Ah, man, that's nasty."

After making sure nothing else is going to come out, I sit up on my own and try to open my eyes again. Looking down at myself, I see my white tank top and gray sweats—they feel damp. My feet are bare except for one sock hanging halfway off. I touch the seat pad on my left and shudder. I'm sitting on a sandy beach. Not ten feet away is the white of water, leading to an aqua blue sea beyond. The ocean. I scramble backward, frantic, determined to get as far away from the water as I can.

"Whoa, whoa. Slow down." The man named Dad tries to hold on to me, but he doesn't have to. My legs are so weak from kicking all night, I collapse before I get anywhere.

I look up, and it's not so bright anymore because a shadow looms over me. "Are you okay?" the shadow asks in Dad's voice.

I open my mouth to speak, but my voice is so raw, nothing comes out.

"Shh." Dad wipes my forehead, and I feel sand falling off my skin. "We're here to help you. Don't be afraid." His skin is brown, a dark bronze that would be impossible to attain even if his Trade involved working out in the sun all day. His hair is dark and cropped short. He wears a beard that is trimmed at the sides, leaving a mass of black and gray facial hair on his chin and above his lips. With dark brown eyes and a collection of wrinkles at his eyes and lips, his face is kind. "Do you think you can sit up on your own?"

I nod, deciding to trust this stranger with dark skin. When I rise this time, a throbbing pain fills my head. I bring my hands to my temples, pressing hard, wanting to drive the ache away.

"Kai, give him—or her—your water." Dad holds his hand out to the boy on my other side.

"This is ridiculous." With an exaggerated sigh, Kai passes over a plastic bottle. "Just ask it if it's a boy or girl already."

Dad yanks the bottle from his hand and knocks it on the top of Kai's head with a stern expression. Dad turns to me, and his face softens. "Are you female?"

For now.

I give him a quick nod.

Dad unscrews the lid from the top of the bottle and hands it to me. I take a small sip. And then a big one. When all the water is gone, I give the empty bottle to Dad and finally glance at Kai.

He seems to be about my age. Eighteen, I guess, like Dad had said. He's already Remade, though—a mature male—with wide shoulders and strong arms. He doesn't wear a shirt, and I see a tattoo on his chest and stomach, covering the left half of his torso. He's tall, like Dad. His skin is a shade lighter, though still bronze. Kai's hair is short on the sides, and tight, black curls sprawl along the top of his head. He bears a slight resemblance to Dad, though I'm sure it's just the strangeness of their skin color that makes them similar. His face is wrinkled also, though not from age. It's scrunched with angry brows and pursed lips. His light brown eyes are cold, not warm and comforting like Dad's. I decide not to trust those cold eyes.

"Do you think you can stand?" Dad asks.

I turn to him and place my hand in his offered one. I rise successfully but fall into him, my legs unable to hold my entire weight.

"It's okay," he says. "Kai, hold her a sec." Though it sounds more like *'older a seek.*

My head hurts from straining to understand their heavily accented words.

Kai grips my elbow with such force I know I will bruise. I don't want him to touch me and try to shake him off, but he stands firm, looking off into the ocean.

Dad stuffs the water bottle into a bag I hadn't noticed before. "We'll carry you, all right?"

I look at Kai. I don't want him to carry me.

He harrumphs.

Dad rolls his eyes and tosses him the bag, then slips his arms under my knees and back, pulling me to his chest. "I've gotcha."

We start to head inland, away from the beach, and thankfully, away from the water. But I remember the floating cushion and begin to squirm in his arms.

"What is it?" Dad asks.

I point behind him to the wet and sandy seat pad buried in the sand. "Don't let go," I whisper, squeezing my hand into a fist.

Dad motions to it with a tilt of his head. "Kai."

"Are you kidding me?" Kai grudgingly retrieves my lifesaver and falls into step behind us. "What a freak."

His words are nothing new.

Dad carries me through a path of dense foliage. Trees and bushes with wide, expansive leaves sprout everywhere, and it's all green. Green below and green above. I've never seen anything like it before in Freedom.

The green on the ground soon gives way to tiny black pebbles that scatter along a purposeful path. At the end of the path is a small wooden building, just one story tall. It's propped above the ground with cement blocks at each corner so I can see under it to the other side.

Kai runs ahead of us, up a short set of stairs and into the building, calling out, "Mom!"

The door shuts automatically behind him with a squeak and a slam. As we ascend the stairs, I realize I can see right into the building because there's a mesh screen on the door that provides no protection from the elements outside.

Kai opens the door for us and cringes as my legs rub against his chest. I resist the urge to kick him in his gut as we pass. Dad carries me to a long set of cushions covered in fabric, like a bed, but made for sitting in comfort instead of lying. He sets me down and calls, "Miriama?"

"I'm coming." A woman's voice echoes from another room. "What's the big surprise, eh?" A beautiful woman with long, dark brown hair pulled into a loose braid and fair, clear skin stops a few feet in front of me. She looks nothing like Dad, but strangely, has the same light brown eyes and pouting lips as Kai.

"We found her on the beach, Miri." Dad puts his hand on Miri's back. "Washed up on shore." They give each other a knowing look, and I wonder if they can communicate through their thoughts, the way their eyes seem to speak their own language.

It reminds me of the way Theron and I can tell what the other means without saying anything. Could tell, I mean. Before.

"The girl's gone and lost her voice," Dad continues. "She's had a rough night, I think. But she'll be fine."

Miri nods and kneels beside me. "Put some tea on, Kai." Her accent is not as thick as the two males, which is a relief.

"Yes, Mom." Kai walks away with a sigh.

I wonder if "Mom" is another nickname for "Miriama."

Miri brushes her hand against my scalp. It's soothing and I close my eyes, too tired to think about where I am or who these people are. I just want to sleep.

"What's your name?" Miri asks.

I open my eyes. "Nine," I try to say. No sound comes out, but a series of coughs erupts from the effort of speech.

"Warning," Kai says from across the room. "I'd get out of the spill zone if I were you."

Miri and Dad ignore him. "Don't waste your voice," Dad says, kneeling by Miri.

"If I ask you a question," Miri asks, "can you shake your head for no and nod for yes?"

I nod, and Miri smiles. I wait a few moments while she looks me over. Her eyes glance over my bald head and the spots on my hands. I bury my fingers in a fold of my tank top, suddenly insecure about my freckles. I wish I had something more to cover up with.

"I know this will seem odd," she says, "but can you open your mouth for me?"

I hesitate, glancing at Dad, who gives me an encouraging nod. I open wide while Miri looks at all of my teeth. When I close my mouth, she shakes her head at Dad.

"Are you a Batcher?" she asks me.

I nod.

"Are you from Freedom?"

I nod again.

"Freedom One?"

Yes.

"Are you alone?"

Every muscle in my body stiffens, from my clenching jaw to my curling toes. I don't know how to answer that one. Yes, I'm alone. More alone than I've ever been in my life. Everyone I've ever known is dead. Theron is gone. I shake my hands out and try to relax.

"She's not alone," Kai says, walking toward us. "She brought a lovely blue cushion along for her trip." He holds out a ceramic cup to Miri and looks at me, then quickly to the floor, as though embarrassed to have seen me so upset.

Miri yanks the cup away from him. "Stop being such a jerk, Kai, and get your sister. She's in the garden."

I don't know what Kai's sister is supposed to be, but I decide I really, really like this Miri person.

Kai opens his mouth to say something, then shuts it again and storms out through the mesh door.

"What's he talking about, Arapeta?" Miri asks.

Dad walks to the front door and brings back my floating pad. Is Dad also called Arapeta? I don't know how "Dad" could be considered a nickname for "Arapeta." These people are strange with their many names and similar appearance. And the way Kai obeys this Miriama and Arapeta so quickly—it's like he's still a child being cared for by Fosterers, not a Remade adult.

Miri examines the cushion carefully before I pull it out of her hands and lay it down next to me. "I think it's from an airplane," she whispers.

She helps me sit up and gives me the cup of tea, telling me to drink. "Did your plane—no—shuttle crash into the ocean?"

I don't have to nod. She knows the answer from my trembling hands.

"And everyone else—"

I shake my head and close my eyes. I want it to be black again. I don't want to remember.

I feel Miri sink into the seat next to me and wrap her arm around me. "Shh. It's okay. Everything's going to be okay."

I hear Arapeta's voice. "If those fools spent more time improving old technology and less time searching for it, this probably wouldn't have happened. All they care about are their awful surgeries and making sure we don't—"

"Not helping, Ara," Miri says. She presses her lips to my ear and whispers, "You're seventeen, aren't you? On your way to the Remake facility?"

I nod, overwhelmed with relief. These strange people in this foreign place don't seem so different anymore. If they know about shuttles, Batchers, and being Remade, surely they know how to get me back home. Back to Freedom. I square my shoulders, ready to be brave and do what I need to do to get home. I take another sip of my tea, look at Miri next to me, and spew the liquid across the room.

"What's wrong?" Miri asks. "Is it too hot?"

I shake my head and point to her stomach, noticing for the first time that it sticks out unnaturally far, like a giant sphere is hidden beneath her clothes.

"I'm not that hideous, am I?" Miri smiles and pats her enormous belly.

"No," says Ara. "You are perfect in every way." He bends down to kiss her stomach. "Be careful what you say to a pregnant woman," he tells me with a grin. "Especially one about to make baby number four." Ara pulls Miri's face to his and presses his nose against hers, inhaling so deeply I think he could swallow her whole. The sight is so foreign and so intimate I blush and have to look away.

I place my cup on the floor and rub my temples again. *Pregnant. Baby.* All these new words are making my headache worse. And these people talk as though they are Makers, ready to give someone a Maker number. Nothing makes sense, and the pull of sleep is too strong for me to resist.

I lie back down and curl into a ball, managing to fall asleep while Ara and Miri argue over what to do with the washed-up Batcher from Freedom.

Chapter Nine

The sound of voices wakes me. My heart sinks as I realize I'm still lying on the fabric cushions with a blanket draped over me. I can feel Theron's absence deep in my stomach, like I haven't eaten in days, and if I do nothing but eat for the rest of my life, I know I'll never feel full again.

"They'll find us in a matter of days," Kai says from somewhere in a room I can't see.

"No one is coming." It's Miri's voice. "I've already checked her. She's clean."

"They'll figure out she's missing and send out a search," Kai says.

"They don't have those kinds of resources," Ara says.

"You don't know that."

"Dad's right," says a new voice. A female one. "They'll

probably assume she went down with the plane along with everyone else."

"I've seen what those people are capable of. You haven't." Kai's voice is beginning to grate on me. "Maybe she's a spy, and she's just posing as a weak, lost victim."

"Yeah, and she's got a locating device hidden in that blue cushion of hers," the new female says. "Don't be such an idiot, Kai."

"The poor girl is lost and alone and doesn't need you to make her feel worse." Ara sounds tired. I wonder if it's later in the day or if I've slept through the night. I can't tell by the low light outside.

"I still don't think she should stay here. It's not right."

"Well, we can't exactly take her back now, can we, Kai?" Miri says.

"I know. But I wish you'd all stop ganging up on me. I'm not an idiot. I mean, look at her. She doesn't have any hair. Her body is . . . She's an overgrown child with a weird bald head. A suppression-junkie has no place here."

I really want Kai to stop talking already. "Hello?" I say, sitting up from my makeshift bed.

"And she speaks!" Ara rushes to my side. "That's Miri's magic tea for ya."

Miri comes to stand next to him, with Kai and another girl close behind. I rub my eyes and yawn, trying to wake up.

"You already know our son, Kai," Miri says. "This is Kai's twin sister, Puangi."

Son. Twin. Sister. I file the words in the back of my brain to ask about later.

"Call me Pua," Puangi says, and I realize I'm never going to remember all these names, nicknames, and foreign words, so I start slow.

"Pua," I say, looking at the girl who moves to sit next to me. She's close in age to Kai and myself. Her hair is dark and falls to just below her shoulders, her skin a light bronze. Like Kai, she's mature, and also like Kai, she bears a resemblance to Miri and Ara.

So. Weird.

"I think everyone's dying to know your name, though," Pua says with her forehead scrunched. She watches my lips, waiting for me to speak.

"Nine," I say. "My name is Nine."

Kai scoffs. "Of course it is."

"Kai!" Miri and Ara say at the same time.

Kai shrugs his shoulders. "What? It's not even a real name— it's a number."

Miri glances at Ara with one of her communicate-without-talking looks. He nods and pushes Kai toward the door. "Kai and I are gonna check the nets," he says, "and let you ladies have some peace."

"And so it begins," Kai mumbles on their way out.

"I apologize for him," Pua says, a little too loudly. "He can be a little . . . neurotic sometimes."

"A neurotic pain in my rear," Miri agrees.

I can't help but smile, but it feels foreign on my face, and I soon drop it.

"You've slept the day and night away, Nine," Miri says. "I hope you're feeling better."

If *better* means not as wasted physically as I had been the day before, then yes, I suppose I'm better. The improvement seems insignificant, though, considering I'll never fully recover from losing Theron.

Miri rubs her hand absentmindedly over her giant belly. "We sent Hemi to stay with his cousins for a bit while we . . . sort things out."

Pua leans over and explains, "Hemi's my little brother."

Cousins. Brother. Yeah, that doesn't explain anything. I exhale slowly. How many people do they have living in this cracked place?

Miri pats my knee. "We weren't sure if you'd have your voice back, so we arranged to have Pua spend the day with you. She's almost entirely deaf, you see, and can read lips."

Pua smiles at me, and I wonder what *deaf* means. Though I assume "read lips" means she can know what I'm saying by the way my lips move. It doesn't matter anymore, though, since my voice is back.

I'm not sure what they expect from me, or why I have to spend the day with Pua. "When can I return to Freedom?" I ask.

Miri inhales sharply and frowns. "We've been thinking about that, Nine." She grabs my hand and holds it in her own. "The thing is, we don't have any way of getting you there. No shuttle or boat. I'm afraid you're gonna have to stay with us for a while."

"But what about a transmitter?" I ask. "Isn't there a way to communicate? Let Freedom know where I am?"

"We don't have that kind of technology here."

"What?"

REMAKE

She must sense my panic because she turns my face toward her and looks into my eyes with serious intent. "Listen, Nine. This is going to be hard for you. Trust me, I know. And I'm sorry." She squeezes her eyes shut for a brief second before continuing. "Life is . . . different here. But my family—we'll take care of you. You can borrow Pua's clothes; we have plenty of food. We'll even set you up in your own room."

I shake my head. This is impossible. It has to be a joke. "You don't understand," I say. "I need to go back. I need to be Remade."

Miri squeezes my hand. "There will be ships. Steamships. They come to our island every few months. Our only option is to wait and see if we can get you passage to Freedom—or near it, at least—on one of them. Until then—"

"Months?" I can't wait months. *No no no.* I'm seventeen now. I need to be Remade as soon as possible so I can start my Trade training and move on with my life in Freedom. Not trapped here, in the middle of nowhere. I stand and turn to face them with my hands on my hips, then drop them because it feels too feminine. "But I don't have any suppression needles. If I can't get to the Remake facility, then I'm going to . . ." I tug at the tank top snug on my immature body.

Miri's eyes go wide as she realizes what I mean. "I'm so sorry, Nine. I don't know what else we can do."

By the time I get home to Freedom in a few—gasp—months, I'll be a fully developed female. This can't be happening. As hard as it was for me to make the decision, I *do* want to become male. I want to be like Theron—more now than ever.

Whatever sick joke the universe is playing on me right now, it's not funny.

I glance at Miri's frowning face and consider my options, then realize I don't have any. But hopefully, under these circumstances, Eri will still let me change. With the shuttle crash and being stranded and all. Surely I'll still have the opportunity to choose for myself. The Prime Maker owes me that much, I think, for her little experiment. I rub at the freckles along my arm and stand tall. If there's ever a time to prove myself, a time to be brave, this is it.

"Okay," I say. "I'll stay here with you until the ships come." I nod, trying to convince myself with each passing second. I've waited my entire life to be Remade, I can wait a few more months.

"Good for you," says Miri. "It'll be nice to have another daughter in the house—level the odds a bit."

Daughter.

Pua stands beside me. "I finally get a sister," she says. "It will be fun, I promise." Her face beams, and for a second it reminds me of the small woman outside my last academic module. Like she really is glad I'm here.

I offer her a weak smile.

"And I bet you're dying for a shower," she says.

Shower. Finally, a word I understand. "Yes," I say. "A shower would be wonderful."

I don't know if there are any showers on the island, but this is definitely not one of them. It's a hose running from the outside, through a window in the toilet room, looped around a hook so that water can pour out at approximately head level into a giant basin below. The water is cold, and I have to use a hard bar for soap instead of it coming through the wash cycle.

Once dry and dressed in what Pua calls jeans and a T-shirt, I admit I feel much better, though. The smell of sizzling food makes my stomach grumble, and I gratefully finish off two plates of onions, potatoes, bacon, and eggs at a table with Pua and Miri. The flavors send my taste buds to another galaxy, it's so unbelievably good. Not like the bland food in our Batch eatery. Theron would have loved this food—he would've loved just smelling this food.

I wipe the moisture from my eyes, stand, and carry my plate and utensils to a sink in what Pua tells me is their kitchen. Miri excuses herself for a nap, and Pua comes to stand by me.

"First thing you'll learn, Nine, is everyone has to work to contribute. Seeing as how you just washed ashore yesterday," she says with a smile, "no one expects you to do much for a couple of weeks. You can tag along with me and learn as I do my chores. When the baby comes, Mom will be out of commission, and your help will come in handy around here."

There's that *baby* word again. "I can wash dishes," I say, grateful for working extra dish hours in the eatery back in Freedom. I want to keep myself busy—my thoughts on things other than Theron and trying to get home. I look around for a dish machine but can't find one.

Pua hands me a sponge and another hard bar of soap.

"No dish machine?" I ask.

"No dish machine," she says with a sigh, watching my lips.

"No lights, no oven, no heat, no cinema, no nothing that involves tech."

I scrunch my brows together. "Why not?"

"Because anything that can be run with electrical power can be—" Pua gives me a sidelong glance. "We just don't use any kind of electrical energy here."

"In your home?"

"On the whole island."

Nothing Techies can detect. I wonder why not. I think of the tracker behind my ear, and my mouth goes dry.

"Not that I really miss any of those things," Pua continues. "I've never seen them. I wouldn't even know about them if my mom—" She bites her lip. "Here, just follow what I do. You'll get the hang of it." Pua rubs her sponge on the bar, dips it in a bucket of hot water, and shows me how to become the dish machine.

She doesn't trust me and is keeping something from me for some reason. Not that I blame her; I don't exactly trust them entirely either. But what choice do I have? At least Pua seems nice.

Actually, everyone seems nice except Kai. I wonder what his problem is. It's like he hates me just for the way I look. Again, nothing new, reminding me of certain people in my Batch. People who *were* in my Batch, that is. If anything, Kai's the one who looks like a freak with his dark skin and giant tattoo. I can imagine what others would say about him, if he were in my Batch. My spots would be forgotten in an instant.

After dish duty Pua leads me outside. "This is our homestead," she says with her arms out, spinning around.

"What's a homestead?" I ask, but she doesn't respond. I look around and see all that greenery again, in every direction. It's beautiful against the blue of the sky. Even the air smells amazing, sweet and fresh and moist all at the same time.

"We have our house," Pua says, pointing to the wood building we just came from. "It's in desperate need of a paint job, and Kai swears he's come up with a formula to make paint. My bet is we'll just have to cross our fingers and wait for the next steamship supply."

Pua walks down the black rock path I remember from the day before, and I follow her.

"This trail will take you down to the beach, where Dad and Kai found you."

I see the trail disappear into dense foliage. I shudder, thinking about the beach and ocean beyond. I have no plans to go farther down that path any time soon. Pua leads me back around the house, pointing out a well that provides fresh water and a pump that connects to it that somehow brings water into the house.

"Except the shower head is broken," she says, "and thus the makeshift hose through the window."

She shows me a fenced area with chickens, pigs, and a cow. I'd never been interested in becoming a Farmer. The animals in Freedom were kept in warehouses and connected to machines. They look so odd out here in the open.

"We keep a herd of sheep, up here." Pua leads me up a short hill. On the other side is a fenced-in pasture with about twenty sheep roaming lazily through the grass. And beyond that is sky. A bright blue that feels like it could swallow me whole just by the expansiveness of it. I've never seen such a clear blue before. It's a far cry from the gray-tinged hazy sky of Freedom. Theron would like this sky, I think.

From our vantage point on the hill, Pua points out a couple of things I hadn't noticed before. Tucked into the foliage near the path that leads to the ocean is a boat made of two long and thin hulls connected by what looks like a bridge between them that has a mast for sails. Pua calls it a double-hulled canoe and explains it is used for fishing, mostly, out on the ocean. Miri said they had no boats, but I guess this one doesn't count. It doesn't look like it'd be able to travel the distance to Freedom.

"We have a few banana trees," Pua says. "Mango, avocado, and lemon, too."

Also, just behind the house is a series of raised beds that make up their garden. Vegetables of all sorts crowd the boxes.

"That's where we'll work today," she says. "Weeding and harvesting green beans. Aren't you absolutely thrilled?"

Her sarcasm rubs off, and I can't help but smile.

It's hot, and my legs are starting to hurt from kneeling all morning, but I don't mind. The work keeps my mind busy, and it actually feels good to see buckets full of food I harvested myself. To feel like what I'm doing matters and will benefit more than just me.

"Where did you get Remade?" I ask Pua as I exchange a full basket for an empty one. With no tech on the island, I wonder if they were shipped somewhere else via steamship on their seventeenth birthdays. Or worse, didn't have the chance to be

REMAKE

Remade at all. Pua doesn't answer though she's right in front of me, pulling beans off the low plants. I don't think she's being rude; she's been nice enough the rest of the day. It's almost like she can't hear me.

I reach forward and nudge her shoulder.

She looks up and smiles. "Yes?"

Strange. "Where did you and Kai get Remade?" I ask again.

"We didn't."

"Doesn't anyone get Remade here?"

Pua laughs quietly. "No, they don't."

This place is a prison, I realize. Where people are expected to labor all day without the help of any tech. I wonder if they've been banished from Freedom for some crime or another. My heart beats a little faster, wondering what sort of people I've landed myself with.

"But what if you want to choose to be something else?" I ask, still unable to wrap my mind around the thought of not having a choice. Of not being equal or free.

"What we are is a gift," she says. "Our hair color, our skin, our family, our gender. Even our ability to see or touch or hear." Pua's eyes fall to her hands; she twists a green bean in her fingers. "They are all things to be grateful for, and we don't try to question *why* things are. We're just grateful that they are." She smiles a tiny grin. "I guess we trust that our first Maker knew what he was doing in the first place."

I wish I had that kind of faith in my own Makers. Maybe they knew what they were doing when they Made a red-haired, spotted girl, but they didn't bother telling me. And I doubt they saw this coming—the shuttle crash, the island. The current has shifted, and I'm left drifting, trying to figure everything out on my own.

I want to ask her what *family* means—Miri said that word earlier today as well—but before I have the chance, a piercing scream comes from the house that makes me drop my empty bucket and fall back on my rear.

"What is it?" Pua asks.

A second scream, louder and more desperate than the first, makes my skin crawl, and I cover my ears to block the sound.

Pua grabs my arm. "What's wrong, Nine? Are you okay?"

I press my hands harder against the sides of my head. "Can't you hear that?"

She shakes me and asks again, "What's wrong? What do you hear?"

A third time the scream comes, and I turn to the house. I feel the blood rush out of my face. It's Miri. "She's screaming," I say, lifting my arm to point.

Pua stands in an instant and sprints toward the house. I get up slowly and, summoning what little bravery I have, follow behind her. I stumble, realizing with equal horror that Pua didn't hear anything I said or the dreadful screaming.

Pua can't hear anything at all.

Chapter Ten

Nine?"

I follow Pua's voice through the kitchen and into a room at the back of the house. The room Miri had gone in for her nap. The house is dark, even though it's the middle of the day. I suppose it's because I've been out in the sun all morning, and the contrast is jarring.

When she sees me, Pua stands and runs to me. Her arms are streaked with blood, all the way to her elbows. I don't want to look behind her, but I can't help it. My eyes confirm it's Miri who's been screaming in pain, though she's silent at the moment. She lies in her bed. There's blood on her. And on the blankets beneath her.

I double over. It's just like that woman, back in Freedom, bleeding on the bed. Only here there are no men at Miri's bedside. Still, all that blood. This can't be good. This can't be good at all.

It takes me a minute to realize Pua is yelling at me. "You need to get Dad and Kai. *Please,* Nine. We need you."

I straighten and nod. "Okay."

"They're at the beach checking the nets," Pua says. "Follow the path to the beach like I showed you, and bring them quickly. I can't leave Mom right now. I need you to do this."

I turn and run out of the room. Out of the house. Grateful to be away from all that blood. I don't stop at the black rock trail, or when it leads into the foliage. Trying to be brave, I keep running and hope I find Ara and Kai as soon as possible. When I run onto the sand, I stop moving. I stop breathing. The water . . . it's wide and blue and never ending. The white water that churns at the shore is so violent, I wonder how I could've ever thought it beautiful that night on the roof of our Batch building. It's anything but beautiful. It's a churning death, the mouth of the ocean itself, the edge of Theron's grave. He's somewhere out there.

I can't breathe. I try to take in a breath but nothing comes.

"Nine?" It's Ara's voice.

I look to my left and see him walking up the shore, holding a mass of tangled rope on his shoulder. Kai is behind him, holding more rope. No—they are holding the same rope . . . a net, draped between the two of them.

Breathe, Nine. Breathe.

"Nine, what's wrong?" Ara asks. "What are you doing here? Where's Pua?"

There's a reason I came here. Something important. I stumble toward him and say the words that strangle me. "Come. To the house." It comes out soft and stifled. "Miriama. Something's wrong."

Ara's eyes go wide, and he drops the net in an instant, sprinting toward the homestead.

Kai comes to me. His eyes rest on my face for the first time since we met. "Your lips are blue. Are you okay?"

I think I'm hyperventilating. My breaths are short, and I feel light-headed. In fact, I think, I might . . .

My knees buckle, and I fall to the ground. Only I don't hit the ground. Kai catches me and lifts me. I don't have enough energy to tell him not to touch me. I don't want him to even look at me. But I just say, "Blood. There's a lot of blood."

Kai gulps and carries me back toward the trail. Once the ocean is out of sight, and I feel a bit more lucid, I take deep breaths and feel my lungs relax. Up close like this, I notice Kai's skin smells woody, like bark. But sweet, too. It reminds me of cinnamon. I tell him I'm fine now, and he can put me down. We both rush back to the house, though I'm afraid of what we'll see and hear when we enter through the mesh door.

Kai runs into Miri's room where I can see Ara and Pua moving purposefully around her through the doorway. "What's wrong?" Kai asks.

I hesitate in the kitchen and strain to hear their answer.

"She'll be fine," Ara says. "Baby's coming a little early, that's all."

"What can I do?" Kai asks.

Ara turns to Kai and sees me behind him, peeking around the kitchen wall. I cover my mouth, hoping I'll keep my breakfast in at the sight of all the blood.

"You can get Nine out of here," Ara says. "Puangi and I have this. It'll be okay, I promise."

Kai sighs heavily and turns to me with a look of contempt. "C'mon," he says, waving me back out of the house. We walk around to the shady side of the building, just under Miri's window. I slide to the ground like Kai and try to hear what's going on inside. Every minute or so Miri's screams spill out of the window, making me cringe every time.

"What's happening?" I ask Kai. "Is she dying?"

Kai rolls his eyes. "No, she's not dying. She's having a baby."

I'd much rather talk with someone else, anyone else, but since staying silent is torturing me, I risk having an actual conversation with him.

"What's a baby?" I ask.

"Geez, you're such a child, Nine. You know that?" Kai rubs his chin and sighs. "A baby is a new human. Brand new. Freshly Made."

"You mean an infant?" I've never heard the word *baby* before coming here. And though I've never seen one myself, I know what a new human is. "Is Miriama a Maker?" I ask.

"Not the way you think." Kai looks at me, his eyes running down my torso and arms, staring at my knees huddled up against my chest. "You're red."

It sounds like he said I'm "rid," and it takes me a minute to realize what he meant. I instinctively brush my scalp and feel the spiky growth there.

"No," he says. "Your skin is red. You're sunburned."

I look at my arms and legs, and sure enough there's a pink hue to them.

"Your face—" Kai reaches out his hand as though he will brush my cheeks, then drops it quickly. "You'll need to wear a hat and long sleeves when you're working outside from now on." His voice is calm. "We don't have any sunscreen, but Mom has some wide-brimmed hats you can borrow."

"The blood," I say. "Is that from the baby?" I know Ara and Kai both said Miri would be fine, but it's hard to believe after seeing all that blood, and I'm worried for her.

Kai watches me for a minute, as though deciding how much he wants to tell me. Or whether to trust me, which I know he doesn't. Much. He exhales and asks, "How are your Batches Made?"

I shrug my shoulders. "I only know that the Makers Make them. Ten boys and ten girls per Batch, every month."

"And you don't know how they do it?"

I shake my head. After seeing what happened in Sub level Two and to Miri inside the house, I'm not sure I want to know.

"I don't know how they do it in Freedom, but here, you need a male and a female, and after—" Kai pauses and his face turns red. "Man, I never thought I'd have to explain this before having my own kids."

I watch him with drawn brows. He must be embarrassed, with his flushed face and the way he won't look at me, but I've no idea why.

"A male and female get together," he says, his words coming out in a rush. "And in the course of making love—"

"Wait," I say, interrupting him. "Making love?"

He looks at me and rubs the back of his neck. "You don't know what that means?"

I shake my head.

"It's . . . um . . . you know." He raises an eyebrow.

"No," I say. "I really don't."

"Uh." He shifts uncomfortably. "Mating. Intercourse."

"You mean sex," I say. "I know what that is."

"Okay, good." Kai blows out a puff of air before continuing. "Well, in that process . . . you know—you know what? I think this is a bad idea. Maybe you should talk to my mom about it. Or Puangi."

A loud scream from the window above us makes me tense. After a minute of silence, I realize Kai isn't going to continue.

"I know about male and female anatomy. I'm not a complete idiot."

His eyes grow wide. "I never said you're an idiot."

"Yeah, but you thought it," I say. "You think it."

Kai narrows his eyes. "I just . . ." He pinches his lips together and doesn't finish.

I don't push him to explain why he hates me and instead shift the conversation back. "So the baby?"

"Um, yeah. Sperm fertilizes an egg within the female, and the baby grows inside of her. It's called pregnancy."

"A human being grows inside a woman?" I've never heard anything like that before, though it explains Miri's large stomach. I touch my hand to my belly. How strange and unnatural, to have something, a human something, growing inside of your body. "And it comes out when it's ready?"

"Basically," he says. "About nine months later. And you've got your brand-new person."

I shake my head. "That can't be right. I've never seen anything like Miri's stomach before in Freedom. Not once."

Kai smirks. "That's because they do something to prevent you from reproducing in Freedom. They alter you when you are first Made, or maybe when you're Remade, I'm not sure. All I know is they take away your ability to have babies so they can control who and what is Made and when."

This whole concept is strange. It takes a male and a female to Make an infant? A baby? Maybe Kai is lying to keep me from knowing what's really going on with Miri. It's no secret he doesn't want me here. Why would he tell me the truth? Everything about it is crazy.

Then why, deep down, do I feel like a pair of hands I hadn't realized were covering my eyes have fallen away? Why does my world look ten times clearer? Maybe the reason I thought there's more to being male and female is because there *is* a reason. A really huge reason. But if that's true, why would Freedom keep it from us?

"What male got Miri pregnant?" I ask.

"My dad, of course." Kai's eyes narrow in anger. "Who else would it be?"

Well, you live here, I think. And then there's this Hemi male, the one Miri sent to stay with cousins, whatever those were. Couldn't it have been either of them? I don't dare ask, though, based on the evil glare Kai gives me. I think about the way Ara looks at and treats Miri, like she's the most important thing in the world. How could he do this to her? She's obviously in a lot of pain. And then I remember something else Ara had said.

"This isn't the first time, is it?" I ask.

"What do you mean?"

"This isn't her first baby. It's her fourth?"

Kai's eyebrows rise in surprise, and he gives me a sad smile. "Me," he says, holding up one finger. "Pua," he says, holding up a second. "And Hemi." He holds up a third. "Miriama and Arapeta are our parents, our Makers. We call them Mother and Father. Or Mom and Dad. The three of us, soon to be four, are their children."

"Does Miri only have sex with Ara, then? And no one else?" I ask. And before Kai can answer, I sit up tall, excited about something else I just realized. "And is that why you all look alike?" If they are Made this way by Ara and Miri, it makes sense that they would inherit traits from each . . . *parent*.

He smirks. "Yes, that's why we look alike. And yes, my parents only . . . with each other."

"And is this what you will do, then? Have sex and make babies with just one female?"

"I . . . yes. I suppose."

"With Pua, maybe?"

"Yikes, no."

"Why not?" She's a beautiful female. I'm certain males with mature hormones feel attracted to her.

"Because she's my sister." Kai shivers.

I sigh heavily. "What is sister?"

"Puangi and I, we have the same parents. That makes us siblings. I call her my sister, because she is female. She calls me brother, because I am male. And Hemi is our brother."

"And you cannot have sex with a sister?"

"No. Definitely not."

How odd to have rules about who you're allowed to have sex with. I've never heard anything like it before in Freedom. Along with everything else we do, if we aren't infringing on another's free will, we can do whatever we want with whomever we want.

"Why did Miri call Pua your *twin* sister?"

"Because we were born at the same time. Two babies at once."

I have a hard enough time thinking about one baby coming out of Miri. But two? It's so weird. "Who came up with all of these names? It's very confusing. Brother, sibling, mother. I can't keep them straight in my head. Your ways are so strange."

"And hormone suppression. Shaving your head. Those are not strange?"

I shrug my shoulders. "It keeps us equal until we are ready to choose what we want to be."

Kai narrows his eyes. "I can't imagine living without a family in such a forsaken place."

"Family?"

"Mom. Dad. Children. All of us together, we are a family."

He knows exactly where he belongs in this world, and I'm sure the rest of his family does too. They are not an experiment.

I lean forward. "Does everyone live this way here, on the island I mean? As families?"

"For the most part. And don't get me started on grandparents, in-laws, and cousins."

I open my mouth to ask about those, but Kai stops me.

"Seriously, I think that's enough for one day," he says with a smirk, standing up. "Stay here, and don't move."

"Where would I go? I'm stranded on an island."

Kai frowns. "I'll be right back." He turns the corner and leaves me alone to absorb all of this new information.

Instead of suppressing my curiosity about this new place and peculiar people, Kai's explanations have made me more curious. There are other words I want to know, like *daughter, son,* and *deaf.* And why is it Pua can't hear anything? Did she have some sort of accident? Was she Made that way? And do they have Fosterers to care for them when they're young, or is that what parents do?

It seems like Miri and Ara take on the Trades of Fosterer, Healer, Farmer, Maker, Cook, Teacher, and almost anything else there is to do. It's a lot of responsibility. Why would someone want to do so much when the work could be spread out over many, making it much more efficient? I wonder how much of it has to do with that *family* word they keep mentioning.

"Nine," a voice whispers through the window above me. I look up to see Pua leaning her head against a mesh screen like the one on the front door. "C'mon in, it's all right."

I stand and walk slowly around the house, realizing the screaming has stopped. And when I enter through the door, I hear laughing and bubbling conversation.

"Come in, Nine." The voice is Miriama's. And she sounds . . . happy.

I walk slowly through the kitchen and peek around the corner, preparing myself for the onslaught of blood. Miri is still in bed, but heavy blankets cover her body. Her hair is soaked with sweat, and Pua stands behind her, pulling it back into a braid. Ara nods at me with a smile, so I dare to step closer. I come to stand by Kai on the right side of the room, by the window, and that's when I see it. A bundle of blankets surround the tiniest of bodies that lies in the crook of Miri's arm. A little brown face with a bald head peeks out from the fabric. Its eyes are closed and its face is wrinkled. It looks so peaceful. Is this the thing that caused so much anguish just minutes ago?

"It's a boy," Miri says, looking up at me. "We named him Tama."

Named him? I figured they'd call him Four until he chose his own name. I look at Pua and Kai. Were they named, too, and did not choose for themselves? I want to think it's unfair, having such freedom taken from them. But is it unfair, really? From the day they were Made, they had someone telling them who they were. You are Tama, and you are male. You are a sibling, a brother. You are my child. And this is your—what do they call it?—*family*.

He won't have to decide on a name, a gender, or how he wants to look. He'll be able to accept it without doubt. I look around at the people surrounding this baby. They are happy and calm and . . . full of love. And for the first time since washing up on these strange shores, I'm not angry, sad, afraid, or confused.

I'm jealous.

Chapter Eleven

I venture down the trail to the beach, past the black rock and onto green grass, daring myself to go farther than I did the day before. The ratio of sand to grass at my feet increases with each step, and I know I'm getting very close, but the dense foliage around me masks any view of the ocean beyond. I turn a corner and see it, a long stretch of sand ahead. Squinting, I try to spot something on the sand, anything. A shoe, a piece of the shuttle. A body. Any evidence of Theron. But there is nothing.

A few more steps, and the blue of the water finds its way to the corner of my vision. I force my eyes down, but it doesn't help. Panic has taken over. A gust of wind blows over my nearly bald head, bringing with it the sharp smell of salt, and I step backwards. The breeze soothes the sting of my sunburned skin but does nothing to appease my fear.

Defeated, I retreat to the homestead and climb into what

Pua tells me is a hammock, tucked into the greenery near the giant canoe. It's dusk now, and the air is getting cooler by the minute.

Nibbling at a piece of fried bread I saved from dinner, I watch people come and go from the house. They're here to visit the new baby born a few days ago and to congratulate Miri and her family. I've had enough new things to last me a while and decide being alone might be better than trying to learn a million new names, nicknames, and titles of extended family and friends.

I close my eyes and continue to swing, listening to the faint sound of waves lapping on the sand in the distance. I've grown used to it, I think, the sound of the ocean. I wonder how long it will be until the sight of it doesn't overwhelm me with terror.

"Where's your hair?" a small voice whispers at my ear.

I open my eyes and see . . . a child. I try to scramble backward on the hammock, but it swings, threatening to dump me over the side. I move back to the center to avoid falling off. I've never seen a child before, at least not since I was one. They're just smaller versions of adults—I know this. But it doesn't prepare me for the oddity of seeing one out in the open instead of inside a Batch tower.

"Are you sick?" he asks, touching my head. His hands are small and sticky and feel peculiar on my skin. "Don't worry," he says with a pat of his hand. "It's growing back nicely."

He crawls into the hammock with me, and I shift to give him room. He's not shy, that's for sure.

"I'm Hemi," he says, pointing to his chest.

"Hemi," I whisper. He's the one Miri sent away for a few

days. I can't help but smile. He looks like a mini version of Kai with dark curls that fall into his face and big, light brown eyes.

"Are you the one?" he whispers. "The one Daddy found at the beach?" His sentences rise up at the end like the rest of his family, but from Hemi, it doesn't sound foreign at all. It fits him.

I nod. "I'm Nine."

He grins from ear to ear. "You came from the sea. Are you a mermaid?"

"Mermaid?"

"Yeah. Mermaids are half fish, half girl. They have a fish tail, but when they come on land it turns into legs."

I shake my head.

"You're too nice to be a mermaid anyway. In some stories they're mean creatures. You don't look mean." Hemi touches my nose. "Your skin is peeling. I don't think mermaids can get sunburned."

"I am definitely not a mermaid, then."

Hemi smiles, and it's contagious.

"How old are you, Hemi?"

"Seven. But I'll be eight in just three months." I like how he's so sure of himself, comfortable in his own skin. It's as though he's exactly who he'd always intended to be.

"And you're a big brother now, no?"

Hemi beams. "Yes. Mom says I need to be a big boy. That's why I'm moving into Kai's room tonight."

Tonight? He's come home to stay, then. I admit, I'm glad. Hemi's little smile helps me relax. Looking into his face, it's as though there's nothing frightening in the world at just this moment. I could get used to this feeling.

114

"Hemi!" Kai calls from the front of the house. He glares at me, and I have the distinct feeling he doesn't approve of me interacting with his younger brother. Just like he glares at me when I wake, glares at me when I'm in the kitchen—or in the garden, or by the water well, or . . . in the hammock. Glares at me when I breathe.

"See you later, Nine." Hemi jumps off and runs to the house.

Kai waits to make sure he gets there before they both enter the building. Not without a fierce look at me first, though. When they're gone, I try to mimic Kai's look—my nose and eyes scrunch together, my shoulders press back and my chest juts out, daring anyone to mess with me. It takes a lot of effort to be so sour, and it kind of hurts my back. I laugh and drop the threatening stance. I think of Theron and wonder if males are prone to violence as a whole.

I'm not the only one fortunate to be on the receiving end of Kai's pleasant manner. He gets angry whenever anyone starts to tell me something he doesn't think I should know. Or if I go missing for more than thirty seconds. Or if Miri asks if I want to hold the baby. It's like I've been sent by his worst enemy to tear his world apart, piece by piece. I don't understand his animosity or what I did or didn't do to deserve it. I thought after our conversation outside Miri's room he would at least start treating me like a human, but no such luck. I plan to avoid him as much as possible. At least as much as one can avoid someone they are forced to live, eat, and work with.

I sigh and sink back down into the hammock. The sky is growing dark. Slowly, one by one, the stars begin to appear. It's a clear night with no clouds, and I realize it's the first time I've

115

been out at night since arriving five days ago. The stars continue to pierce the black, and with a gasp I realize Theron was right. There are thousands of stars here in the middle of the ocean, away from electric lights. I try to pick out patterns in the lights, but there are so many, it's overwhelming. I wonder if Theron is up there, somewhere among them, looking down at me.

"I miss you," I tell the night. I inhale and can almost smell him, the scent of his skin next to mine. Feel the beat of his heart with my head on his chest. Hear the familiar snore-breath-whistle that used to lull me to sleep. "I miss you so much." I wipe at my face and sit up on the hammock. I look toward the house and gasp, holding my hand to my chest to calm my racing heart. Kai is there, not ten feet away from me.

His eyes widen, and he looks at his shuffling feet. "Sorry. I didn't mean to scare you." He hesitates, looks at me with drawn brows, then turns to head back to the house. "My mom asked me to get you," he says as he leaves. "Everyone's gone now."

I watch him walk into the house before I finally stand and follow.

"We've set you up in Hemi's old room." Miri fluffs a pillow at the head of a bed covered in blue and yellow sheets. An old quilt sits folded at the foot end.

"I'm fine on the couch," I say.

"Don't be ridiculous. This is your home now . . . for as long as you like." Miri pulls a black shade over the window on the far side of the room. They do the same thing to all the windows at night, though I've no idea why.

She catches me staring. "It's safer this way."

That explains nothing, only makes me afraid of what they're trying to hide from.

"If you want to open it while you sleep, you can. Just make sure the light's out before you do." She points to a lantern on a corner table. "Hemi's in Kai's room, across the hall. And though the baby's still with me, once he's sleeping through the night he'll move in with Pua."

I look around the room and smile. It does remind me of Hemi, and I'm glad of it, though I feel bad for kicking him out. On one side there are boxes stacked in no particular pattern, each overflowing with balls, toys, books . . . things I remember having loved once, as a child.

"We'll get his stuff moved over soon."

"No, don't." I smile at Miri. "I like it full like this. It will feel so empty with it gone."

"Okay," she says, coming to stand by me and putting her hand on my shoulder. "We'll leave it for now. But maybe one day you might want to put things you've collected in here."

I nod, but knowing I'll be leaving in a few months, I won't bother. All I have right now is a trunk full of clothes from Pua and my blue cushion. I smile to see it propped beside my bed.

Looking across the room to the other wall, I see it's covered in paint, a mural of the ocean. There's an island with trees and mountains on one end that meets up with the saltwater. The scene is painted so I can see under the water to the creatures that lie beneath. A few are familiar. A crab crawls along the bottom of the ocean among drifting greenery and coral. Striped fish, bloated fish, stick fish, fish from every corner of one's imagination, swim through the water. A half human, half fish with long flowing hair swims above a reef—a mermaid. I smile at a sea turtle floating in the blue, then touch the graceful form of an animal I do not know.

"It's a dolphin," Miri says. "They're extinct now, but my father-in-law still tells the story of one he saw as a little boy, just outside the reef. It's beautiful, isn't it?"

"It's all beautiful," I say.

"Kai painted it for Hemi a couple of years ago." Miri smiles, studying the mural. "Kai was so excited when he traded for a new set of paints during a steamship visit. He spent two whole weeks in here, all day, painting the scene."

My hand glides along the wall to the picture of a canoe, an exact replica of the one that sits outside. Beneath it, a creature with eight long and twisted legs floats next to a swarm of jellyfish. The mural ends on the right side with a giant creature breaching the surface of the water. Its mouth is full of what seem like a thousand small and sharp teeth.

I pull my hand to my chest and scream. Shaking my head, I stumble backward and into the bed. I slide off the edge of it, hit the floor, and scream again.

On the other side of the house, I hear the baby start to cry. Ara and Kai rush in my room to see what's wrong. I can see Pua holding Hemi to her just outside the door.

"Nine?" Miri asks. "What's wrong?"

"Monster." I say it in a gasp and point to the creature on the wall.

"The shark?" Ara raises his eyebrows in confusion.

"Shark," I whisper and bring my hands to my mouth,

trying to stop myself from screaming again, but it still comes out, muffled and painful. My shoulders begin to tremble, and my arms shake uncontrollably.

Miri gasps. "You've seen this animal, haven't you? Did you see a shark, Nine, when you were in the water after the crash?"

My hands move from my mouth to my stomach. I clamber to my feet and stumble to the bathroom, heaving over the toilet. *Oh, Theron.* I'm a mess, and I can't stop shaking. I run the water at the washbasin, rinsing my mouth and face and letting the cold of it numb me.

After a while, I walk into the family room and collapse on the couch next to Miri. She holds Tama to her breast, a sight I've grown used to these last days. Her milk calms him, and I apologize for my behavior, for disturbing the baby.

"Don't be sorry, Nine." Miri's eyes are sad. "It's not your fault. None of this is your fault, do you understand?"

I nod, somehow knowing she's not just talking about waking the baby. It's not my fault the shuttle crashed. It's not my fault the shark took Theron and not me. That I'm the one that got away. It's not my fault Kai hates me so much. I want to believe her, but what if it *is* my fault? Not the crash, but everything else. Maybe there was something I could've said or done to appease Kai's disappointment in me. Maybe I should have swum toward Theron, not away. Maybe if I weren't such a coward, I would be with him right now. Brave in death, and not running away from it like a child. Like the child Kai believes me to be. I don't know how to make it right, because with Theron gone and me here, away from Freedom, things can never be right again.

"Kai is taking care of the shark as we speak. You won't have to see it again." Miri stands and takes Tama to his crib—the baby bed with bars on the sides so he cannot escape. Only for him it's not a prison, it's protection. I don't know if I'll ever feel that way here, protected as opposed to imprisoned, at least not if Kai has anything to say about it.

Miri returns to the room with a large blue sphere in her hands. "Careful," she says as she sits next to me. "It's very old." She hands me the sphere, and I hold it carefully.

"It's a globe," I say. I turn it around and see the familiar land masses and bodies of water that make up our Earth. The features are familiar, but the names are not.

"Here is Freedom One." Miri points to the southeastern coast of the smallest continent. Except it doesn't say Freedom One. It's labeled SYDNEY instead.

I remember the day I sat in the Prime Maker's office and watched her run her finger across the ocean to the Remake continent. I mimic her motion and draw the path of our shuttle, the intended path of our shuttle, if it had completed its course.

Miri points to a pair of long islands off the coast of Freedom, then a smaller one just east. "This is where we are." MAHAWAI.

I don't remember its name from the maps I studied in my academic modules, probably because there's no Freedom province here.

I crawl my fingers from Mahawai to Sydney. "It's not very far," I say. On this map, in fact, it seems very close indeed. Could it really be that difficult to get me there? Compared to the distance between Sydney and the Remake continent—the

United States, according to this dated globe—it seems like a short skip across the water.

"I know it looks close, but the ocean is a big place." Miri sighs. "And even with the steamships that cross the seas, it could take weeks to get there."

"But it *can* get there," I say, confident my trip home will not be as difficult as I had thought.

Kai comes out of Hemi's room, *my room*. "What are you doing?" He holds a bucket of light blue liquid and a bristled brush that drips some of the blue into the bucket. His face is red and twisted.

"How did your homemade paint work on the shark, son?" Miri stands and walks toward the bedroom.

Kai puts his bucket and brush on the floor, then snatches the globe out of my hands with a scowl. "Might as well paint a target right on us, Mom."

Miri ignores his snipe. "Oh, Kai," she says with a frown, looking into the bedroom.

Kai tucks the sphere under his arm and glances at his mother. "Doesn't matter." He storms out of the room, and I'm left wondering, again, what I did to upset him so much.

"Will you be okay, Nine?" Miri asks, walking to her own room.

"I'll be fine, thanks."

She nods and shuts the door behind her. I could've sworn I saw her brush a tear from her face.

I walk to my new room, afraid to be alone again. I consider calling for Miri, telling her *no, I'm not okay*. I haven't been here long, but already I crave the comfort her words give me. She has a way of putting me at ease the way no one else can. I can't explain it. I bite my lip and push my shoulders back, entering the room, sloughing off my cowardice.

"Oh, Kai," I say, echoing Miriama's words. The shark on the wall is gone all right, along with the rest of the mural. The wall is now a solid light blue color, all evidence of Kai's masterpiece only a memory now.

I don't want to disappoint everyone all the time, even Kai. But I can't seem to help it, can I?

I drag the bed to the far window and push it against the wall there. After blowing out the lantern at the bedside table, I raise the shade and lie down to look at the thousands of stars outside. I try to count them one by one, wondering each time, if that one is Theron. And wondering, each time, if he is searching for me too.

Chapter Twelve

Whenever my name comes out of Kai's mouth, it sounds like he's trying to spit out poison. I've been here for five weeks, and it sounds the same every time.

"But Nine is not a part of this family," he snaps at Ara. "Don't you get it? I don't even want her here, and now I have to be her babysitter?"

From my spot on the couch, I watch Ara pack a bag on the kitchen table. He's going hunting for a couple of weeks on the islands just west of us with his father and two brothers. I'm not thrilled with Ara's proposal either, but I'm decent enough not to bite at him for suggesting it. It's such a strange combination, the fighting that members of the family endure which doesn't seem to affect the way they care for each other. I can't imagine caring for Cree or Bristol the same way.

"Quit talking about Nine like she's not in the room," Ara

says. His voice sounds so similar to Kai's. The way his phrases turn up at the end and how he extends his vowels. I wonder how one can feel like a cool hand on my humid skin and the other like a sunburn that refuses to heal.

"I don't care if she hears me." Kai glares at me from the kitchen. "This isn't fair."

"Listen, Kai. While I'm gone, your mother's gonna need Pua to help with the baby and Hemi. Nine's been shadowing your sister long enough. I think she's learned everything she can about gardening, cleaning, and cooking. And we've all learned never to let her in the kitchen ever again." Ara turns to me and smiles to take the sting from his words.

My face reddens, but I smile at the suffering the family has had to endure from my cooking disasters.

"It's time you teach her about your work too." Ara throws his bag over his shoulder and smacks Kai on the back of his head. "And don't be a jerk about it." He leans in and presses noses with his son, breathing in each other's breath.

Kai mumbles something to him about being careful.

"I will. I love you." Ara turns to me and waves. "See ya, Nine. Don't let him kill you while no one's looking."

"Bye," I say, waving back. I scowl at Kai. It'd be funny, what Ara said about Kai killing me, if half of me wasn't afraid of that very thing. I sigh and wait for Kai to storm out of the house before grabbing my large straw hat and falling in step behind him.

I cross my arms and try to ignore the soreness in my breasts. They've grown significantly these last few weeks—evidence that the suppressant is wearing off. Every day that passes means

I'm one day closer to getting off this island, one day closer to heading home and being Remade. But with these changes in my body, it feels more like I'm moving farther away from Freedom. From becoming male. A panic grows inside me knowing I won't be able to hide the fact that I'm female much longer.

Kai heads for the beach, like I knew he would, and I lengthen my stride to match his, determined to take on whatever he decides to throw at me.

We walk through the path of foliage and emerge on the other side onto sand. The sight of the ocean doesn't frighten me like it once did, though I haven't gone in the water since I've been here. I follow Kai down the shore, avoiding the tiny blue jellyfish that scatter along the beach, brought in by the morning tide. The beach ends at a series of black rocks that jut out into the sea.

Kai walks into the water to a floating red buoy twenty feet in. He turns to me and yells, "Don't just stand there, come and hold this end while I swim around."

Is he serious? I step back and shake my head.

"I can't do this by myself, Nine. Get over here."

I grasp my hands together behind my back. I'm not getting in the water.

Kai curses and walks out of the water toward me. He must see the fear in my eyes because his face softens just a little before he says, "See the white water out there?" He points to a line of white waves in the distance. "That's the edge of the reef. Between here and there, it's too shallow for sharks to swim. Do you understand?"

I peek at him from under the shade of my hat but don't say anything.

"Sharks can't get past that white water. You're safe here." He presses his lips together and looks me up and down, hesitating. "You can do this," he whispers. He walks back into the water to the red buoy and waits for me without glancing back.

The water barely comes to his waist, and I decide if this is what it takes to prove to him I'm not completely worthless, I'll do it. I take a deep breath and walk into the water. It's colder than I thought it would be, and I panic as my feet begin to sink into the wet sand. I keep moving forward anyway. When I reach him, I can't help but grasp his arm for balance.

Kai peels my hands off him and puts them on the red buoy. "Just hold on, and don't let go."

I nod and watch him swim farther out to another buoy thirty feet away. As he pulls it inland, kicking his feet behind him in the deeper water, I realize the buoys are connected to a net that lies beneath. I wonder how long it's been out here. The net rises as Kai continues swimming to shore. I try to stand still, but the waves move in and out and throw off my balance. My feet are pulled out from underneath me and away from the beach.

Don't let go, I tell myself. The water comes to my neck when I finally manage to plant my feet.

"Bring it in," Kai calls.

I try to walk toward the beach with the buoy in my hands, but a wave comes up from behind and washes over my head. I swallow salt water and panic, frantically kicking but sinking. *Don't let go,* Kai said. I don't let go and try to stand again, knowing it can't be that deep where I am—I had been standing a few seconds ago—but I don't feel anything solid and let go of the buoy, flailing my arms in a panic.

Opening my eyes under the water, I can't tell which way is up or down. My hand hits sand, and I try to push the other way, but another wave washes over, and I'm twisted all over again. Just when I don't think I can hold my breath any longer, something grabs me around the waist and lifts me out of the water. Kai drags me to the sand and collapses next to me. I cough out water and bring my hand to my nose. It burns, and I realize I must have inhaled salt water.

"What happened?" Kai asks.

"A wave came, and I . . . I couldn't touch the bottom anymore." My throat feels raw from the salt.

Kai appraises me. "Can't you swim?"

I shake my head.

"But your plane crashed," he says. "And you survived. How did you do that if you don't know how to swim?"

I think of Theron and the effort he went through to save my life. The forethought of a flotation device, pushing us away from the sinking shuttle, making sure Bristol didn't drown me, telling me to kick away from him. Forever away.

I look up at Kai and shrug. "I had the cushion and I just kicked."

"You just kicked, eh?" Kai laughs and shakes his head. He stares at me for a minute as though thinking something through. The open space between us seems to shift, like the air molecules are no longer stretched in a taut line that could snap at any moment. The air still feels tight, but if I could press against it, I think it would give. Bend.

Kai bites his lower lip and looks out to the water. My hat floats in the shallows, and he stands to retrieve it. He puts the dripping hat on his own head and turns to me with a sigh. "Well, like it or not, Nine, you live on an island now. And no one lives on an island without knowing how to swim." He walks into the water and waves me in. "C'mon."

I really don't want to go back in, and I lower my head.

"You're not gonna make me drag you in, are you? Let's go."

I rub my neck and walk into the water until it hits my knees. Kai grabs my hand and leads me toward him, where the water comes to his waist.

"I won't let go of you," he says. "I promise."

His eyes narrow but under the dripping hat they are warm. I decide to trust him, but hang on to his arms as though my life depends on it, which in this case, I suppose it does.

"So you can kick, huh?"

I exhale and nod.

"Pretend my arm is the cushion and show me." He holds out his arm, and I grasp it hard, slowly lowering myself into the water, extending my legs behind me. I kick slowly at first, then stronger, remembering the ferocity of the action from weeks ago.

"Whoa," he says. "Kick from your hips, here." He moves my leg up and down from my upper thigh. "Good. Keep your legs straight. You don't have to make a huge splash. Try to get your feet to barely break the surface of the water with each kick."

I do as he says and feel my body relax.

"Yes. Just like that." Kai glides his arm in a circle so I kick around him. After a few minutes, he has me stand in the water and mimic his arms, bringing them up out of the water in an arc, and back around again and again, alternating left and right.

"Okay." Kai grabs my waist. "I'm going to hold you here, at your middle, and have you go around me again. But this time I want you to use your arms *and* legs. Ready?"

I nod and let him lift my feet off the sandy bottom. He ducks low in the water and pulls me close against him, his arm wrapping around my waist. I try to move my arms and legs like he showed me, but my limbs feel like they're just flailing in desperation. When I splash water into my mouth and feel my head sink, I panic and grab hold of him, wrapping my arms and legs around him so tight I knock the hat off his head, and he complains that he can't breathe. I loosen my arms around his neck, just a little, and he sighs and carries me back to shore. Sitting me down on the sand, he puts the hat back on my head.

"It's okay. We'll practice a little every day." He pulls his wet T-shirt over his head and shakes his curly hair to get rid of what water he can. "Your heavy clothes don't help, either. Tomorrow, wear a swimsuit."

"But I'll burn."

"I'll find you a rash guard to protect your shoulders. You'll be fine. Stay here, I'll be back in a minute."

I watch him jog down the beach and enter the trail back to the house. He returns after a few minutes holding a thick, bright orange vest with black straps.

"Don't worry, Nine. You'll be a fish in water in no time. Until then you can wear this." He slides the vest over my head and straps it tight across my chest and waist.

I try to ignore the tenderness in my breasts. "What is it?"

"It's a life vest," he says, smiling. "Like your blue cushion, only your hands will be free to help me pull in the nets."

It's a relief to see him smile at me for once. Anything's better than his standard scowl, but it makes me wonder what changed and if it will last. I'm not sure how I feel about this shift.

We spend the rest of the morning gathering three different nets from the water. After tossing fish and crabs into a bucket, we set the net in the water again for the next day's catch.

With a full bucket, we return to the homestead, where Kai shows me how to slice and gut the fish. We put them in a large pot with holes along the bottom and then suspended them from a rack. Kai starts a fire underneath, adding water every so often to create smoke that rises up into the pot. He tells me it helps preserve the fish. We toss the crabs, which are still alive, into a tank under the house until dinner.

After lunch, I watch Kai climb a tree and toss down several golden brown coconuts. We carry them into the shade of the giant mango tree on their property. He picks up a tool with a long wooden handle and a double-pronged top. One side of the metal head ends in a sharp point, the other in a flat blade. Kai calls it a pickax. Bringing it high above his head, he sends the flat end into the ground with force, leaving the sharpened point sticking up in the air.

Grabbing a coconut, he brings it down onto the pointed tool and twists the fruit so that an entire chunk of the husk peels away from the hard shell beneath. He rams the coconut onto the point a few more times, each time twisting off the husk until the bulk of it has fallen to the ground. After picking off a few loose strands, he holds the hard shell up to me and points to one end.

"Two eyes and a mouth," he says, pointing to three dots on the shell. He pulls something out of his pocket, a flat stone with a sharp tip. "You want to hit it between the eyes."

He knocks the coconut with the stone, and it splits into two perfect halves. He offers half to me, and I drink greedily, already addicted to the taste of coconut water from my weeks on the island. He pries off a piece of coconut flesh and gives it to me, then chews on a piece himself. He tosses the rest into a bucket, ready to be taken into the house. There the white meat will be grated off the shell and wrung to harvest coconut milk.

Kai bends down, picks up another coconut and hands it to me with a nod. Then he sits against the trunk where he can see me, nibbling on his coconut piece.

I shake the coconut and hear water sloshing around inside. I bring it high above my head and then down onto the pickax. The fruit bounces off and flops to the ground.

Kai snickers from his resting spot. I glare at him and pick it up again, determined to get it right this time. I gather all the energy I have and ram the coconut into the sharpened point. The fruit doesn't fall, but sticks in the metal. Not very far, though. I press down, jumping up and putting all of my weight into it. Nothing.

I don't look up, but I hear Kai give an exaggerated sigh. I despise the reminder that I'm weak. If I'd already been Remade, I'd be stronger, like Kai. I'd be male. It's not fair for him to expect me to do something that comes so naturally to him.

Cursing, I lean my body into the coconut, pressing with my

arms and chest. The coconut slips off, and the pickax slices me inside my upper right arm. I gasp and pull away, revealing a long gash from my armpit to my elbow. Blood gushes all over me.

"Holy—" Kai jumps up and tears off his shirt. "This is deep, hang on." He wraps it around my arm and struggles to cinch it tight.

"But it doesn't even hurt." Streaks of blood move down my arm from beneath his makeshift bandage to my hand. I watch as drops fall to the ground from the tips of my fingers. "I can't feel anything."

Kai gulps. "Nine, I . . ." His eyes go wide as the cloth on my arm soaks through with blood. "Come on." He hustles me to the house, and we plow through the mesh door.

"Mom!" He pulls me to the kitchen table and lays me on top.

"What is it?" Miriama walks into the room, takes one look at me, soaked in blood, and heads straight for the bathroom to throw up.

"Really?" Kai runs his hand through his hair and wrinkles his forehead at me, unsure what to do. I don't think it's a good time to tell him there's blood on his face and hair now, in addition to the streaks across his bare torso.

Puangi walks in with the baby in her arms.

"Pua, help." Kai puts pressure on my arm and holds it over my head.

When she sees the state I'm in, she looks desperately at Kai. "But Grandpa Rongo isn't here."

"I know."

Grandpa Rongo is Ara's father and is trained as a Healer.

132

But he left this morning to hunt on the western islands with Ara and his other sons.

"Get me some water," Kai tells Pua.

She nods and hands Tama to his mother, who has come out of the bathroom with a stack of fresh towels and a glass bottle of clear liquid. Pua turns on the kitchen sink and fills a large bowl with cold water.

"What happened?" Miri asks, keeping a distance.

"The pickax," Kai says through gritted teeth. I can't tell if he's mad at me for being so clumsy, or at himself for letting it happen.

"What were you doing? Trying to hack her to death?" Miri asks.

I let out a laugh, and Kai's face relaxes.

He gives me a crooked smile. "Yes. But only because my attempt at drowning her this morning failed miserably."

I can't help but smile at the irony.

Pua brings over the water and soaks a towel in it. She wipes it along my raised arm.

I can feel the wretched wound now. I hiss at the pain and Miri gasps, leaving the room.

"It's not so bad," Pua says, pouring the clear liquid Miri brought over the gash.

Bubbles form along the cut, and it stings tremendously. I squeeze my eyes shut and try to push through the pain. It's gone in under a minute, and I open my eyes to see Kai with his arms folded, staring at me, shifting his weight from foot to foot.

"She's going to need stitches, though," Pua says.

"What are stitches?" I ask.

133

Pua frowns at me but doesn't answer my question. She looks at Kai and shakes her head. "I can't do it," she says with a gulp.

Kai curses under his breath. "Find me a needle, Pua." He moves to the sink and washes his hands with soap.

"Needle?" I ask. I don't know why he needs a needle, but I'm sure *I* don't need a needle. "What's the needle for?" I sit up and wait for him to answer, but he doesn't. I glance at my arm and try to ignore the logical place in my brain that knows what's going to happen next.

Pua comes back into the room holding a small needle in her hand with a match to the tip. She cuts off a length of string and threads it. She gives it to Kai and takes a step back from the table.

Kai examines the cut.

"What's the needle for?" I ask again, desperation lacing my words.

"The cut is too deep," Kai says. He climbs onto the table with me, facing the opposite way. He lays my arm in his lap and ties a knot in the string.

"It's not too deep," I say, shaking my head. "It'll be fine. It doesn't even hurt anymore. Really." I start to pull away, planning to dismount the table on the other side, but Pua is there, climbing onto the table with us. They look at each other as though agreeing on something without speaking aloud. It must be a twin thing, and for a brief moment I wonder how much weight this table will hold.

Kai rubs a towel across his forehead, wiping away the sweat that has built up. "It's going to hurt," he says, looking at me. "A lot."

I feel like a fool, throwing a tantrum over a tiny needle after being mauled by a pickax, but I am genuinely terrified. "I can't do needles."

"Yes, you can, Nine." Kai's face is firm, determined. "You've done a lot of hard things. You can do this, too."

I recognize the resolve in his face, and I know he means it. He thinks I can do it. For some reason, I don't want to let him down. A male wouldn't cower in fear, would he? I give a slight nod.

He holds my arm tight and presses the needle into my skin just above my elbow.

I cry out. "AH!"

Pua puts her hand on my face and moves it so I'm looking at her. She watches my mouth as she says, "Tell us about your family, Nine." She bites her lip and shakes her head slightly, probably not sure if that was the right word to use. "Tell us about your life in Freedom."

I whimper as I feel the needle pierce my skin again.

Pua squeezes my hand. "Keep looking at me," she says.

Her voice is calm but unassailable. It reminds me of Miri's voice. I think of how Pua told me she started to lose her hearing five years ago. How it just slowly faded away and no one, not even Grandpa Rongo, could do anything about it. She can barely hear through her right ear, and only if you press your mouth against it to speak. Pua has lived through hard things. I squeeze her hand back and try to absorb her strength.

I watch her face, my eyes focusing on her big brown ones. "My family," I say, trying to think what my Freedom equivalent would have been. "Theron was my family."

"Yes?" Pua smiles. "Tell us about Theron."

"Theron was in my Batch," I say. "He was the only one who cared about me. Who didn't care that I was different. No—who loved me for being different." I do my best to ignore the painfully slow, careful draw of thread through my skin and think of Theron. I picture his bald head and blue eyes. The way one side of his mouth rose when he heard something funny. Or the glint in his eye when he had a secret he couldn't hold in any longer. I remember the feel of his hand in mine and the sound of his snoring every night as we drifted to sleep. The comfort of knowing he would always be there when I woke. Smiling. Happy. A smiling and happy that was always meant for me and no one else.

"He was my best friend." I clench my teeth as the needle stabs my skin again. "But more than that. He was my brother, my father, my son. He was everything to me." A painful ache spreads through my chest, and I know it's not just because of the needle anymore. "Theron saved me. Every day he saved me. And the night of the crash . . ."

Pua puts her arm around me. I slide my hand between my knees to stop it from shaking.

"He got me out of the shuttle," I say. "Away from everything that could hurt me. He risked everything for me."

"Theron sounds like an amazing person." Pua's voice is soft but encouraging.

I want to stop the story there. I don't want to remember what comes next. But I take a deep breath anyway. "Then the shark came."

Pua holds me tight, and I lean into her, taking whatever strength I can find.

"It pulled Theron under, and I couldn't see him in the water. When he finally came up, he told me to swim away. He said to keep kicking and never stop, so that's what I did. I knew he was hurt, and I left him there, left him to die."

I welcome the pain of the needle this time. There's a satisfaction in the stinging, punishing bite. An atonement for things I've done. Or should have done.

"It's not your fault," Pua says. She's emotional too, her lip quivering as she speaks. "You are incredibly brave."

Brave is the opposite of what I am. Brave wouldn't have left him. Brave wouldn't be sitting here, feeling sorry for herself over a needle when her best friend was torn to pieces by a sea monster. I am a coward and a weak, pathetic little girl.

Kai's face is lowered, his eyes wide. He stares at his hands in his lap. My arm is all sewn up.

"Thank you," I say.

He doesn't look up but makes a sound deep in his throat before sliding off the table and walking out of the house. I wonder what he thinks of me now, the girl he thought could do hard things—running away from her best friend.

So much for not letting Kai down.

Chapter Thirteen

Kai opens my door and tosses a black rash guard on top of my head as I try to sleep in. "Five minutes," he says.

"But why do I need this?" I ask.

"No more baggy clothes, remember?"

"I'm going in the water?" I sit up, look at my newly stitched arm, and frown. There's slight bruising along the stitches, and my entire upper arm feels swollen.

Kai walks in and lifts my arm. He runs a finger along the stitching, examining the wound.

A chill runs through me at his touch, and I pull back slightly.

"You'll be fine," Kai says, narrowing his eyes. He turns and shuts the door behind him.

I crawl off my bed and hold up a swimsuit Pua gave me last night after I was stitched up. I slip on the bottom piece. It's small—nothing more than underwear, really. I try to put on the top, but it is a tangle of strings and straps, and I have no idea how to get it on.

"One minute," Kai yells at me from the kitchen.

I toss the top of the suit aside and slip on the rash guard. I don't know why I need it if I'm wearing this top anyway. I glance at myself in the mirror and take in a quick breath. I know my body has been changing these last few weeks, but I guess I haven't had a chance to really look at myself.

My hips have spread significantly, and my rear end has filled in. I have definition at my waist, and my legs seem longer. Was I growing taller too? The rash guard fits tight against my torso, and I can see my breasts creating two significant bumps. They still feel tender. It's a little annoying how they get in the way of things like lying on my stomach, or how they bounce up and down if I do anything more than walk.

I frown at the reflection in front of me. There's no denying I've become a mature female, and it's a little unsettling.

"Nine!"

"I'm coming." I tie a fabric wrap around my waist, slip on a pair of flip-flops and a straw hat, then follow Kai out of the house. I grab the life vest from its drying spot on the stairs and turn toward the ocean, but realize he's headed the opposite way, flinging a backpack over his shoulders.

"Where are you going?" I ask.

He doesn't answer but tosses me a pair of sneakers. "Put those on," he says. "And you won't need the life vest today."

I toss the flip-flops aside and slide my feet into the shoes. They are a little big, and I silently wish I had socks. "But I thought we were going in the water." I tug at the rash guard as evidence.

"We are." He grabs a bicycle leaning against the side of the house, steps over the seat, and pats the wide handlebars—his way of telling me to sit.

I hate it when he does his vague minimalist routine. I sigh and climb onto the metal bar, pulling my fabric wrap to my knees to keep it from tangling in the spokes.

Kai pedals us through town on the worn street. Tall poles with wires strung across the top line up along the road. I wonder what they had been used for in another time. Houses like Kai's emerge once in a while, complete with small livestock, wells, and garden plots. Others are empty, abandoned. If I squint I can almost picture them full of people, envision what this town used to be like before the Virus diminished its population.

I can't imagine it ever being like Freedom, though. Without electricity, the islanders *could* still gamble or run cage fights. Even brothels. With all their rules about sex and the time they spend on chores, though, I'm not surprised those things don't exist. It's like what Pua said about dish machines, ovens, and heat—they don't understand what they're missing. But if they did, I'm not sure they'd choose it anyhow. These people seem happy without it. I've never lived outside my Batch tower before coming here, but each day that goes by, I realize I don't miss those things as much as I once did either.

We turn onto a dirt track that heads toward the mountain. Large sheep pastures extend away from the road on both sides. On the right, the pasture gives way to a banana grove filled with floppy leaves and bunches of green fruit that extend above my head.

The road ends at the base of a trail that winds up the mountain. Kai ditches the bike there and leads me through the trees and bushes. After twenty minutes, I'm about to say something to him about how we are as far as anyone can get from the ocean, when I hear it. A loud surge of water ahead. We turn a corner and walk into a clearing where a large rush of water falls on the other end. It descends in one large sheet into a giant pool surrounded by wet rocks.

"What is that?" I ask.

Kai turns to me with a frown. "A waterfall," he says.

"It's beautiful."

Kai tosses his backpack on a dry boulder, pulls off his shirt and shoes, and runs into the water. "Come on."

I take off my fabric wrap and shoes and walk carefully into the water. It's cold but refreshing after our hike. I tiptoe in until the water is at my waist, then lower myself slowly to my chest. The frigid temperature numbs my aching arm, and I sigh with the relief it brings.

Kai swims toward the falls, becoming fuzzy as he moves farther and farther into the misty spray. He dives down and resurfaces with something in his hands. As he swims back, I see that it's a metal cage, and inside the cage are hard-shelled animals crawling over one another.

"Crayfish," he says, putting the cage down in the water near the rocky shore.

I instantly fold my arms and gasp, wondering how many more of those are crawling around at my feet.

Kai smirks. "Don't worry, they hang out around the falls. And I won't make you go over there. Promise."

"Is that why we came? To harvest crayfish?"

"Nope. That's just a bonus. I'm gonna teach you how to swim if it takes all day."

That's why he said no life vest. "But why here?" The ocean is a few minutes' walk from the house. It seems a more logical place for lessons.

"Because the fresh water will make it harder," he says.

I raise an eyebrow. That makes no sense.

"The saltwater is more buoyant. But here, you'll have to work harder to stay afloat. You'll become a stronger swimmer." Kai grabs my hand and pulls me into the deeper water. "And there are no waves, and definitely no sharks, so I'm hoping you'll be able to relax a bit."

No sharks. Still, it's hardly reassuring, learning my sinkability factor has increased. Okay, maybe a little reassuring.

Kai pulls me farther away from the shallow water, and I can't touch the bottom anymore. I panic and grab hold of him around his neck, ignoring the stiffness in my stitched arm. "Kai!"

"It's okay," he says. "Just hold on." He pulls us even farther until I know he can't touch either, and he is treading water to keep both of us afloat. When we've gone several more feet, he peels me off and holds me at arm's length. I can tell he's struggling to keep us both up with just his own legs kicking, and it does nothing to calm me.

"Nine," he says. "I won't be able to hold the both of us forever. So you're going to have to start keeping yourself up."

"What?" My eyes widen with anxiety.

"Don't worry, I won't let you drown." He grins at me. "But I'm depending on you to forget what a jerk I am and care enough to not let *me* drown."

"What?" I ask again. All of this drowning talk is definitely not helping.

"I want you to kick from your hips, just like yesterday, with your legs straight. Only point them straight down in the water." Kai shows me what to do, with his hands still at my waist, holding me at arm's length in front of him.

I do what he says and resist the urge to go for his neck. His hands are definitely keeping me up, not my kicking.

"Good," he says. "Now move your hands forward and back, as though you're pushing the water each way with the palm of your hand." He releases one hand from my waist to show me the movement. When his head sinks below the surface for a second while he adjusts his balance, my heart races. Surely he's kidding about the letting him drown part. Right? "You do it," he tells me.

I move both of my hands together, forward and back, pushing the water with my palms like he showed me.

"Good. Don't forget to kick."

Oh yeah. I add my kicking, and though it still feels awkward, it's almost as though I'm more in control of myself than Kai is.

"Slow down," he says, keeping only one hand on my waist.

I slow down and start to feel a balance in my movements. Arms forward, kick, kick, arms backward, kick, kick. It's tiring, but at least I'm in control. And the pain in my injured arm is completely gone now. I look up at Kai, who smiles and holds both of his hands above the water next to him. He's not holding me anymore. Oh no. No no no.

"Kai!" I move toward him and grab hold of his neck, but the motion sends both of us under the water. He's going to drown, and it will be my fault. I let go and rise above the water. *Arms, kick, kick. Arms, kick, kick.* I focus on my movements while looking around frantically. He's still under the water. I can't see him. "Kai!" I scream. It's like Theron all over again. I panic, and my motions become rushed. I'm afloat, but Kai is still under the water. I killed him.

Then suddenly a head pops up right in front of me and says, "Boo."

"Kai!" I grab hold of him again so fiercely, I know we will both go down, but I don't care. At least I'll go down with him this time. At least I won't be left alone.

But we don't drown. Kai pulls us to the shallows and helps me to my feet, frowning at the terror on my face. "I'm sorry, Nine. That was really dumb of me."

I jump into him, wrapping my arms and legs around him so tight I almost knock him over in the knee-deep water. "I don't care," I blurt out. "I'm just so glad you're still alive." I hold him tight, grateful I have something to hold and that he's not lost at the bottom of the pool. He lets me bury my face in his neck, then I feel his arms move around me, slowly, holding me against him.

When I no longer feel anxious, I loosen my arms a bit. He stands me in the water and steps back, looking away before muttering something under his breath.

"What?"

"I said, let's grab something to eat. I know you didn't eat breakfast."

Funny—I thought he had said something like *maybe baggy clothes were better.*

He pulls out kiwi fruit and sweet bread to share. After eating, we go back in the water. In the deep end, after a promise from Kai for no more teasing, we work on treading water again. After mastering the straight kick, he teaches me how to tread water by alternating circles with my legs. It takes me a while to get it right, but when I finally do, it's much easier to maneuver than the straight kick.

I feel like a fool when Kai has me blowing bubbles in the water. When he holds me to swim this time, I don't feel quite as disoriented. We practice kicks and strokes, and by the late afternoon I can swim decently across the pool. I amaze myself by swimming out to the deep end, treading water for a minute, then swimming back to the shallow.

"See, just like a fish, eh," he says when we're back on dry ground. The late afternoon sun casts a shadow across his face.

I can't help but smile. "Thank you," I say, "for teaching me."

"How do you feel?" he asks, stuffing the crayfish into his backpack.

"Good. I'm tired—exhausted, really. I'll probably collapse as soon as we get home."

Kai comes to stand in front of me and examines my stitched arm. "And the rest of you?"

"I've forgotten all about my arm," I say, "but my breasts are killing me."

Kai's jaw tightens and his eyes go wide. He must not understand what I mean, being a male and all.

"They've been so tender lately," I explain. "Do you think they're filling up with milk like Miriama?" I start to lift my rash guard to show him what I mean.

"Gah!" Kai grabs the hem of my shirt to stop me and curses. "Pull your shirt down."

"What's wrong?" I glance down at my covered chest and frown. I wonder if they are developing incorrectly.

Kai looks at me with a red face, gulping. "You can't do that, Nine."

"Do what?"

"Flash your . . . your . . . you just can't show anyone your bare chest. Don't ever do it again."

"Why not?" I ask, angry at his unsolicited outburst. "You do it all the time." I slap his bare chest right in front of my face.

"That's different."

"Why?"

"You're such a child," he mutters to himself.

I hate it when he calls me that. "Why is it different?" I ask again.

"Because I'm a guy and you're a . . . a girl."

Grr. I'm getting really tired of these gender rules I don't understand. I crouch and angrily put my shoes on. When I stand, Kai's holding out my fabric wrap. I tear it from his grip and toss it over my shoulder.

Kai exhales slowly and glances down to my bare legs. Through gritted teeth, he says, "Put it on, Nine. *Please.*"

I don't want to do as he says, but I'm starting to feel cold under the glare of his icy eyes, so I put it on and storm away back through the trail. It feels like it takes a lifetime to get to the bike, and even longer to reach home. When we do, Kai tosses the bike to the ground and tells me he's hitting the reef. He grabs his fins, mask, knife, and spear and heads for the beach, but not before telling me I am definitely not invited.

I'm too tired to argue. I stumble into the shower, letting the water wash away my anger. I don't understand what I did wrong this time. Just when I think we're getting along, maybe even enjoying each other's company, Kai has to muddle things with his senseless loathing toward me. I'll never know where I fit if he keeps confusing whatever this is between us.

After I'm dressed, I eat a dinner of some kind of fish stew and collapse on my bed before Kai has returned from diving. My entire body is spent, and I am asleep in an instant.

It's later that night, in the dark, that I vaguely realize someone is standing in my doorway for a few minutes before coming in and draping a blanket over me. I'm too tired to say anything, but I'm aware enough to realize *that someone* has a mass of black curls on the top of his head.

Chapter Fourteen

No one wakes me early, and I'm glad. My body is so tired, the extra sleep feels absolutely blissful. When I finally do roll out of bed and head for the kitchen, I realize why no one woke me. It's pouring rain, which means we'll spend the day inside.

Hemi runs to squeeze me around the waist. "I don't have to go to school today, Nine." His smile, as always, is contagious, and I play with the curls on his head. "Kai's gonna paint me something in our room."

"Neat," I say. I glance at Kai at the kitchen table, stirring whatever it is he's having for breakfast. He used to complain about having to share a room with Hemi because of me, but I can't remember the last time he's mentioned it.

"What's he going to paint?" I ask Hemi.

"I don't know yet," he says. "It's a surprise. What are you going to do?"

"Um . . . maybe I'll do some reading." The family has a few books on a small shelf that seem very old. Miri told me I'm welcome to them any time, and maybe it will keep my mind off things. Like Theron. And a certain someone's irrational behavior around me.

I join Kai at the kitchen table and peel a banana. "Did you catch anything in the reef yesterday?" I ask him, tentative.

He shakes his head. At least he's not ignoring me.

I eat in silence, and Kai disappears into his bedroom with Hemi. I volunteer to hold the baby while Miri takes a shower, and when she takes Tama back later, I put away the dry dishes and clean the bathroom. I offer to help Pua knead dough for rolls, but she shoos me away. Sighing, I scan the small bookshelf, picking up an old book with thin pages and the word *Bible* on the cover.

Sitting at the table across from Pua, I open it to the first pages. The language is ancient, foreign. But after a few lines, the words become familiar. Sort of.

> *So God created man in his own image,*
> *In the image of God created he him;*
> *Male and female created he them.*

"Pua?" I ask after getting her attention. "Is God another name for the first Maker?"

She smiles. "Yes."

I read on to more familiar words.

> *And the Lord God formed man of the dust of the ground*
> *And breathed into his nostrils the breath of life;*
> *And man became a living soul.*

149

Then I read things unfamiliar. *Adam. Eve.* The names of the first male and female. I reread the passages over and over, trying to understand their meaning.

> *And the Lord God said, It is not good that the man should be alone; I will make him an help meet for him.*
>
> *And the Lord God caused a deep sleep to fall upon Adam, and he slept: and he took one of his ribs, and closed up the flesh instead thereof;*
>
> *And the rib, which the Lord God had taken from man, made he a woman, and brought her unto the man.*
>
> *And Adam said, This is now bone of my bones, and flesh of my flesh; she shall be called Woman, because she was taken out of Man.*
>
> *Therefore shall a man leave his father and his mother, and shall cleave unto his wife: and they shall be one flesh.*

After waving my arm in the air to get Pua's attention again, I ask, "What is a wife?"

She pours more flour on the table and rubs it into her hands. "Mom and Dad are married. That means she is his wife, and he is her husband."

"What does married mean?"

"When a male and female decide they love each other very much and want to spend the rest of their lives together and with no one else, they get married." Pua begins to roll the dough out with a wooden rolling pin. "Our cousin Liko is getting married next month. There is a ceremony and friends and family attend, to help celebrate their love."

"So they vow to be lovers with only each other?" I think about what Kai said the day Tama was born. That he planned to have sex and make babies with just one female. Well, those were my words, not his, but he affirmed them.

"Yes," Pua says. "But it's more than that. They promise to love each other for always, no matter what happens. They are bound as one, always caring for the other more than anything else in the world."

I look back down to the book in my hands. "What does it mean to be fruitful and multiply?"

Kai walks out of his room with a bucket full of paintbrushes.

Pua winks at me. "It means to have lots of babies."

Kai growls, turns around, and walks back into his room again.

Pua laughs.

I had thought Pua and Kai would be similar in the way they behave toward me because they were born at the same time, but it's the complete opposite.

I lie on the couch and think about the words in the book and how similar yet different they are from the words we memorized as children back in Freedom. I've never heard of marriage before, and although most people in Freedom have sex with whomever they want, a few choose to be with primarily one other person. Not with any promises to stay together forever, though. And certainly not having babies together.

I thought I understood why they have strange rules about sex here. Because for them it's not just for recreation, it's how they reproduce. But I'm starting to realize it's more than that. It's . . . special. Pua's words drift through my head—*promise, love, always.* I let them cover me like a blanket, bringing a warmth that surprises me. Because I hadn't realized I was cold.

The spattering rain outside lulls me to sleep on the couch. A tiny hand shakes me awake. It's Hemi. I look outside but cannot tell how long I've been asleep. The rain continues to fall heavily.

"Nine," Hemi says. "Come and see." A blue moon and star are painted on his face.

I smile at his excitement and let him pull me into his room. Kai kneels on the floor, gathering his homemade paints and brushes onto a tray. Hemi lets go of me and rushes past him to the wall behind him. It is a solid black background with colorful spheres and rings standing out from the dark. It's our solar system, complete with sun, planets, moons, and an asteroid belt. Hundreds of tiny stars dot the black sky. Hemi jumps and points to what looks like a shuttle in space, with fire spewing out the back of it. A tiny face with curly black hair peeks out of a window.

"It's me," he says. "Flying in a spaceship. Did you know there used to be spaceships that traveled from planet to planet?"

It's a ridiculous notion, but I smile at Hemi and his wild imagination. "It's wonderful," I say, glancing at Kai. He raises one side of his mouth and continues to gather his supplies.

"I'm gonna show Mom my moon face." Hemi runs out of the room.

I walk toward the wall, in awe of how grand the scene is, and how small it makes me feel. The Earth is painted at my eye level, and I get a close look. It's amazing how much detail Kai was able to include. I can see Freedom One, and just off the coast, two long islands with a smaller one to the right. Mahawai. Our island.

"Kai?" I ask without turning around.

"Mm?"

"Why do you hate me so much?"

He doesn't answer for a long minute, and as I'm about to leave the room in frustration, I hear him whisper, "I don't hate you."

I clear my throat to prevent myself from laughing out loud.

"I don't," he says. "I hate Freedom. I guess for a while I took it out on you, because you were Freedom to me."

"And now?" I turn and look at him on the floor.

Kai sighs. "And now, I don't know what to think about you."

It isn't exactly reassuring. "Why do you hate Freedom?"

"Because it's anything but freedom." His face twists in anger. "They make you think you're free, choosing your hair color and gender and whatever else you people change. But it's just a way for them to control you . . . giving you a false liberty."

"But we are free," I say. "We are equal."

"They take away one of the greatest gifts of all mankind—the ability to have children. Where is that choice for you to make? They don't give you the chance to be raised by people who love you. There are no families. It's not right."

Being here these past weeks, I've learned the appeal of a family. Everyone working not just for themselves, but for the benefit of all. It's a place to belong that's not a place at all, because I imagine that feeling of family would still remain even if they were apart. It reminds me of Theron, and the way we'll always be connected, no matter what. Those in Freedom don't know any other way. Maybe when I go back, I can tell the Prime Maker about families. Then people will have an opportunity to choose that too.

I turn back to the mural on the wall. The strip of ocean between Freedom and Mahawai seems so narrow, but, like Miri had explained, I know it's a vast distance—far enough to have kept this island hidden for a long time from Freedom.

"Why not forget them, then?" I ask. "Let Freedom live as it wants, and you live here. Why worry about what the other is doing?"

Kai stands and comes up behind me. "I wish it could work that way. But Freedom has already attacked other rebels." He pauses. "Last year I went hunting with my dad on the west islands, and while we were out on our canoe, we saw people from Freedom on the shore. They were attacking a rebel village there. We managed to sail away and hide the boat, but by the time we reached the village on foot, it was abandoned. The houses were empty with plates of food still sitting at tables. Clothes and toys and medicines were tucked away on shelves. Those people didn't just decide to move away."

"You think they were killed?"

"Or taken."

"How do you know it was Freedom?" Maybe the people became sick—possibly from a form of the Virus. Maybe he's confused about what he saw.

"It was Freedom." His words aren't harsh, just pensive. "They won't be satisfied until everyone is under their control."

"But why attack families?" I ask. "They seem like the least likely target. What threat do they hold?"

"Families have something to fight for, and Freedom is threatened by that."

I glance at the vast ocean on the Earth painting. "Do all rebels live on islands?"

"A lot of them do." Kai puts his hand on the small of my back and hesitates, as though trying to decide how much to tell me.

I turn to him, but his hand doesn't fall. "I would never give you away," I whisper. "I would never tell them where you are. I'd die first." And I would, if it meant protecting this family that I have come to love.

Kai nods toward the mural. "Many rebels live on islands for weather reasons, really. We can't use electricity if we want to evade Freedom's Techies. In a temperate climate, it's easier to not have to worry about heating or cooling. Growing conditions are ideal here, and living near the ocean provides an endless supply of food. And of course the isolation helps."

It's a good thing my tracker doesn't work outside of Freedom. "Is that why you block the windows at night?" I ask. "To avoid being seen?"

"Yes. Their Techies can't find us if we don't use electricity, but after what I've seen on the nearby islands, it's obvious their soldiers have come close. We can't take any chances. No visible fires at night. Darkened windows. We even have several lookouts along the mountain ridge; islanders take turns scouting for unfamiliar boats out at sea."

It's a lot of trouble to go through just to maintain their way of life.

"But there are rebels everywhere," he says, pointing to

Freedom One. "Even in Freedom. They call themselves the Rise, and they are trying to unite all of the rebel camps around the world."

Rebels in Freedom? Is it possible?

"But Freedom could fix Pua," I say. "They could make her hear again. They could make her perfect."

Kai's hand tightens against my back, and for a moment I think I've upset him, but he pulls me closer so our bodies almost touch. My heart begins to race, and my stomach soars. I can't explain why, but I have this desire to move in closer. To erase the space that remains between us. The feeling is new and confusing.

"Pua is fine," he says. His brows narrow, and he looks conflicted. "She's accepted her condition and has no desire to change it." Kai moves his hand from my back to my hair, fingering the end of a short strand. "Why would you want to change anything about you?"

I don't think he's talking about Pua anymore. I can barely breathe. Kai's hand drops to his side, but his eyes look at that same lock of my hair with such concentration, it feels like he's still touching it. No one's ever looked at me so intensely before besides Theron. But this is different. So different.

His attention moves to each stitch along my injured arm, settling on the freckled hand at my side. He reaches forward and grabs my hand. His face is so close I can feel his rushed breathing. This time the space between us hasn't just shifted, it's become this erratic yet pliable thing. Like I can shape it into whatever I want. I lean forward slightly. I have the strongest urge to reach up and kiss him.

"Nine." Hemi comes running into the room.

Kai lets go of my hand and steps back so fast I feel like I will fall over from a loss of balance.

"Is Kai going to paint on you too?" He looks between Kai and me with excitement.

"I don't know," I say. I look at Kai and grin at his flushed face. "Are you going to paint on me too?"

"Um . . . sure." Kai exhales and picks up a brush and tray of paint. "Have a seat."

I sit on the edge of his bed, and Hemi climbs into my lap. "Are you going to paint a spaceship?" Hemi asks.

"No spaceship. It's a surprise." Kai pulls my arm to him and starts to paint small red dots on my skin. He paints with his left hand, the same one he eats with. I smile at the way his tongue sticks out between his teeth as he concentrates.

"Are you giving her the measles?"

"No measles." Kai winks at Hemi.

"Good," I say. "I wouldn't want to be contagious or anything."

Kai coughs and dips his brush into the paint again. He begins to connect the dots he painted on my arm. Soon, simple pictures appear along my skin. For a moment, I think of Theron when he gave me my temporary tattoo. My stomach twists in a not so pleasant way at the reminder.

"What did you paint?" Hemi asks.

Kai points to a figure at my shoulder. "This is Matariki, and here is the Southern Cross. They are constellations in the night sky."

"Why did you paint stars?" I ask, my eyes narrowing at the pictures on my arm. I don't have a good feeling about this.

Kai blushes. "The freckles on your skin. They just . . . they remind me of the stars. It's silly, I know. But I like to think of them as stars in the night sky, hundreds of them."

I push Hemi off me and leave the room. I head straight for the bathroom and turn on the sink. Scrubbing at my arm, I'm grateful when the paint comes off easily, not like the temporary tattoo. I grasp the sides of the sink and stare at my reflection in the mirror, forcing myself to stop shaking. I will not let him replace Theron. Not with his touches or painting or calling my spots the stars. Not with his telling me I don't have to change. That I'm perfect the way I am. He is not Theron and never will be.

I leave the bathroom and head straight for my room. Kai watches me from his doorway with a hurt look on his face. But I don't care. I close my door and flop onto my bed, bringing my knees to my chest and holding tight, trying to convince myself between desperate breaths that I don't care.

I. Don't. Care.

Chapter Fifteen

The next day, I begin to bleed in my underwear. My stomach hurts, I have a headache, and my lower back is on fire. I tell Miri, and she makes me a special tea.

"It's your period," she says. "And it's a good thing. It means you can have babies now."

My chest feels like it's expanding and constricting at the same time. "I thought I couldn't have babies, since I'm from Freedom." I didn't know carrying babies was a part of being female until I came here, and thinking I might have that potential now feels surreal. Like it's the final step in my transformation of becoming *not* male.

Miri flashes a conspiring grin at me. "Coming from Freedom doesn't mean you can't get pregnant, not if you haven't been Remade yet."

I don't think I want to get pregnant, especially if it means going through what Miriama had to. I won't volunteer for that kind of pain. It doesn't matter anyway. I'll be gone on the next steamship. Back to Freedom. Back to being Remade. And it will be a moot point.

"Nine." Miri rests her hand on my shoulder. "I know things haven't been easy for you here, but I think you've handled it remarkably well. I'm proud of you."

"Really?" I feel like I've been more a burden than anything, so the thought that someone is pleased with me is surprising.

"Yes, really." She smiles. "You need to give yourself credit. You've had to adjust to a new place, new people, new way of life . . . even a new body. And losing everything you've ever known and people you've loved on top of that—it's nothing short of a miracle you decide to wake up each day, ready to take on what's thrown at you next. I am *very* proud of you."

I feel like a weight I'd been carrying has shifted, and though it's still there, I'm not the only one having to hold it up anymore.

"If you have questions about anything," she continues, "you can always come to me, okay? I can't promise I'll always have the answer, but I promise to help you the best I can."

"Thank you," I say. Because I don't doubt for a minute she'll help me when I need it—like today and the tea in my hand. It feels good to trust someone so completely again.

Miri tells Kai I don't have to work with him for the rest of the week. It's mostly so I can adjust to this period thing, but I can tell Kai is hurt. I remind myself I don't care. Serves him right for all the times he complained about having to babysit me—the child. He should be grateful.

By the next week though, surprisingly, I'm itching to get in the water. I want to see how I fare in the ocean after my intense swim training at the falls.

On the tenth day since Ara left on his hunting trip, I dress for the beach and fall into step behind Kai without a word. I enter the water as soon as we reach the first net and help him pull it in with ease. I am so excited, I want to thank him again for teaching me to swim, but he hasn't glanced my way once all morning, and I'm not sure how to break the uncomfortable silence that has grown between us.

When we return home for lunch, Hemi runs into the house. "School is canceled the rest of the day," he says, excited. "A steamship has come to Castle Beach."

"A steamship?" I ask, unbelieving. I hurry into Miri's room. "A steamship has come, Miri. Can I go? I don't want to miss it." Castle Beach is only five miles away. We could be there in twenty minutes by bicycle.

"Calm down," she says. "The ship will be here for a few days. There's no rush."

My face falls. Freedom feels so close, and I want to be there this instant. "Please?"

Miri sighs. "Fine. Kai, you take her. The rest of us will gather trading supplies to take to the ship tomorrow."

Kai has to take me. I wait for his complaint, but it doesn't come. I turn to see him across the kitchen, watching me. He turns away, not upset like I expected. Instead he wears more of the hurt look I've seen lately. I grumble against the feeling deep in my chest. The one that tells me to quit pretending that I don't care about what Kai thinks or feels. That I don't care about him.

I sit on the handlebars as he pedals us to Castle Beach. The wind feels good on my face and through my short hair. My hands are inches from his on the handle grips, and I want so badly to touch his skin.

There's a crowd down by the beach. It's the first time I've seen so many islanders in one place. They are dressed similar to us: casual swimwear, loose dresses, thin shirts, clothing that has been altered or patched to fit. But the variety in their skin and hair is hard to believe. I've never seen skin so many shades of brown, from the darkest chocolate to the barely there tinge of cream. Combined with an endless assortment of hair colors and textures, it's overwhelmingly beautiful. But it's not like the diversity in Freedom. It's more natural, almost. Genuine.

I was a little worried about what others would think of me: the spotted girl from Freedom with blazing hair. Fingering my locks, I realize no one has even looked my way. Emboldened in my present company, I lift my chin and wander through the crowd to find the steamship. It's pulled up to a dock jutting out to sea. Men and women unload boxes of supplies. I step closer to get a better look.

Boxes labeled MEDICINE and TOOLS receive a lot of attention. But my eyes immediately find one labeled CHOCOLATE. I haven't had chocolate for weeks, and I decide to ask Miri what we can trade for it.

I look around for someone in charge, but everyone unloading looks like they could live on the island. I turn to Kai, and by the roll of his eyes, he knows I need help.

Kai walks down the dock and onto the ship. I climb aboard with him. It's smaller than I imagined, with wheels and turbines crowding the deck. Every other inch of space is filled with metal boxes and containers holding items for trading. The crew must eat and sleep below, though they have to be crowded down there, considering the cramped conditions. A large pile of black stones is stacked near the edge of the boat where it must be fed to fuel the fire that burns on that end. I don't know what the black stuff is, though.

At that far end, Kai speaks to a woman with black skin and hair almost completely sheared off. What's left is shorter than mine and matted against her head.

"Are you captain of the ship?" Kai asks.

"Yes."

Kai holds his hand out and motions for me to continue talking to the woman.

I stumble forward. "Um . . . I'd like to gain passage on the ship."

"Where you headin'?" Her accent makes the end of each phrase fall.

"Freedom."

Her eyes widen, and she looks me up and down. "There's a lot of Freedoms, sweetie."

"Freedom One," I say. I turn around, but Kai is gone.

"Why would you ever want to go there, girl?"

I don't want to tell her it's my home. No reason to bring suspicion on myself. "I just have some business there," I say.

She looks me up and down again and glances behind me—probably to find the boy that brought me to her. After a heavy exhale, she says, "I'm heading the opposite way. To the other islands in the Pacific and on to South America."

All her words mean nothing to me. Nothing except *opposite way*. Those are the only words that matter, I think.

She must see the despair on my face because she adds, "Be back this way in four months. I could probably swing it then."

Four months? It's a lifetime. I nod at the woman and walk slowly off the boat. I pass Kai on the dock. He grabs my arm and makes me pause.

A question is on his face. He's trying so hard to look uninterested. Uncaring. Yet I know he wants to know what the woman told me. I look at him long and discerning. Does he want me to go? Does he want me to stay? A week ago I would have said go . . . definitely go. But now I'm not so sure. I guess it doesn't matter though. I'm staying whether he wants me to or not.

Kai keeps his hand on my arm and waits for me to say something. Well, I'm not going to, so I wait for him to speak. But he doesn't.

After a minute, he narrows his eyes at me and drops his hand. He's so stubborn he can't even bring himself to say one word. I storm away, and though I know he watches my retreat, he doesn't follow.

I go to the bicycle and sit on it. I wait. Looking up, I see Kai slowly walking my way. What is the look on his face? Relief? Amusement? The corners of his mouth twitch as though he might actually smile. Surely he's realized now that I'm not going anywhere real soon. Is he laughing at me about it? I don't need this right now.

I put my feet to the bike pedals and take off without him.

REMAKE

It wobbles at first, but I'm in control soon enough, thanks to weeks of practicing on the island. Once I'm down the road away from the beach, I turn back and see Kai watching me leave with a frown. And I don't care.

I continue to pedal the five miles to the house, but I don't want to face anyone yet. They might be frustrated to learn they have to keep me for another four months, and I'm not ready for any more disappointment today. Besides, I have a long time to see them still, apparently.

Passing the road to the waterfall, I am farther away from home than I've ever been, but I keep going through a maze of streets that must have once been populated greatly, considering the number of houses. They are all empty now, though. I pass a series of low, run-down buildings and turn right. The road here is overgrown with weeds, and I jump off the bike to walk it for a while.

I veer toward a large building, toss the bike to the ground, and walk in through a still-functioning metal and glass door. It would be dark inside if it weren't for the giant hole in the ceiling letting in afternoon light. Warped wooden alleys run in one direction across the building, with low rails along the side of each strip. A painted sign across one wall reads BOWLING, whatever that means.

I walk down one of the wooden planks to where a low hangover covers the end of it. I crawl inside, so I can still see the light, but it's secluded enough that I feel protected. Protected from the world, from Kai, from the time I will need to wait until I go to Freedom. To be Remade. To the rest of my life.

Everything I've known from my life in Freedom feels like a

dream. Not because I'm a far distance away, or because so much time has passed since I left, but because everything I've learned as a Batcher seems to go against the way these people live on the island. What if I forget how to live in Freedom? What if I lose sight of what I really want to be—what I've already chosen to be? Sometimes I worry I've already started to forget.

I watch the afternoon sun cast a shadow on the wooden planks, shifting across the floor as the time goes by. Maybe I can wait in here until the steamship returns.

It's dark out too soon, and I can barely see anything from the light of the moon. I find my way to the entrance, and as soon as I open the door, Kai is there, about to walk in.

"Geez, Nine," he says, doubling over with an exhale. "What do you think you're doing?"

I don't answer but just stare at him.

His eyebrows narrow at me. "We've been looking for you for hours."

I assume *we* means his family, though he's alone. "Why?"

"For some unknown reason my family seems to care about you. Do you not understand that?" His family cares about me. Does that include him too?

"But . . ."

"We thought you were lost—when you didn't go straight home. My mom chewed me out a good one for losing you." He rubs his forehead like he's tired after a long day.

I'm not lost, but I feel bad that I didn't think about Miri or how worried the family might be about me. I've never been accountable to anyone before. "How did you know I was here?" I ask softly.

REMAKE

Kai huffs in frustration. "I saw the bike." He turns away and walks toward the bicycle. "You are such a child."

I close the door to the building and lean against it. "Quit saying that." I grit my teeth. "I am not a child." I fold my arms and stomp my foot, just like a child would do.

He doesn't even turn around to acknowledge I had spoken, but mumbles something under his breath.

"Stop ignoring me!"

Kai turns abruptly and reaches me in three long strides. "Ignore you? How can I ignore you? You're everywhere—my house, my work. You're there when I wake and there before I fall asleep." He runs his hand through his hair in frustration.

I'm used to his angry outbursts, but with him in my face, in front of me like this, there's nowhere I can go.

"I can't get away from you," he continues. "You're in my thoughts. My dreams. I see you in everything."

Kai puts his hands on the door behind me at either side of my head. He looks at me so fiercely, I can't look away. His breath comes short and quick, and I realize it mirrors my own short breathing. The air between us doesn't shift, doesn't bend. It disappears altogether, and now there's nothing left to keep us apart.

"I could never ignore you," he says. "Even if I wanted to." He slips a hand to the side of my face. "And you're right. You're not a child."

He squeezes his eyes shut for a moment and gulps. When he looks at me again, I feel like I will melt into the ground right at this spot if he wasn't holding me in place.

His voice is a low whisper when he says, "You are definitely

167

not a child." Lowering his head, he pauses just before my lips, giving me a chance to pull back.

I don't.

And he kisses me.

When our lips part, he presses his nose against mine, keeping his hand at the back of my head. He inhales so deeply, I feel like he has stolen my breath. He steps back and reaches for my hand, curling his fingers over mine. A wide smile spreads across his face.

"I've never done that before," I say.

"Kiss someone?" he asks.

I nod.

"Well, I'd never know. You did it perfectly."

I touch my lips and think of how it felt to have his pressed against mine. Would they feel that way if I had new lips? Remade lips? I look up at Kai. "You have?"

He raises his eyebrows. "Kissed someone?"

I nod.

"Um . . . yes," he says.

I frown.

"No?" He shuffles his feet and adjusts his hand on mine. "I mean . . . yes, but—not like that."

I bite my lip, wondering if I've done something wrong, despite his assurance.

"Definitely not like that." He grins and steps closer again. His hand brushes my chin, and after a sigh, he says, "We need to get back."

I nod, not wanting to worry the family any more than I

already have. As I ride on the handlebars on the way home, I slide my hands over his on the bars.

When we get to the house, I pull him to the side of the front steps—not ready to let him go. He wraps his arms around me, bringing me in for an embrace. I rest my head against his shoulder, inhaling the cinnamon scent of him that makes my stomach flip. The thought of me and Kai together like this seems so ridiculous yet so perfect at the same time, it makes me laugh out loud. He leans back and smiles, his eyes laughing along with me. I reach up and press my lips to his, smiling as I kiss him, unable to contain my happiness.

"Mom!" Pua's voice makes us jump. We both look up to see her standing on the front porch, bending over the railing, grinning at us. "I think Kai found Nine," she yells into the house. Pua walks down the steps toward us. "Or were you just hiding her, Kai, to keep her for yourself?"

"Shut up." Kai grabs Pua around the neck and pulls her into his chest.

"I knew it," she squeals. "I knew you liked her." She punches him in the ribs, and he lets her go. She looks at me and winks before running into the house ahead of us.

Kai gives me a shy smile. I smile back, feeling the blood rush to my face. He slides his hand into mine with a nervous exhale, then pulls me behind him up the stairs and into the house. Today, it feels really good to be a girl. I decide four more months on the island might not be such a bad thing after all.

Chapter Sixteen

I settle my head into the crook of Kai's shoulder as we swing lazily in the hammock. He reaches over, pulls my arm across his chest and slides his fingers up and down the stitches of my upper arm. The cut is no longer red or bruised, but the bump of a scar is beginning to form.

He kisses the top of my head. "You are so beautiful."

Only one other person has called me beautiful before. I wonder if the day will come when I'll stop comparing him to Theron.

Kai's fingers are rough and calloused, evidence of the life he's led. One in which hard work and labor—providing for the welfare of his family—is considered a privilege and not a burden. What would it be like to have such strength, as a male? Would being strong physically make me strong inside too?

"Kai?"

"Hmm?"

"What does your name mean?"

"It means the ocean."

I smile. Of course it does. I smooth over his shirt, mimicking the rise and fall of water. The gentle rocking of the hammock beneath us adds to the illusion.

"Whereas you, Nine," he says, pausing for a moment. "You are more like *makani*—the wind."

"Because I'm full of hot air?"

Kai laughs. "No."

"Because I blew you over?" I say it like he would: *ovah.*

"Kind of," he says. "You are *makani*, but maybe more like *ani*—a peaceful wind that catches you by surprise. It rolls over the surface of the ocean and creeps up on you."

I redden at the thought of me, like a wind, rolling over Kai. I know he can't see my face, but I move in tighter to hide my blush anyway.

"From the moment you told me you couldn't swim, yet you spent the entire night in the ocean . . . I knew you were different. You were more than I gave you credit for." Kai sighs. "A wind that creeps and winds and fills your entire being," he says.

That day I told him I couldn't swim was the first time I noticed the shift in the air between us. And now I know why. It was the moment he began to see me as more than just a Batcher from Freedom. I was a wind trying to find somewhere to settle. A new place to belong. And though Kai fought against that shift for a while, I think he really has, finally, given in.

I look up at him and smile. His eyes smile back at me, and it reminds me of the way Arapeta looks at Miriama, like I'm the most important thing in the world. I'm about to reach up and kiss him when I hear a voice from the beach trail.

"Well, that's something I never thought I'd see."

"Ara," I say.

"Dad!"

Kai and I try to hop off the hammock but end up falling onto the ground on top of each other.

I stand before Kai does and find Ara grinning at us and walking closer.

Kai stands, brushes off his clothes, and gives his father a hug. "We've missed you," he says.

Ara extends his arm out to me, and I hug him too. "And it looks like I've missed a lot," he says.

I smile shyly, but Kai stands tall and holds my hand in his.

Ara beams. "Maybe I should've put you in charge of Nine sooner—saved us weeks of torment from your blabbering complaints."

Kai smiles and squeezes my hand. He pulls me close to his side, and I sigh in contentment, finally feeling like I know where I belong in this foreign place.

"Go and help your uncles unload, Kai," Ara says, his eyes shifting between Kai and me.

Kai nods and winks at me before jogging to the beach trail.

Ara turns to me and grins. "Everything go okay these past couple of weeks?"

I nod. "Kai taught me how to swim. And you just missed a steamship visit."

"And yet here you are."

"Here I am." For a few more months anyway. "The boat

was heading the opposite way. But Miriama traded for some chocolate."

Ara smiles widely. "Let's go see that bride of mine. Come on."

In the house, I take the baby from Miri's arms. I blush as Ara kisses his wife so passionately I feel like I'm intruding and walk back out with a smile on my face.

I take Tama to the beach, and we watch the men unload three deer off the canoe. Kai grins at me every once in a while. I bounce the baby on my hip and move his hand in a wave at his big brother.

When all the gear has been unloaded and taken to the house, Kai brings his grandfather, Rongo, over to us.

"How are you, Nine?" Rongo asks, bringing my face to his, nose to nose in greeting.

"I'm good."

Kai takes Tama from me and shows Rongo my arm.

"And you did this?" Rongo asks, with one eyebrow raised. I wonder if he means the damage or the stitching.

Kai nods, tight-lipped.

"It is good," Rongo says. "And it's healing nicely."

Kai sighs in relief.

Rongo pats a hand on Kai's shoulder. "You should consider being a Healer."

I gasp and pull my arm away, taking a few seconds to compose myself and then finally look up. Kai and Rongo watch me, waiting for me to say something.

"Sorry," I say. "I think Kai would be an excellent Healer." I smile and take Tama back, adjusting him in my arms, trying to avoid their gaze—and trying not to think about Theron and how he wanted to be a Healer.

"I think I'll stick to the ocean," Kai says. "A fisherman is more my thing, although it's good to learn a little of everything."

"Are you good at dancing?" Rongo asks, and I know by the way he grins the question is meant for me. "Because we're having a bonfire later on, before it gets too dark. Food and music required."

Dancing? The only dancing I've done is in Freedom, and in the time I've been here, I haven't heard any kind of music except for Miri's humming to the baby. I have a hard time thinking they'd listen to any of the music I've heard in Freedom Central.

I shrug at Rongo. Kai puts his arm around my waist and pulls me to his side. "I'm a good teacher," he says.

Rongo smiles and nods, taking his baby grandson from me and heading back to the house.

"Are you a good dancer, then?" I ask.

Kai takes my right hand with his left and holds it out to our sides. He pulls me close with his other hand at the small of my back. "I am an excellent dancer." He spins me around, kicking sand into the air. He stumbles on the incline of the sand bank, sending us both to the ground.

"Well if that's what you call dancing," I say, "then no, I'm not a good dancer."

Kai laughs and grabs a handful of sand, letting it fall through his fingers. "I have a feeling you'll pick it up fast—you're good at everything you try."

"I have the best teacher," I say, trying to catch some of the falling sand.

"Hmm. Let me teach you something else, then." He wipes his hand clean on his shirt and leans in so he's only an inch from my face.

"What's that?" I ask, wanting to close the distance and press my mouth to his.

"How to make a fire."

I move in to give him a quick kiss, then pull back and tug on his shirt, thinking how he once told me he'd wait until he was committed to someone—married—before making love. What if that someone was me? What if he chose me to be his family? Is that something I could choose too? I'm not in Freedom anymore . . . that's for sure.

Kai shows me how to gather branches of different thicknesses, separating them into piles by size. Starting with the smallest, we build a tripod of wood at a spot near the house where a hole is filled with sand. Kai rubs a stick back and forth along a thicker and longer one on the ground that is split down the middle. A tuft of coconut husk sits at the base, and soon it begins to smoke. He picks up the husk and lets me blow on it until an orange flame engulfs it. He places the husk at the base of the tripod of wood and continues to blow until the small sticks come aflame.

We add larger pieces of wood around it, and soon a solid fire burns before us. It's something I hadn't seen much of in Freedom, but here on the island I see a fire at least once a week. I've never helped anyone make one before, though. It makes me feel stronger and proud, somehow. Capable.

I help Kai bring chairs and logs around the fire to serve as benches. The smell of meat cooking on a spitfire makes my mouth water. Late in the afternoon, the extended family arrives. Ara's brothers and their own families bring plates and bowls of food to share in celebration of their return. We enjoy a feast of strange fruits and vegetables that, after almost two months on the island, don't seem so strange anymore. We eat fish Kai and I caught that morning in the nets. Mixed with greens and coconut milk slowly cooked in the fire, it is absolutely delicious.

After eating as much as my stomach will hold, I join the adults around the fire while the children run through the fields and trees and sand. They hide and chase one another until their sides hurt so bad, they collapse to the ground in fits of laughter.

I sit next to Pua and listen to a group of musicians. A man plays a low wooden hollow log in lieu of drums, and a few others play small instruments of different shapes and sizes. I'm surprised when I see Kai pick up something Pua tells me is a guitar. Even though his fingers fly up and down the neck or strum at the strings, Kai rarely takes his eyes off me, always smiling.

"Come on, Nine." A tiny hand pulls me to my feet, and Hemi leads me to an open space. We hold hands while we kick and spin and jump in ways that are unfamiliar to me but undeniably fun. I try to follow others around me, including Pua, who dances even though she can't hear the music, but I soon realize there aren't any rules for what to do. We just move as we feel the music directs us.

Kai taps Hemi's shoulder, and Hemi squeezes my hand, then puts it into Kai's, letting his brother have a turn. I look back at the musicians and see someone else has taken over Kai's instrument.

He pulls me close and whispers to me. "I want you to relax," he says. "And let me do all the work. Just follow as I lead . . . and have fun."

"Okay," I say nervously, not prepared for what he has in store for me.

Kai holds my hands with his and proceeds to push and pull, spin and twirl me. I feel at one moment I will fall away from him the way he pushes me so hard, but his hands are there, holding on tight, ready to pull me back into him so fast my head spins. Then I'm gone again in another direction—and it's so thrilling I can't help but shout and laugh at the same time.

It's the most fun I've had in a long time, this dancing. And so different from the nightspots in Freedom, where everything is flashing lights and loud music and buzz drinks. Here it is motion and rhythm and happy—the kind of happy that seeps into me, and I know it will never find a way out. It'll stay with me forever, resurfacing whenever I hear another song, or feel his hand in mine.

The music ends, and I fall into Kai's arms, laughing and breathing hard.

"Did you like that?" he asks, out of breath.

"Very much," I say, leaning into him for strength. "You're an adequate dancer."

"Just adequate?" he asks, wrapping his arms behind my back.

"I'll let you practice on me anytime," I tease, "so you can get better." I slide my hands around his neck.

A much slower song begins to play, and Kai begins to sway to the lazy beat, pulling me close. He buries his face in my neck and inhales deeply.

"Kai," I say, glancing to his parents on the other side of the clearing. I'm still unsure how they feel about this change in our relationship.

He angles his head to where I look. "I've already talked to them," he says, bringing his face in front of mine. Both of his hands frame my face as we continue to sway back and forth.

"You've talked to your parents about us?"

He smiles. "They're my family. I can talk to them about . . . anything. They teach me. Answer my questions. Give me advice."

I remember Miri telling me I could go to her with any of my questions. How would it be to have someone like that your entire life? Someone to turn to—who loves you unconditionally in return?

I lift my head and raise an eyebrow, waiting for Kai to answer my unasked question.

He laughs. "And they're happy for me. For us."

"Really?" A smile grows across my face.

"Really." His lips find a place against my mouth, and I feel like I'm home.

*   *   *

Kai tosses his head back and laughs out loud, his body shaking against the cushions on the couch. "Blue?"

"Yes," I say, sitting next to him and rolling my eyes. "Dark blue. Like the ocean." I've been telling him and Miri about life in Freedom, and Kai seems to find humor in things people choose for their Remake. Like the Healer and her deep-blue teeth. "I saw one man who had his teeth sharpened into points, like some wild animal."

Kai makes a face and turns to his mother on the other side of him.

She pinches her lips together to suppress a smile and shakes her head. "I think I've had enough Freedom for today," she says, standing up from the couch. "I'm going to bed."

The rest of the family is already asleep, the house mostly quiet except for Kai's periodic laughter. I yawn, about ready to turn in myself.

"Don't stay up too late," Miri says, retreating to her room.

"We won't. Good night, Mom." Kai squeezes my hand and turns back to me. "What about skin color? Do people change that, too?"

"Yes," I say, shrugging. "But they choose colors like pink or green, not natural shades of brown like people on the island." I glance at my hand in his, his darker fingers intertwined with my fair and freckled ones.

He shakes his head. "That's so weird."

"Not as strange as this woman I saw once. Her skin had patches of bumpy, leathery skin. It was dark green, like she was part lizard or something. And she had these spikes jutting out from her brow and in a line down the back of her head."

"Like a dinosaur?" Kai's mouth falls open in disbelief.

"What's a dinosaur?"

His eyes widen and he forces a small smile. "It's like a giant lizard, I guess. But they're extinct."

I wonder if anyone's ever seen these dinosaurs in person. Like the dolphin Rongo saw as a boy in the ocean—they're extinct now too. I think of the Virus and how close humans came to extinction. Living as Batches keeps us safe, since over-population won't bring the disease back. But what does that mean for those who live as families outside of Freedom? If the Virus were to return and wipe us out one day, would there be any creature left to remember us?

"What about you?" Kai sinks lower into the couch and leans his head back against the cushion, turning toward me. "What do—did—you want to change? For your Remake?"

I catch his shift in tenses. I tread just as carefully. "I wanted to get rid of my red hair and freckles," I say. I don't add that I likely still want to. I also don't tell him about my choice to change gender—I'm having second thoughts about it myself.

He rubs his thumb back and forth along my knuckles. "Change your freckles? Wouldn't that have been a shame."

I feel my face redden and give him a shy smile. He makes me feel proud to look the way I do, and I glance at his black curly hair, light brown eyes, and pouty lips. I wouldn't want Kai to change anything about himself, either. I rest my head against his shoulder and finally understand what Pua once said about the way we look. That it's a gift. And for the first time, I start to feel grateful for being different.

Chapter Seventeen

When I wake, I hear the distinct breathing pattern of someone *not me*. I find a hand on my stomach and realize it is Kai's. I cover his hand with my own.

I lift my head and glance around, confused for a moment before I realize we're lying on the couch. We must have fallen asleep here last night by accident. I drop my head back down and yawn.

I shift onto my back and shake his shoulder. "Kai," I whisper. "Wake up."

"Mmm." Kai moans in his sleep.

I laugh and kiss the side of his face. "Time to get up."

He responds by pulling me tight against him and smiles, his eyes still closed. "Mmm. Nine," he says, making my heart beat faster.

It still feels strange to me that people save themselves for marriage, but I know how important it is for Kai to wait. It's a promise he's committed to, and I respect that, because a part of me kind of wants to make a promise too. I sigh and move his arm off me, pushing away from him.

"Nine?" Kai opens his eyes and looks at me, confused.

"Yes," I say, giving him a half smile.

"How——?"

The sound of steps echoes along the floor, and we both turn to see Miriama standing above us.

"What the——?"

"Mom?" Kai looks from me to his mom and back to me. "Nine." His eyes widen, and he scrambles backward over the high end of the couch, falling to the floor behind it. He stands, red-faced, holding his hands up in defense. "Nothing happened, Mom. I swear." He runs his hands through his hair, which sticks up all over the place after a night of sleep.

"Yeah, looks like it," Miri says with a glare. "What else am I supposed to think when I find the two of you——" She pauses, glancing nervously around the room. Her voice is low but heated, like she's upset but doesn't want anyone to hear her in the house. "You're lucky I'm the one who found you and not your father."

"I don't understand," I say, wondering what we did wrong. "We just slept together."

Miriama's jaw drops.

"Not like that, Mom." Kai rubs the back of his neck. "It was an accident. We were just talking, and . . . we must have fallen asleep. It's just a big mistake. I promise." He glances at me, a smile twitching at the corner of his lips.

"Yeah . . . right," she says, moving around the couch and giving him a swift kick, aiming for his rear end.

He dodges her foot and runs around the furniture, trying to get away. He leaps over me and the couch, sprinting toward his room. I hear him shout, "Good morning, Nine!" before slamming his door shut to save himself from his mother.

I'm left laughing on the couch. I sit up as Miri retreats from his door and turns to me with a straight face, her lips pursed.

She comes to sit by me and sighs. "I consider you my daughter, you know that, right?"

I smile and nod. I know she cares for me, and everyone in the family has made me feel so welcome, like I'm a part of them. But hearing Miri say the word "daughter"—especially now that I know what it really means—makes me want to dance, and I feel like I might never stop smiling.

"I love you, Nine. There's a place for you here—always." She puts her hand along the side of my face. "But if you pull a stunt like that again, you're out."

My smile grows, and I lean into her hand, relishing the solid feel of it against my face.

"What's so funny?" she asks. "I'm trying to scold you."

"Nothing. I just . . . I'm so happy."

She raises one eyebrow at me.

"No one's ever cared enough about me to worry about what I do or to scold me for doing something wrong." I pause and look up at her shyly. "It's a nice feeling."

"Oh, Nine." Miri pulls me into an embrace. "I admit it *is* nice to see you and Kai getting along—just don't get along *too well*, eh?"

"No sleeping together, then?"

She coughs, and it turns into a laugh. "Right. No sleeping together."

"Okay."

She kisses my hair and stands up from the couch.

I think about how Miri and Ara would never let Kai sneak into the nightspots in Freedom or jump into a cage fight. But it doesn't mean they don't care about him. It's because they care that they'd advise against it. Of course he'd still have a choice; they wouldn't force him. They wouldn't take away his freedom. But I'm starting to feel that it's better to have someone to teach you, to guide you—someone who actually loves you—instead of wandering in circles trying to figure it out all by yourself. My heart swells at the thought that they'd make the same effort for me.

I lean back on the cushions with a huge grin and listen to Miri pound on Kai's door, rattling off the list of punishments she's about to unleash if he doesn't open up right this second, mister.

Kai and I help Ara load food into the underground oven behind the house. Pork, chicken, deer, and fish meat are scattered among hot rocks, along with taro, breadfruit, sweet potatoes, onions, and greens. We cover the food with ti leaves, then layers of heavy cloth, weighed down by more rocks. It will all cook slowly for the next twenty-four hours in preparation for their cousin's wedding celebration.

"Liko wants octopus for tomorrow, and we're all out," Ara says.

Kai's eyes brighten, and he smiles widely. "I'm on it." He turns to me. "Are you ready to go diving?"

I smile and nod, not really caring what I do, as long as it's with Kai.

"I don't need to send a chaperone with you two, do I?" Ara raises one eyebrow, and I think he is only half kidding. Miri and Pua have taken the younger two children to Liko's homestead for other wedding preparations, so there's no one to send with us anyway.

We both say, "No," and Kai pulls me to the house to gather supplies for spear diving in the reef. When our arms are loaded with everything he says we need, we hike through the beach trail and down the shore. Near the black rocks, we put on as much gear as we can and walk to the edge of the rocks. Hanging our feet into the water, we prep the final items.

"Snorkel?" Kai asks.

"Check." I lift the thin tube into the air.

"Mask?"

"Check."

"Fins, knife, bag?"

"Check. Check. Check."

"Spear?"

I hold up Kai's extra spear. "Weird spear with three prongs and an overgrown rubber band—check."

Kai gives me some green glossy leaves to clean out my mask. "It's called *naupaka*," he says. "Its flowers are only half of a blossom. It is said the other half lies in the mountains, two lovers separated."

"How romantic."

Kai spits into his mask and rubs it with the leaves. I do the same, changing my mind about the whole romantic part.

"Then you toss the leaves into the water," he says, "to see which direction the current is flowing." We both discard our leaves and watch them flow hard to the right and out to sea.

I struggle to get my nose into the mask. "I feel like we should do some kind of ritual dance and blood handshake before diving in." When I finally get my nose in, my lips stick out from beneath the black seal of rubber.

"Don't make fun," Kai says. "Besides, blood would just attract—" He bites his lip and turns his face away.

"Attract what?" I ask.

"Nothing." He gives me a puckered grin. "You look adorable."

"Not so bad yourself," I say, kicking water at him with my fins.

"Ready?"

"Yes."

We dive in and veer left. I'm content to follow Kai through the water, holding my spear at my side. We swim around the hills and valleys of the reef. I spy a sea turtle swimming beneath us in the crystal clear water. I try to shout at Kai through my snorkel, but it comes out muffled, so I pull on his waist to get his attention. He smiles at my fascination, and I begin to understand why he likes coming out here so much.

Something bright and reflective peeks out from a layer of sand. I let Kai swim on without me, and I poke at the object with the sharp end of my spear. It's a metal square about the size of my palm, and a strand of shredded dark fabric hangs from one side of it. I take a deep breath and dive down to retrieve it, blowing water out of my snorkel when it breaks the surface again.

The silver square is rusted and worn, but there's no doubt in my mind what it is. The memory of Theron shoving me into a seat in the falling shuttle flashes through my head. His hands fumbling with the straps at my waist. Tightening my safety belt. Making sure I was secure—making sure I was safe.

I turn the buckle over in my hands, waiting to feel the panic. Waiting for my breath to quicken and my heart to race. But it doesn't come. Instead, a sense of calm settles over me. A sense that even though Theron's not here, he'll never truly be gone. It means I can move forward living without him. Finding happiness in my life isn't a betrayal of his.

Kai swims up and pulls out his snorkel. He mouths to me underwater, *Are you okay?*

I turn the buckle in my hands one more time before letting it go. It falls slowly to the floor of the reef, settling into the sand near my fins. I glance back to Kai and nod.

Yes, I think I'll be okay.

I follow Kai through the water again, and after a few minutes, he sees something that gets him excited. He motions for me to come up out of the water. We plant our finned feet on the bumpy coral beneath us and breach the surface. Kai pulls the snorkel out of his mouth, and I do the same.

"What is it?" I ask.

"Do you see anything strange down there? Just in front of the coral ledge," he says, pointing with his spear to a spot several feet in front of us. We both duck our heads under the water, and after a few seconds I squint in confusion. We breach the surface again.

"There's a small pile of rocks in front of that hole," I say. "It doesn't look natural."

"That's right," he says with a smile, seemingly impressed that I spotted it so fast. "Rocks would never pile up that way in the water on their own, would they?"

"No. It's kinda fishy."

"Ha, ha."

I think about it for a moment. "Octopus?"

Kai nods. "They stack rocks in front of a hole as camouflage while they lie in wait inside. They wait patiently for an oblivious crab or lobster to pass by, and then . . ."

"Surprise attack." I grin.

"Exactly."

"They eat crabs and lobsters?" I ask. "How do they get through the hard shell?"

"They have a beak to break through it. And nothing can escape the suction cups on its tentacles."

"So you're telling me there's an octopus behind that pile of rocks?"

"Most likely."

"Well, then. Show me your magic, Kai."

Kai replaces his snorkel, takes a deep breath, and dives down to the hole under the coral ledge. I lower my face into the water from where I stand to watch him. In the dark behind the stacked rocks, I see a flash of movement. Is that the octopus? My heart beats faster in excitement.

Kai prods the hole with his spear and waits patiently. Tentacles come out and wrap around the metal prongs. Kai quickly reaches with his other hand and holds the tentacles to the spear, drawing the creature closer to him at the same time. He grabs the back of its head and frees it from the spear, careful to keep his hands away from where the beak must be.

He shakes the octopus vigorously in the water, and we are immediately encompassed in brown-black ink. Suction cups pull on his hands and arms, but he continues to shake the animal. After a few minutes, the ink stops coming out, and the water slowly turns clear again. Kai motions for me to open my net bag and carefully puts the octopus inside, cinching it tight.

"Ta-da," he says when our heads are above the water again.

"That was amazing," I say. "And a little bit terrifying. I'm genuinely impressed."

Kai smiles. "Are you okay to keep going?"

"Definitely."

The next two hours pass in a flash. I see countless colorful fish swimming in and around the reef, and even a slithering eel. Kai catches three more octopuses, letting me do most of the work on the last one.

"You must be good luck," he tells me as we walk back to the house with our spoils. "I've never caught this many before on one dive."

We set our gear at the utility sink behind the house. I throw on a sundress over my suit, and Kai pulls the first octopus out of the net bag.

I touch one of the tentacles, still enthralled by the strange sucking sensation I'd felt from it back in the water. "It's pulling on me," I say, surprised. "I can't believe it's still alive."

"Not for much longer," Kai says. He flips the octopus's head inside out and pulls off the slimy guts and ink sack.

"Ugh." I wince and step back. "That is so, so wrong."

Kai laughs and reaches down to unsheathe the knife strapped to his calf. He uses it to cut out its eyes. He pops out the black beak, and I inch closer again, curious.

I touch the sharp, hard piece and ask, "Aren't you afraid of it biting you? That is one nasty beak."

"It's happened to me before." Kai lifts his right hand and points to a scar just below his thumb.

I finger the white line of healed skin and feign shock. "Seems dangerous. And you let me handle that thing in the water?"

Kai smirks. "I knew you'd be fine."

After cleaning the octopuses and disposing of the unwanted parts, we take our catch to the kitchen. Kai finds some rock salt and shows me how to massage it into the animal, tenderizing it. After blanching the meat, we slice it into small pieces and cook it in a skillet with butter and onions, adding herbs and sugar to the concoction. Kai dishes each of us a small portion before putting the rest away for tomorrow's feast.

"Mmm." I open my mouth while I chew to cool off the food inside, not wanting to wait for a more reasonable temperature to eat it.

"Not bad, eh?" Kai asks, eating his own at a more leisurely pace.

"Actually," I say with a mouthful of food. "This is disgusting." I lift the plate to my face and shovel the rest of it into my mouth. "Seriously, Kai. Probably the worst thing I've ever tasted." I lick the plate clean, not caring who sees me do it.

"Uh-huh," Kai says with a wry smile. "Sorry to disappoint." He spoons some of his own portion onto my plate.

"It's all right," I say, happily eating more. "We can't all be master chefs."

He coughs a laugh away, surely thinking about my amazing skills with all things culinary.

I smile at the line still visible on his face where his diving mask had been. "It's a good thing you've got your looks."

Kai takes our plates and puts them in the sink. "I smell like fish," he says. "I'm taking a shower."

"Oh no you don't," I say, running for the bathroom before he gets very far.

"Hey." He chases after me, and we tumble over each other to get to the shower first. We land in a heap in the tub, Kai tickling me in my ribs.

I squirm away and stand, turning on the hose so that a rush of cold water pours over Kai.

He pulls me back down, and we get drenched in the flow of the water. I try to shove him out of the tub, but he makes his body go limp, and he's just a blob that won't respond to any of my efforts. The tub drain is stopped, and soon we are sloshing around in a pool. We splash each other until the bathroom floor is covered in a layer of water. I know Miriama will have a fit about it, but I can't stop laughing.

Then Kai brings his fingers to my lips to quiet me. I hear the familiar squeak and slam of the screen door followed by voices. Miri and the others are back. We're in so much trouble.

And not just for the flooding. I don't think Miri will be thrilled to find us in the bath together, even if we are fully clothed.

He reaches up to turn off the hose and slowly settles back into the water. We sit in silence for a moment, frozen, just looking at each other.

He is the most beautiful thing I've ever seen. It's not just his curls or his skin or his tattoo. He's beautiful on the inside too. He is smart and decisive and curious. He is strong. He has a good heart. I decide, then and there, I don't ever want to be apart from him. Where he goes, I want to go. I want to be by his side always, even if it means never returning to Freedom. Even if it means staying female. Being Remade is not worth it if I can't have Kai by my side.

As I lean forward, wanting to move in closer and feel his touch, Miri's words push to the front of my mind—*If you pull a stunt like that again, you're out*—and I hesitate.

"What is it?" Kai asks.

I shake my head. "We shouldn't be here, alone like this . . ."

He opens his mouth to speak when Hemi comes racing into the bathroom.

"Hey, Mom never lets me have a bath." Hemi turns around and begins to walk out. "I'm telling—"

"No." Kai calls him back into the room.

I grab Hemi's hand. "We made it for you, Hemi."

"Really?" he says.

We both nod, and Hemi jumps into the water with us, sending another wave of water over the edge of the tub. We all splash one another until Miri hears and comes to scold us from just inside the bathroom door. Then we splash her too.

REMAKE

Soon we have a room full of bodies intent on getting everyone else wetter than they are themselves. When Ara tosses a bucket of water in through the bathroom window, we take our water war outside and splash and play until we are all soaked through. Even Tama joins in the fun, first as a shield, then as the prize. The laughs are contagious, and the smiles the family gives me as we collapse from exhaustion are the best prize of all.

Chapter Eighteen

Unless it comes from a steamship trade or altered from other fabrics already on hand, the clothing we wear is made of wool. And the dress Pua slips over me is no exception. It's an off-white knit wool, undyed, with a cowl-neck collar—that's what Pua calls it. It drapes low on my neck while the rest of the dress is fitted, coming to just above my knees. Looking at myself in the mirror, I realize it's the most beautiful piece of clothing I've ever worn, and undeniably feminine.

"I don't know, Nine," Pua says behind me, sitting on the edge of my bed. "It's not right to upstage the bride at her own wedding."

I turn, knowing she's teasing. "Are you sure I can wear this?"

"Of course." She sits me on a chair in front of the mirror. My dresser rests below it, a collection of shells I've accumulated lining up along the surface. I count them, even though I know there are twenty-two exactly.

Pua tugs at my fire-red hair that is now finger-length after months on the island. "We need to do something with this hair, though."

She brushes through it and adds an egg white gel to mold it this way and that, scattering tiny white blossoms throughout. With a little dark ash on my eyelids and a tinted balm on my lips, she declares me perfectly suitable for an island wedding.

I thank her and watch as she braids, twists, and pins her own hair into a complicated updo, which, combined with her beauty, will definitely upstage the bride. She slips on a sleeveless gray wool dress with a V-neck and flowing skirt. While she finishes with her own makeup, there's a knock at the door. Kai walks in wearing a white collared shirt and fitted black pants. His hair is newly trimmed and his face freshly shaven. His jaw drops when I stand and step toward him.

"You look amazing," he says, looking me up and down. "I mean . . . seriously. . . . I can't even—"

Pua slaps him on the shoulder. "I'm in the room too, you idiot."

Kai rolls his eyes at his sister. "Yes, you look good too, Pua. I'm sure all the boys will drool over you all evening, as always."

Pua smiles brightly, satisfied with the compliment. She winks at me and leaves the two of us alone in my bedroom.

"But you, Nine." Kai slides his arms around my waist and pulls me close. "I'm not sure I want to share you with anyone else today."

"Too bad," I say. "I heard several good-looking boys are coming and I'm not missing out." I waggle my eyebrows so he knows I'm kidding. I'm actually anxious to see what this whole wedding thing is all about, and Pua made me wear a swimsuit under my dress for a surprise later tonight. I've no idea what it is.

Kai half laughs and half groans before stepping back and biting his lip. "I made something for you." He slides a hand in his shirt pocket and pulls out a white strand of tiny shells. They are strung together to form a necklace.

"You made this?" I ask as he fastens it behind my neck.

He nods shyly.

It is delicate and surprisingly light against my skin. "It's beautiful."

"You make it beautiful," he says, sliding his fingers along the necklace. With a sigh, he leads me out of the room.

Liko and Ronan, the bride and groom, stand before a holy man in an open grass area at Liko's homestead. The area is decorated with flowers, flowers, and more flowers. Even the guests wear fragrant blooms in their hair or around their necks. The air smells like a blossoming fruit orchard at the start of spring. The holy man talks to the couple about marriage and family, devotion and sacrifice. He mentions the word "God" several times as he speaks.

I press my lips to Kai's ear and ask in a whisper, "Why does he tell of the first Maker?"

Kai smiles and whispers back in my ear. "Because God is the one who sanctions marriage. He is sacred. And so is the promise they make today, to love each other always."

Sacred. I like that word. It's as though this wedding, this commitment they make, is more than just a promise to each other. It's a promise to God, their families, and the entire world. It transcends this moment in time, this place, and expands beyond their reach to somewhere we cannot see.

"So marriage is sacred?" I ask.

He nods.

I pause. "And sex, too?"

"Yes."

"Because making babies is sacred?"

Kai gives me a discerning look, glancing from my eyes to my nose, my mouth. I cannot tell what he is thinking.

"Yes," he says against my ear. "But it's not just that. It's a way to show your spouse you love them. That you are devoted to them. It's not just procreating that is sacred." Kai gulps. "It's the act of lovemaking, too."

I think of the day I read from the Bible book, when Pua first told me about marriage. It was the first time I suspected sex was more than just recreational—more than just for reproduction. That it was something special. And I think today, I finally understand why.

"And God," I say. "He is the one who commanded it to be so?"

Kai nods and wraps his arm around my shoulder to pull me close.

"This is now bone of my bones," says the holy man. "And flesh of my flesh." I lift my head at the familiar words I had read in the Bible book. "Therefore shall a man leave his father and his mother, and shall cleave unto his wife: and they shall be one flesh."

With a match, the bride lights a candle in her hand

and waits while the groom does the same. Using their own candles, they light a third one at the same time. And two lives become one.

Several people in the audience are in tears. We stand as Liko and Ronan walk up the aisle, and we all follow to a banquet set up with more food than I've ever seen in one place in my entire life.

I sit next to Pua and across from Kai, who tosses tiny pieces of bread at me every once in a while. I swear I must have ten pieces stuck in my hair among the white blossoms.

"Kai's got it bad for you," Pua whispers to me.

"Got what?"

She laughs and covers her mouth as she whispers into my ear. "He's madly in love with you."

I feel heat rise to my face. "Why do you say that?"

"He has a plate full of sautéed octopus he hasn't even touched because he's too busy watching you."

We both laugh as another piece of bread flies into my hair. I stand and switch my plate with Kai's. I happily finish off what's left on his plate.

After food there's music. I let Kai practice his adequate dancing skills on me until I'm so tired I collapse into him.

"Come with me." He half pulls, half carries me toward a grove of trees, far from the music and dancing of the crowd. A guitar leans against the trunk of a tree.

We sit on the grass, me behind him with my head against his back and my arms wrapped around his waist. He spends a few seconds tuning the guitar and plays me a song without words. I peek over his shoulder and watch his fingers dance

198

on the strings. One hand moves up and down the neck of the instrument so fast I can't keep up. The other uses a combination of strumming and picking at the strings across the guitar opening in a pattern so complex my jaw drops in awe at how talented he is. When he finishes, I can't help but clap.

Kai smiles and motions for me to sit in front of him. He places the guitar in my hands, and with his arms wrapped around me, he puts my right hand on the strings. His left hand cups the neck of the guitar lightly, so that as I strum, no sound comes out.

"Down-down-up-up-down," Kai says. "Down-down-up-up-down. Good." He moves my fingers across the strings until I strum the pattern on my own. "Keep going," he says. His right hand moves from mine and hits the body of the guitar on its side, creating a rhythmic pattern to complement my strumming. His left hand makes purposeful shapes on the neck of the guitar, and suddenly my awkward strumming sounds like a song.

I keep strumming, nervous about messing up the melody Kai created. When I finally relax and feel it come naturally, he starts to sing. The words speak of love lost and found. Of kisses and touches and forever. He sings softly behind my ear, but in the dim light of a sunset, here in the copse of trees, the sound of his voice penetrates through my whole body. It is piercing and beautiful at the same time.

My fingers stop, and my hand lays frozen against the strings. Kai takes the guitar out of my lap and puts it on the ground. He turns me to face him and brushes a lock of hair behind my ear.

"I keep thinking," he says, "about the day we found you on

the beach." He exhales slowly. "I can't even begin to understand what that experience was like for you. Lost, alone. I'm sure it was the worst day of your life."

I open my lips to speak, but Kai's fingers silence me.

"Nine, it was my best day," he says, moving in close. "I didn't know it at the time, but you washing up on this island was the most meaningful thing to happen to me." His fingers fall from my mouth. "Does that make me a monster?"

"I'm glad you found me." I breathe in his musky sweet scent. "Any story that ends like this—with me, here, in your arms—is one I don't regret." For the first time, I realize it's true. I don't regret the journey that brought me to Mahawai. To Kai. But would I do it again? I think of losing Theron. I don't think I could. I hate that the loss of one is tied to gaining the other.

Kai's hands cup my face and bring me in for a soft, ethereal kiss.

"Come on, Nine, Kai." Pua taps both our heads at the same time. "We're going to jump off Turtle Rock." She runs by with a handful of teens our age.

Kai holds my hand tight, and we follow behind them toward the beach. As we move from grass to sand, I catch a glimpse of the bride and groom leaving in the distance, a crowd of people cheering them off.

When we reach the edge of the beach, we hike along a sandy trail through black rocks until we come to a large rock cliff jutting out into the water. It's curved, like a turtle shell, explaining how it got its name. A stretch of sand spreads out before it. I stand at the edge of the water, feeling the gentle waves flow in and out across my feet. I stay in the same spot for as long as I can, trying to resist the current's push and pull. Beneath my feet, the sand washes away around the edges and leaves a bumpy yet solid support directly under each foot. It's a strange but comforting feeling.

"Feel like jumping?" Kai asks, pulling his white shirt over his head.

I look at the top of the rock and see a line forming as one by one the jumpers fall over the edge. It must be forty feet in the air from where they leap. I see Pua run and fly off with the loudest scream so far. When she comes out of the water, she heads straight to me.

"Nine, you have to try this!" She drips water all over Kai and me. "You're falling," she says, "and then you think to yourself: I'm still falling. There's that much air time. It's incredible." She laughs and runs back to the base of the rock to start her hike up again.

Kai pulls off his pants and is left standing in his swimsuit, like the rest of the jumpers. "Nine?" He holds a hand out to me and waits.

I look up at the rock and down to the water. It's a really far drop. Higher than from where Theron and I jumped from the shuttle, I think.

"Take a chance, Nine."

I know a challenge when I hear one. And I didn't wear a swimsuit for nothing. I slip my dress off before I can change my mind and race past Kai toward the rock. He speeds up to me, and we climb together. At the top, the wind is cool, and it looks much farther to the water than it did when I was on the sand. I swallow; it's a far drop. Pua jumps off again with a bloodcurdling scream. I look wide-eyed at Kai. I'm not sure I can do this.

As if reading my thoughts, he says, "You've got this." He rubs the skin bumps on my arms. "Wait for a wave to come in. The water will be deepest then. But don't worry, you'll be fine either way."

I nod and watch three others jump before me. Their heads pop up from the surface below every time. I convince myself this means it's perfectly safe—even without Kai's hand holding mine. I can do this.

I take a few steps back and see Kai's face drop for a split second. Without hesitating, I run forward, push off into the air, and fall fall fall. The wind whistles at my ears, and my stomach feels like it will fly right out of my throat. But my lips—my lips are turned up into a smile because it is the most thrilling thing I have ever felt. It's as though I'm flying. Free. I hit the water, and it stings my skin. Water rushes up my nose, and I swallow a giant gulp of seawater. But when I surface, I'm laughing. I swim away from the base and look up to see Kai jump off, doing a front flip before he lands in the water with a splash.

I swim toward the beach until the water is chest-deep and then wait for him. When he reaches me, he pulls me close and presses his nose against mine. He breathes in deeply, closing his eyes for a brief second.

"Well?" he finally asks.

"It was amazing."

"That was brave of you, Nine. I've never seen anyone jump off that fast their first time."

"Brave like a boy?" I ask.

Kai's brows furrow, and he pulls away, shaking his head. "No, brave like a girl."

I give him a salty kiss. A splash from a fellow jumper forces us apart. I laugh and drag Kai out of the water and up the rock face for another go.

Chapter Nineteen

What should I paint?" I ask.

"What do you wish you could have in your room? What would you want to look at every day?"

I dip the brush in brown paint and put it to the sky blue wall. I draw a simple stick figure of a person with brown eyes. Adding black to the brush, I squiggle curly hair on the top of his head.

Kai laughs. "Nice." He stands to my left and paints another figure, more detailed and realistic than my stick version, with red hair sticking out all over the place. Using his left hand, he paints details of what I'm wearing, adding curves to my hips and chest.

"Hmm." I glare at his grinning face and look at my rendition of him. I add two bumps on the straight-lined arms to mimic a more muscular build.

Kai steps closer and holds my left hand with his right while he continues to add to the picture. I lean against him, in awe of how naturally the lines and shapes come together to form something so beautiful. He adds details to his own portrait then connects his and my arms between us, so we're holding hands in the picture as well.

I squeeze his hand and dip my brush in red paint. I add color to my lips on the wall, and in tiny impressions, paint silhouettes of lips across Kai's face, as though I had kissed him a hundred times.

Kai laughs and looks at me with his light brown eyes. After a lifetime, he finally looks away and, with a shaking hand, alters the clothes I'm wearing in the picture. No—he alters the way I look in them, making my stomach stick out like a ball. I look like Miriama did when I first came to the island. I am pregnant.

I put my brush down and press my hand flat against my stomach. I look down and try to picture myself with such a tummy, harboring life within me. It's scary to think of that experience—frightening to remember Miri giving birth. But then I think of Tama and how absolutely wonderful and perfect in every way he is. It'd be worth it, wouldn't it?

I don't dare look at Kai, but I keep my hand squeezed tight against his. Picking up my brush, I add something to Kai's arms in his picture. A bundle of cloth with a tiny face peeking out, tucked just against him.

Kai sighs next to me, and he brings our entwined hands to his lips, pressing my fingers with a kiss. With his paintbrush, he draws a large circle next to his face that starts and ends with a point at his lips, as though the picture Kai is speaking. He writes the words *I love you* in shaky letters in the top of the circle.

I take in a short breath but still can't bring myself to look at him.

He adds more words below the first three. *Please don't go.*

I take the brush from his hand and put it down on the paint tray. Slipping my hand out of his, I turn to face him, finally looking up at his light brown eyes. I slide my arms around his waist and move in close. I tell him the words I've wanted to say for a long time but haven't had the courage to admit. I haven't been brave enough to truly decide. "My place is here now, with you. With all of you." I smile, thinking about Miri and Ara. Pua, Hemi, and Tama. They are . . . my family. And Kai. I look up at him and say, "I love you, Kai. And I want to be a family, with you."

He brings a hand to my face and holds it. "I love you, Nine. I love you a thousand times a thousand. And I'm so sorry. For every hateful word, every terrible look I've ever given you." He closes his eyes and gulps. "For every hurtful thought I've ever had about you. I'm sorry, Nine. Can you ever forgive me?"

I melt against him and know this is where I want to be. "Yes. I forgive you. Everyone knows you can't help being an idiot, Kai."

He laughs and lowers his face to mine, kissing me. His hands press at my waist, and I place mine over his, wanting to keep them there forever. Holding me in place. Keeping me exactly where I belong in this world. Connected to him and never letting go.

He pulls back and traces his finger in a line across my

forehead from one side of my face to the other. Connecting the dots. Tracing the pattern of me.

It reminds me of the day in his room when he painted stars on my freckles. If I'm the stars then he's the line that connects every piece, changing me into something beautiful. Something memorable. A constellation that tells the story of us. By myself I am fragments and parts, but with Kai I'm complete.

The thought of him painting on my skin gives me an idea. I bring his lips back to mine and fumble at my side for a paintbrush, bringing it to his face and dragging a line of black across his cheek while I kiss him.

He pulls back, eyes wide. "You didn't—"

My laughter tells him yes, I did.

He grabs for the brush, but I hide my hand behind my back. "Nice try," I say.

Without hesitating, he dips his fingers in the red paint and reaches for my face, determined to get me back. I turn around in a flash and collapse into myself, protecting my head. His hands wrap around my waist and press into my sides, his tickling fingers trying to break my resolve while staining my clothes. It's hard to breathe.

A vibrating shock shoots through the right side of my head. It's not painful, but it's so unexpected and jarring, my legs buckle, and I fall to my knees on the ground with a loud gasp.

I'm still wheezing short breaths as Kai comes to his knees behind me. "Nine, are you okay?"

"I think so." Then the shock comes again, and my hand flies to my right ear, where the buzz originates.

"What is this?" he asks. I feel his finger, still wet with paint, at the back of my right ear.

My hand brushes over the metal stub there, touching the spot he asks about. I spin around and open my mouth to say something, but no words come out.

"Is that what I think it is?" His eyes widen, and his chest rises and falls violently. He's out of breath like I am. "Is it a tracker?"

I nod. What else can I do? "Yes, but . . ."

Kai runs out of the room. I hear the mesh door slam and Kai's voice yelling for Miriama. I sink down the wall of my room, hoping against hope I haven't gone and ruined things all over again.

I sit on the couch, holding Tama tight against my middle. Hemi snuggles up to my side as the rest of the family paces back and forth in front of us.

"You said she was clean," Ara says pointedly to his wife.

"She was," Miri barks back at him. "I guess they stopped installing 'em in their teeth. How was I supposed to know?"

Pua lifts my chin and looks in my eyes. "So it hasn't buzzed until now?"

I shake my head and touch the tracker behind my ear. The vibrations come every thirty seconds and are barely noticeable now, but I feel like they echo with a roar in the small house every time—even though there's nothing audible about it, even for me.

"It's not supposed to work outside of Freedom," I whisper. "I thought . . ."

"What if they aren't tracking you?" Miri taps a fist against her lips. "What if it's in some kind of self-destruct mode? A sort of fail-safe, to terminate the host and others nearby?"

I wring my hands. Both options are equally terrifying.

"Can't we just yank it out of her and destroy it?" Kai looks at me with brows furrowed. If he keeps biting at his lower lip the way he is it will fall right off.

"It's fused to my brain," I say, remembering the words of the Seeker who tested it. "Taking it out would kill me."

His eyes fall, and I look away.

I grab fistfuls of hair at the sides of my head. I'm sorry for frustrating them like this. I'm sorry for putting them in danger. I don't want to hurt them, but I don't know what to do either.

"There's a gun," I whisper.

"What?" Ara asks.

"A gun," I say louder. "Well, it looks like a gun. It has a long plastic barrel that kind of attaches to the tracker. Pull the trigger and the tracker comes free." The Seeker said it's the only way to remove it without killing me.

They look at me for a moment before talking all at once.

"Too long to get it."

"Steamship gone."

"Can't wait."

"She can't stay here."

"Must be another way."

I pass the baby to Pua and stand. "Everyone, just shut up." The family turns to me and waits.

"We can't take it out," I say, avoiding Kai's gaze. "And so I can't stay any longer. They'll come and find you, or you'll get hurt—either way it'll be my fault." My voice shakes, and I see Kai crumble into a chair at the kitchen table through the corner of my eye.

"I need to leave," I say. "And get as far away from here as I can. Now."

Pua slips her arm around her mother. "But they can take it out in Freedom, right?" she asks. "What if we can get her there, find a tracker-removing-gun thing, and get it out? Then bring her back home."

Kai shakes his head and buries his face in his hands.

"It wouldn't be the first time someone's escaped from Freedom. It's possible, isn't it?" Pua looks to Miri as though she would know the answer to that more than anyone else.

"Kai can take her," Miriama says.

Kai stands, knocking over his chair. "No! I won't do it."

I let Pua wrap her arm around me as Miri walks to Kai.

Kai shakes his head over and over. "I won't take her there, Mom." He swipes at his face, and I hang on Pua, too weak to keep standing on my own.

"They'll take her," he yells, anger eclipsing the despair in his voice. "They'll take her away from me. I can't let that happen."

"Kai, listen to me." Miri puts both hands on her oldest son's shoulders. He towers over her, but with his hunched frame and her steadfast posture, it's as though he's a little boy seeking comfort from his wise and protective mother. "Do you love her?"

REMAKE

Kai narrows his eyes at her, as though upset that anyone would question it or suggest otherwise.

"Is she the one?" she asks, her voice cracking.

"Yes," he says, strong and sure and without hesitation.

"Then you have to do this. Take it out ourselves—she dies. Do nothing—we could all die. Take her to Freedom—and we might *all* have a chance." She brushes a curl out of his face. "You don't have any other choice."

Kai looks at me, and his gaze is so full of emotion, I don't think I can take it. I would die, right here, right now, for this family, if that's what it would take to protect them. The thing that burns straight to my heart is that they would do the same for me. They are willing to sacrifice their own son to save me. I don't deserve it, but it's the most wonderful feeling in the world to belong to this family. Pure sacrifice. Pure love.

I throw my arms around Pua.

"You'll take the canoe," Ara says. "We can have it ready in an hour. You'll need to leave then and no later."

Hemi grabs my waist and buries his head in my side. "Don't go, Nine."

I collapse to the ground, unable to stand anymore. How can one body, one person, hold on to so much love and so much despair at the same time? I feel like I could melt away just by willing it.

"It's too far for the canoe to travel." Pua frowns.

"It's our only option," Ara says.

"Plus, it takes two grown men to sail that canoe," she adds. "At least. Nine's never even stepped foot on it before."

"She can do it," Kai says, strong and loud.

211

I lift my head to see him nodding at me. He's brave and confident now that the decision has been made. I reach my hand out and grasp at the air, as though I can catch some of that brave and keep it for myself.

The canoe is loaded with more coconuts than I can count, fresh and preserved fruits, vegetables, and meats. Miri has filled every available container she can with water. The tiny amount of space not taken up by food or water carries a few tools, blankets, clothing, and fishing gear, including Kai's diving spear.

"How long will it take?" I ask, my voice strained.

"Weeks." Kai won't look at me. I want so badly to reach for his hand, but I'm weak and don't think I can take any kind of rejection right now. He must hate me. I'm tearing his family apart, and who knows when we'll see them again. *If* we'll see them again.

Miriama comes up behind us and puts an arm around our shoulders. "We need to talk," she says. She leads us to a dry spot in the sand, and we sit while the rest of the family finishes loading and prepping the canoe.

"First off," she says turning to me, "you need to know something about me. Something I've made the family keep silent about until now."

Kai doesn't look surprised. He watches me with swollen eyes.

"I'm not from Mahawai," she says. "I'm not even from another rebel island."

My eyes widen, but am I really that surprised? She's much

fairer than the rest of her family. I noticed it on the first day I arrived. Her skin is light and clear. I wonder if she arrived on a steamship. From a continent far away, maybe. With her dark brown hair, she blends easily enough with her family, and diversity among the islanders is common. Her milder accent is more proof she's from somewhere foreign.

And then it hits me. Dark brown hair. Light, clear skin. Whenever anyone in the family has a question about Freedom, they ask Miri.

"You're from Freedom," I whisper.

She nods and puts her hand on my knee. "Freedom One, actually."

"But how—?"

"I was fourteen when I escaped. I ran away one day, upset about something. I'd had a scuffle with another Batch member, but beyond that I don't even remember why I was so upset. I ran to the concert house. The one that sits at the edge of the ocean."

"Yes," I say, thinking of my conversation with Theron about shells versus sails. "I know it."

"I ran there, thinking . . . Oh, I don't know what I thought. It just seemed so magical to me, somehow. I'd hoped it would be the perfect place to hide and be lost forever." Miri brushes a lock of hair behind my ear. "I met a woman there. When I confessed that I'd run away, she convinced me to follow her to a secret place, somewhere I really could get lost forever. Escape from my Batch. Escape Freedom. But first, she had to remove my tracker."

Miri opens her mouth and points to a gaping hole on the

left side where a tooth should have been. "It hurt like death coming out, but I figured I could get my tooth back when I was Remade, eh." She grins but quickly grows serious as she pulls a folded paper out of her pocket. "The woman took me to a rebel camp on the other side of the harbor. I have no reason to believe it's not still there." Her voice is shaking as she unfolds the paper. It's a hand-drawn map of Freedom One, complete with the concert house and harbor. Detailed instructions are written on one side. "Here, on the north side of the concert house is a bridge with a red rail over the water. When you've reached the third section of the bridge, there's a section of the rail painted orange. It's subtle, only noticeable if you're looking, but you'll see it." Miri shakes her head, and her voice cracks.

Kai wraps an arm around his mother.

Miri takes a deep breath and continues. "That's the spot where you'll need to jump. Night is better, but go when you think you won't be seen, whenever that chance arises. Jump and swim down. Keep going, even when you think you don't have enough breath for the return trip up, keep diving down." Her lips tremble. "There, at the bottom, you'll see a light glowing around a trunk. Inside the trunk will be rebreathers. Insert one in your mouth like you would a snorkel and bite down. Inhale to breathe. There's a round, metal door to the right of the trunk, as though it leads straight into the ocean floor. Open it, and swim down into a chamber, closing the door behind you. It will be dark, and you'll be frightened. It was the most terrifying thing I've experienced, feeling trapped like that, and I was with someone who knew what she was doing. You two are going to have to trust me . . ." Miri shudders.

I hold her hand and press it against my face, thinking how brave she must have been then. As a Batcher, she wouldn't have known how to swim. She was only fourteen and ready to trust a stranger. Ready to take on a new and scary world.

"Make sure you close the door behind you. It's the trigger to let them know someone's there. They'll drain the chamber for you. Follow the tunnel until you come to a grate at the end. There's a ladder, set into the wall leading up. Take it. When you come up, there'll be a guard stationed there. Tell him you're part of the Rise. Do you understand? The Rise."

I nod. "The Rise. We'll remember."

Kai takes the paper from his mother and zips it into a pocket.

"They'll be able to get your tracker out, Nine." She reaches into another pocket and pulls out small shiny stones that glimmer in the sunlight. She opens my hand and pours them in. "This is gold," she says. "It's very valuable among the rebels. You can use it to barter passage on a steamship so you and Kai can come back home."

"Thank you," I say, closing my hand over the gold. "For everything." My voice trembles, and Miri pulls me into an embrace.

"I love you, Nine." She pulls back and presses her nose to mine, stroking my cheek with her thumb. "You take care of my Kai, okay?"

I nod. "I promise."

After too short a time, and too few hugs and kisses among the family, Kai and I are standing on the edge of the canoe, drifting into the ocean while his family waves, standing in the water, soaked through.

"My necklace," I whisper, running my fingers along my bare collarbone. I forgot the necklace Kai gave me. I close my eyes and picture it, lying on the dresser next to my shell collection. I see my bed, still unmade, with a blue cushion leaning against it. And the pale blue wall, now with a picture of me and Kai, holding hands with a promise of love and family hanging between us. I wonder if I'll see any of those things again.

I watch his family, *my family*, become smaller and smaller until they are only tiny dots in the distance. I watch the island shrink until it seems a hiccup of land over the blue of ocean, and then even that disappears. I watch until dark replaces the blue of the sky, and piercing stars shine through the black. I watch until Kai pulls me into his arms, kisses my forehead, and lets me fall into his chest.

PART THREE

Chapter Twenty

Hold it tighter," Kai yells at me after the boom slips from my grip for the third time.

"I'm doing my best," I snap back at him.

"Well, it's not good enough."

I grit my teeth and grab the wooden boom, leaning back with all my weight to hold on to it while Kai straps it in place. I feel another gust of wind at my back and cringe, knowing it will slip again. I refuse to let go, and the sail makes a snapping sound as it tightens against the wind and pulls me along with it.

Kai curses and turns to where I am dangling over the water, trying to grip the boom with my legs and arms, desperately hoping to avoid falling into the ocean. "What do you think you're doing?" he says, laughing at my scrambling limbs.

"I held it tighter," I say, my fingers slipping.

Kai pulls me in with the boom and hands me the rope. "I'll hold; you tie."

I pull on the length of rope and secure the knot in place, collapsing when I'm done. My arms ache from working the sails these past weeks. Kai says we are halfway to Freedom, but I'm not sure how much more my muscles can take. It's hard work, sailing this canoe. And there's no escape from the energy-draining sun. We sleep during the day, mostly because Kai navigates easier by the stars at night. But it's much more pleasant in the cool air too. I'm ready to collapse into sleep to escape the oncoming daylight as soon as possible.

Walking along the crossbeam that connects the two hulls of the canoe, I spy our food supply and sigh. Kai is going to have to dive soon. Tomorrow at the latest. I hate it when he does. All I can think about are the sharks that roam the waters. Kai doesn't have the protection of the reef out here, and our attempts at net fishing haven't proved successful yet.

I sit on my bed: a pile of clothes and blankets stuffed between our dwindling coconut supply and water jugs. Kai's bed is on the other side of the boat, but he sits next to me, which means he's not ready for sleep yet.

"I'm going to stay up a little longer," he says. "I want to make sure this wind heading holds before I fall asleep." He sits cross-legged and I lie back, my head in his lap. "How is your head?" he asks.

"It hurts," I say. As much as I wish I could ignore the buzzing in my head, it's still a constant reminder of the danger we're in. It makes me think we could be found at any moment, and Kai could get hurt and it will be my fault. It reminds me we are not free. Every vibration is a countdown to the moment we are killed, destroyed.

"Do you need a distraction?" he asks.

I know what that means. "Yes," I say with a sigh of relief.

Kai leans over and kisses my eyes, my cheeks, my ears. He kisses my mouth upside down, which feels so good my lips tremble. He kisses my chin and jaw and neck. I don't notice the buzzing anymore. There is only Kai.

I lean over the edge of the canoe and count. *One. Two. Three. Four.* I spot the fluorescent orange strip of the top of Kai's snorkel in the distance. Too quickly, he dives back under. *One. Two. Three. Four. Five. Six.* When he surfaces, I realize he's too far.

"Kai!" I call, but he cannot hear me from this distance.

He goes under again. The sails are down, but the canoe, caught in a current, drifts away from where he dives. *Kai, you're too far.*

When Kai comes up this time, he holds his spear above the surface to show me the large tuna he caught. I can tell when he realizes how far out he is by the way he immediately swims for the canoe. *Come on come on come on.* I bite my lip, wondering how long it takes for a predator to smell blood in the water. He reaches the canoe an eternity later and tosses the spear on board with the fish still attached. I reach for his hand, but he shouts and goes under the water.

No. No, no, no. Where is he?

His head surfaces, and his face twists in pain. "Nine—"

I jump in immediately. I don't care if there's a monster

under the surface, I will not abandon him. I'll go down with him. I'll not leave him the way I left Theron. Wrapping my arm around his neck, I pull him to the boat. He is stiff and grasping his leg in pain.

"What is it?" I ask, one arm holding him in the water, one arm on the lip of the canoe.

"My leg," he says through clenched teeth. "Muscle cramp."

I somehow manage to get myself into the boat without letting go of him. I am surprised how easily I'm able to get him on board. It might be from becoming stronger these weeks on the canoe, but more likely it's from the rush of adrenaline that surges through me. I stretch out his leg onto my lap and massage where he says the pain is. His rigid form begins to relax, and he drapes a wet arm over his eyes.

"You aren't drinking enough water," I say.

"If we run out of water, cramping muscles will be the least of our problems."

"If I lose you, it doesn't matter how much water is left."

Kai sits up and grabs my chin. "If you lose me, you can't give up."

I shake my head. I don't want to talk about this right now.

"Listen to me, Nine. If you lose me—whether I die out here on the water or am captured by Freedom or whatever—you can't stop fighting. You can't stop trying. Keep living, and stand up for what's right. Fight for what's worth fighting for."

I swipe his hand away from my face. "No." I can't believe he mentioned me losing him. It's not the most comforting thing to say when I just dragged his body out of the water. "Life is not worth living if I don't have you."

Kai's eyes go wide, and I know he's mad, but I don't care.

My words tumble out of me. "I don't care if it's in Mahawai, in a rebel camp, or in cracked Freedom itself. As long as you're with me, it doesn't matter where I live. I just . . . I can't lose you, Kai."

"It does matter," he says. His eyes narrow at me, angry and confused. "It matters."

"I don't want to talk about this anymore," I say. I turn away and hunt for a knife to clean the fish.

Kai's fingers can't keep still, and I feel them on my side. One hand takes a position on my upper arm where they form what feel like guitar chords, while the other mindlessly strums at my waist. He hums a tune that echoes off the surface of the ocean in the still night. Water laps against the side of the canoe in a steady beat, as though the sea wants to perform along. The flapping of the sails as they catch wind gusts completes the symphony, and I smile, promising myself to always remember this moment.

I'm not afraid of the ocean anymore. It's still filled with monsters and a vast unknown, but here, with Kai—whom I wouldn't argue with if he claimed to be born from the sea himself—it's different. Now I welcome the taste of salt on my tongue and wake early to see the shades of the water under the light of every sunset. Sometimes the sea seems to hold its breath, creating a glass finish on the surface so perfect that I think I could walk on it, and I can't help but hold my breath too.

"Have you always loved the water?" I ask.

"Always."

"You've never been afraid of it? Ever?"

"Not really."

"What about the Virus?" I ask, thinking about what we learned as children back in Freedom.

"What *about* the Virus?" he asks, confusion in his voice.

"It killed most of the population of Earth. And it came from the sea."

"It didn't come from the sea. That's just something they tell you in Freedom to make you afraid of the ocean."

I frown. "Why would they make us afraid?"

"To keep you in Freedom. To give you second thoughts about trying to escape."

I've never met anyone who'd wanted to escape, not before Miriama, but I'd heard rumors of people doing such things. I think of how Theron wished he could sail the ocean like the explorers of old. I wonder how many more people there have been with dreams of escape. Of being free and exploring the unknown.

I think about the main cause of the Virus, not just its fabled origin. "Do you want to have lots of babies, Kai?"

His nervous laugh shakes my body against his. "Yes, I want to have lots of babies."

Be fruitful and multiply . . .

"And you aren't afraid of overpopulation?"

"The Virus spread fast and easily because there were a lot of people back then, yes. But that wasn't the *cause* of it. It was no one's fault—the disease. Overpopulation of Earth wasn't to blame." Kai continues to strum his fingers against my side.

"Without a cure, our ancestors could only sit and wait it out. Luckily, a few survived. Maybe how we live on the island started as a way to avoid Freedom's Techies, but connecting with the land and sea the way we do—"

I look up and see the waves reflected in his eyes.

"I wouldn't want it any other way," he says. "Having children is a gift. A blessing. Our family is a part of the rhythm of the planet."

I smile, thinking of the symphony I hear on the water. Kai's words create a harmony with the music that makes me feel like a part of that connection. "I want to have lots of babies too," I say. It seems so trivial a thing to speak of, out here on the water with no one around. Yet with every buzz in my head it's as though we are crowded out by those who would tear us apart.

"Good to know," Kai says with a smile on his face.

I punch him in the arm, and he laughs out loud. I bring his face to mine. "I love you," I say, kissing his salty, chapped lips.

"Mmm," he moans.

A large splash of ocean water sprays over us.

"What the—?"

We both turn and gasp at the same time. The eye of a giant animal stares back at us, rolling backward into the water. I open my mouth to scream, but Kai pulls me close.

"It's okay," he says, anticipating my terror. "It's just a blue whale. It won't hurt us."

I nod, holding his arm tight. The whale breaches the surface again, this time knocking the side of our canoe. The sheer grandness of it is hard to fathom. I know what we see is just a portion of its massive body, and I can't comprehend how it can

225

move through the water at all. And so stealthily, it seems, by the way it surprised us.

A spray of water bursts from a spout on the top of its head, falling on us like a misty rain. I laugh nervously as its giant eye blinks at us.

"It's checking us out," Kai whispers. He extends his arm, pulling my hand along with his to touch the whale.

I hold my breath, and my heart feels like it's beating in the tips of my fingers. I bite my lip as the hard but slippery surface of its body moves beneath my touch. "Wow."

"I know." Kai's face is illuminated under the light of the moon. "I've never seen one this close before."

"It's beautiful." Suddenly I feel so tiny. Insignificant. Like a breeze that is here one moment and gone before you have a chance to ask where it came from or where it's going next. Before you're able to *really* feel it.

I think of all those places I've only seen in pictures. Jungles and deserts. Forests and mountains. It's suddenly all so magnificent compared to how small I feel. But instead of making me feel unimportant, I feel grander. Blessed. Honored to be a part of the giant puzzle of our planet. A puzzle that connects me and Kai, here, together on the water. It's a humbling feeling. A happy feeling.

"Tell me about Theron." Kai passes me a coconut, and I take a giant gulp from the hole he drilled into it. It's still dark out, but dawn approaches on the horizon.

"Theron?"

"Yes," he says, chewing on a piece of coconut flesh. "He was your only family, and I want to know about him."

It's a good distraction from the buzz in my ears, thinking about Theron, and for that alone I'm glad Kai brought him up. "Theron liked to fight," I say. I picture him in our training room, with gloves strapped to his fists, hitting and kicking the practice bag over and over. "I got a lot of comments from other Batchers about my freckles. Since we were all bald and wore the same clothes, I guess that's the only thing they had to pick on. Sometimes I think Theron became my friend just so he'd have an excuse to beat others up every once in a while."

"I like this guy already," Kai says, smiling.

"Despite his love of pain," I say with a grin, "he wanted to become a Healer."

"Even though he'd have to use needles?" Kai asks with feigned shock.

"Yes." I laugh. "Apparently it didn't leave him in tears when he was in the same room as one."

I tell Kai of how Theron and I would steal chocolate from the eatery kitchen at night, and how we planned to live together after we were Remade, in our own apartment. Kai cringes when I mention us showering and sleeping together, but I explain that was just how things were in Freedom—no sense of modesty or restraint like that among the rebel families of his island. I didn't know any other way.

I speak of our excursion into central Freedom, of Theron getting knocked out trying to keep me from cage fighting. Kai laughs at that, sending a warm tingling through my body at the sound. It's a strange feeling, placing Kai and Theron together in my thoughts. It's almost like I've lived two separate lives. Life with Theron versus life with Kai. I realize as we approach Freedom, those worlds will blend, blurring the lines between life before the crash and after. I'm not sure if I'm ready for that.

"He was so nervous he put the wrong shoes on my feet," I say as I tell Kai about the shuttle crash. I don't know why I remember that small detail. It seemed important at the time, somehow. Flustered Theron was not the norm, and it scared me. I tell Kai other details of that night: the beeping in the plane, the impact with the water, holding onto Theron as we jumped out. And the sound—the awful, awful sound—of dying metal.

"There were bodies in the water," I say. I look up and realize Kai is at my side, holding me. I don't remember him coming to sit beside me. "Cree. Cree was dead. Debris floated everywhere. And Bristol." I rock back and forth as I tell of how Theron killed him to save us. "It was terrible, Kai. All of it. Somehow I knew—I knew we would die. Theron was certain we'd be rescued because of our trackers, but they don't work outside of Freedom."

"But your tracker is working. Whether it's so they can find you or . . ." His words trail away. "Right now it's buzzing."

I'm frustrated Kai brought it up. I'd forgotten all about it while talking about Theron. "I don't know why," I say, bringing my hand to my ear.

"You didn't see Theron die, did you? That day I stitched you up . . ." Kai touches the long scar on the inside of my arm. "You said he told you to swim away."

I don't answer. I didn't see Theron die, but what I did see

was just as bad. He couldn't swim and was terribly injured yet I left him there with that beast. He was as good as dead when I abandoned him.

"Were there other survivors?" Kai asks.

I nod, remembering the voices of others in our Batch, frantic and hopeless in the water. I wonder how long it took for them to die. Hours? Days?

"And then you found me," I say.

Kai pulls me close to him.

"I miss him, Kai. I miss him so much."

"I know," he says, running his hands through my hair. "I'm so sorry, Nine."

It will be strange to be in Freedom, or close to it, at least, without Theron there. Change is hard, terribly hard. I hold on to Kai and inhale his sweet, earthy scent. Change can be a good thing too.

The sun has fully cleared the horizon now, and I see something in the distance. "Is there a storm coming?" I ask, pointing far to the northwest. It looks like a mass of low-lying gray clouds hovering over the ocean.

Kai squints and looks where I point. He purses his lips together and inhales sharply. "Those aren't clouds," he says, standing up to adjust the sails of the canoe. "It's smoke."

Chapter
Twenty-One

It's a long day of waiting in the water. Kai thought we should wait until dark before approaching the smoke. Less chance of being spotted.

As soon as the stars are visible in the sky, we move in.

"We're too far south for Freedom," he says, glancing at the sky. "But it's definitely Australia." If it's not Freedom One, then it must be a rebel camp.

After an hour of sailing, we reach land. We tie up the canoe on a rocky shore and disembark, keeping close to the trees in the dark to stay out of sight. Before long, we come to the outskirts of a village, but tents dot the landscape, not permanent homes. As though the people are only here temporarily. As we follow the smoke, the tents come more frequently, some bigger than others, and only then do I notice they are empty.

We carefully step into one of the larger tents. The space

smells like a small animal crawled in here to die and no one bothered to remove it. I cover my nose and mouth then spin around to take it all in. Tall and deep shelves line the walls with ragged fabrics piled haphazardly on them. They almost look like . . . beds. As though people were stacked in here to sleep, taking up as little space as possible. I imagine it to be the kind of place prisoners live, not rebel families.

"I don't like this." Kai pulls my hand away from my face and leads me out of the tent.

We travel farther within a copse of trees, following the direction of a road thirty yards to our left. It's not long before I hear something. Kai brings his fingers to his lips and motions for me to get down. The red of fire looms in the distance, but I'm not sure what's burning. The smell of smoke and ash is overwhelming. I squint my eyes and see a crowd of people huddled against a brick building closer to us. Uniformed guards patrol around them, wearing black jumpsuits with large firearms strapped over their shoulders.

"Seekers," I whisper. If I squint hard enough, I can see the symbols on their shoulders. A red star in a white circle. The symbol of Freedom.

Kai turns to me and raises an eyebrow.

"The ones in black," I say, pointing to the guards. "They hunt for the lost by their trackers."

Kai's eyes go wide in an instant. "This was a bad idea," he says, grabbing my arm. "Let's go back."

"Wait," I say. I look back at the mass of people. Fear is evident on each face—men, women, and children. And from what I've learned about life outside of Freedom, I know they are fathers, mothers, families. "They need our help, Kai."

He drops my arm and groans because he knows I'm right. He puts his hand to my ear.

"Nothing's changed," I say. "The vibrations are the same. They don't know I'm here. Or they just aren't looking for me here."

Kai nods and leads us through the trees until we're close enough to hear voices. We lie on the forest floor and strain to hear what they say.

" . . . gave you a chance to live here under generous conditions. We let you stay together as long as you followed a few simple rules. But you weren't grateful for that freedom." It's a female Seeker who speaks, turned away from us. Her words are harsh. I think of the Seeker who spoke so kindly to me when he tested my tracker the day I boarded the shuttle. He was nothing like this woman. "You disobeyed," she continues. "You squandered that freedom. So now you will be punished."

Other Seekers grab the children from the crowd and pull them to the open space in front of the Seeker in charge. Men and women scream and scramble for their children, but there are too many guards, and when they don't stay against the building on their own, the adults are beaten into obedience.

I don't understand. These people aren't free-breakers. I can't imagine they've done anything to infringe on the free will of Freedom citizens. Not hundreds of miles away.

"You were told not to breed," the Seeker shouts. She holds one of the children in front of her by his neck, a boy of about eight. His hair is dark and curly, and I think of Hemi, crying for me back home on the beach. "These children are evidence you have disobeyed a direct order from the Prime Maker. They no longer belong to you." She turns to the other uniformed Seekers and says, "Take them away."

As the children are dragged away, an eruption of cries follow from the adults still huddled against the building. One man breaks free of his restrainers and runs for the children. He hasn't gone ten feet before a loud shot rings through the clearing.

I open my mouth to scream, but Kai's hand is there before any sound comes out. The man's body drops to the ground with a loud thump. I am shaking when the other Seekers aim their guns at the rest of the adults, ready to fire should anyone else attempt to go after the children. I grit my teeth and push Kai's hand away. I'm not going to make a sound. The vibration in my head is a warning siren now. We have no weapons, no way to fight back. I don't know what to do. I lie there, too shocked to move.

"Grab the adult females," the woman Seeker orders the others. "Eridian wants more surrogates. Take the rest to the commuter for transport."

"Eri," I whisper. Is the Prime Maker behind these attacks? I don't know what a surrogate is, but it can't be anything good. What will they do to the rest of the adults? To the children?

I turn to Kai. "The empty village on the west island—" I don't have to finish because he knows what I'm thinking—he was right. The people from the rebel village he found were taken, not killed, and likely brought here to be stored and sorted like animals.

"Let's go," Kai says.

I let him drag me through the forest and back the way we came. His grip on my arm is so painful, I want to hit his hand away, but I'm too weak to move anything but my stumbling feet.

"Did you see the baby?" I ask, the sound barely escaping my throat. "They took the baby too."

"I know." His hand tightens on my arm, and I wince.

I've never felt so helpless. How can we do nothing? How can we let these people be treated this way? It's not right—but what can we do? I dig my heels into the forest floor and pull my arm back. "We have to do something."

Kai tugs on the collar of my shirt and pulls me to him. His face is practically in mine when he says, "I'm getting you out of here, Nine. Back to the boat."

"And then what?"

"I don't know. I just . . . I have to think." He shakes his head. "Something's wrong here."

"Of course something's wrong," I say a little too loud. "They're tearing these families apart. Kidnapping them."

"Exactly." He rests his forehead on mine and whispers, "Didn't you hear that woman? They let these people continue to live here in this . . . prison camp. Why would they do that? Where are they taking them? It doesn't make sense."

"Are you really complaining that the Seekers didn't kill them instead?"

"No, I just . . ." He pulls back and bites his lip. "Maybe we can sail to the rebel camp in Freedom, like my mom said. Organize an army to come back here—"

"They could all be gone by then."

Kai shakes me by my fisted shirt. "I'm getting you away from—"

The sound of nearby laughter makes us turn. Quickly, Kai pulls me with him behind a tree, and we peek around the corner to see who made the sound.

Three male Seekers drag a woman to a spot not ten yards away hidden among the trees. They throw her to the ground, and I can tell from where we are that she is very pregnant, her stomach evidence that she's close to full term.

"You like making babies?" One of the men spits at her. "Yes? You like making them?"

The other two Seekers hold the woman down. Her screams of panic are too much to bear. I don't know what they plan to do, but I can't stand aside and let her be hurt by these monsters.

I try to run to them but Kai holds me back. "Let go," I say, but he's too strong for me.

"Nine, *please.*"

If he won't let me go, I'll have to get their attention another way. "Stop!" I scream at them. "Stop!" My voice echoes through the forest, and I've no doubt they heard me. I don't care if I die. I can't stand aside anymore and let these innocent people be hurt, let them be killed.

The spitting Seeker aims his firearm at Kai and me. "Who are you?" he snarls.

I glance at Kai, my tongue frozen in my mouth. I hadn't thought about him when I jumped out from behind the tree. I was ready to give my life to save this girl, not Kai's life. Suddenly

I'm in a panic, trying to think of a way to salvage my idiotic outburst.

"Speak now, girlie, before I blow your friend's head off." He aims the gun at Kai, and I jump in front of him.

"I'm from Freedom," I say. "My shuttle crashed on the way to my Remake, and I was lost in the ocean."

The Seeker's eyes narrow, and a grin starts to form at the corner of his mouth. "A Batchling with red hair? I don't think so."

"Look," I say, turning my head and pointing to my tracker. "See, I *am* from Freedom. I'm just trying to get home." I don't dare look behind me at Kai. I hope he's sane enough to go along with my story. I can't see any other option right now.

The Seeker pulls me by the ear to him. He touches the metal nub, and I cringe at the pain in my head. My body knocks against his gun. "Hey, Cael," he calls behind him. "You got a tracker gun on ya?"

Cael brings a familiar plastic firearm to the Seeker. The third man stays with the woman, pushing her arms down to keep her still. My heart beats so hard the sound of it almost drowns the vibrations in my head.

The Seeker brings the plastic barrel to my head, and I gasp as it connects to the tracker with a snap. He pulls the trigger. "Hmm. It's defective. Probably corroded from ocean water." He presses the red button on the barrel and yanks the tracker out of my skull. Out of my head.

The vibration is replaced with screams. My own screams. I fall to my knees, and my hand flies to my ear, the pain almost more than I can handle.

"Bron, you idiot," Cael says. "We don't have any bandages. She's gonna bleed out all over the place."

Bron points his gun at Kai. "You, take your shirt off."

Kai does as he says and kneels next to me, pressing the fabric against my head.

"Get away from her." Bron kicks Kai's arms away, and I dare to turn to him. His face is pale, and his hands ball up in fists. His chest rises and falls in labored breathing.

Don't do anything cracked, Kai. I am screaming in short outbursts now. My arm is covered in blood that flows down from my head.

"Don't worry," Cael tells me. "We'll get a new tracker installed soon enough. It's a good thing you found us. We never would have been able to find you with that defective tracker."

A sharp pain grows within my stomach. The buzzing wasn't a countdown, wasn't Freedom searching for me. It was just my tracker breaking down. They wouldn't have found me. I wouldn't have been hurt. We left the island for nothing. We left Miri and Ara. Pua and Hemi and Tama. We left our true freedom.

Bron kicks Kai to the ground and grinds his boot into his head. "Doesn't look like your friend has a tracker, though." He bends down and spits in Kai's face. "You're not from Freedom, are you?" Bron's voice is a snarl, and he pushes the barrel of his gun into the side of Kai's head.

"Remember what I said, Nine," Kai says in a rush. "It matters. You can't stop. It matters."

No. I won't let this happen. "He's with me," I say, pushing the gun away from Kai's head. I stand and look Bron right in the face. "I am under special assignment by the Prime Maker herself. If you kill him, you'll be compromising that assignment."

Bron hesitates, and I can see Kai's eyes go wide for a brief moment, confused. Doubting. The air between us becomes so tight I can almost hear it. Like the tiniest vibration would make it snap. *Don't let go of me yet, Kai. Please, trust me.*

Bron flips his gun around and brings it down on Kai's head, knocking him out. "You better be right about that, girlie, or you'll regret not letting your friend die peacefully."

I nod like one with authority. "I demand to see the Prime Maker as soon as possible."

"I think that can be arranged." Bron smirks. "Get rid of her."

I think he is talking about me and brace myself to be dragged away from the forest. But instead the third Seeker releases the woman on the ground. She scrambles up and runs. I slump my shoulders in relief. At least I was able to save her.

And then Cael brings up his firearm and shoots at her as she runs away.

I drop the fabric from my ear, screaming—and the blunt end of Bron's gun flies into my face.

Chapter
Twenty-Two

When I open my eyes, a shining light blinds me. My head is pounding, my right ear is on fire, and I can feel a large bump forming on the left side of my head. As I try to turn away from the light, my head and neck resist. Sticky, wet blood has run down from where my tracker used to be. I try to touch it, but realize my hands are tied behind me, pinning me to the chair I sit in.

"Hello?" I call out. I can't tell if I'm indoors or out, alone or not, with this cracked light shining right in my eyes. The echo of my own voice is the only answer. I'm indoors but alone.

I can't get away from the light so I close my eyes and pull at the rope around my hands. "Kai," I whisper. "Please be okay."

"What is this?" A commanding voice comes from behind me, followed by the loud click-click-click of shoes with heels.

I feel the light in my face turn away, and I open my eyes, blinking to adjust to the dimness of the rest of the room. Cold hands behind me untie the ropes.

"This will not do at all," the voice says, moving in front of me. I would recognize the red hair pulled back into a tight bun anywhere.

"Eri," I say in a breath.

"I'm so sorry about how you've been treated here, Nine," she says with a tsk. "I'm going to have a long talk with Bron. And after all you've been through, you poor, poor dear." I can tell she attempts to make her words warm, like she did the first day we met. But this time I see right through them. She can't mask the cold of her voice with a variation in pitch or careful word selection anymore.

"Where is he?" I ask. "The boy . . . the one that was with me. What have you done with him?"

"Kai?" she asks, her saying his name giving me a chill right to my bones. "Kai is fine. He is recovering from a blow to his head in the next room."

"I want to see him," I say. "*Please.*"

"Kai can't be disturbed right now. I think we should talk first, anyhow." Eri reaches for the bump on my head. "The crash was most unfortunate, but we were under the impression you didn't survive. We searched for you for days, and nothing."

"My tracker was defective," I say, repeating what Cael had said. "I washed ashore on some island, and Kai found me there."

"Do you know where this island is?"

I shake my head. "I don't think Kai does either. We were the only ones there."

"No one else on the entire island?"

"It was very small."

"And how did Kai get there?"

"He can't remember," I say. I need to stop her questions before she catches me in my lies. "I told him about Freedom and how we could both be Remade, if he helped me return. He's been eager to go ever since."

"Hmm." Eridian purses her lips. "The Remake is reserved for those Made in Freedom. But this is a special circumstance, I think." She taps her red lips, deciding something. "It's an interesting turn in our little experiment."

I wonder if she's glad I was found, so that she can continue testing me—that I wasn't a complete waste of years of observation.

"We'll need to take you two back to Freedom first, get you cleaned up and healed. And we'll need to install a new tracker in the both of you."

I nod in agreement. "Can I see him now?"

Eri ignores my question. "Let's talk about what you've seen here with the rebels today."

"Here?" I didn't know we were still in the prison camp. I wonder what the Prime Maker is doing here, so far outside of Freedom.

"Yes, here. Among these . . . savage people." She spits the words out like a bad taste in her mouth. "You need to understand why we must gather and control them. They've taken it upon themselves to populate without regulation."

"I know how infants are Made—outside of Freedom, that is." I watch her face carefully, trying to read what she thinks of

241

that. I dare to say one more thing: "And I have a feeling they are Made the same way in Freedom."

Her eyes flash with surprise for the briefest of seconds.

"That's why I couldn't become a Maker, isn't it? Because I don't have fair, clear skin or dark brown hair. I don't have the right genetic makeup. You couldn't risk passing on my traits to another Batch member." For the first time in my life, I wonder what my real parents looked like. What traits did I inherit from them? My father's hair? My mother's freckles? What parts of my personality were passed down from those before me, and which were learned? Which are just . . . me?

Her mouth opens to say something, but I speak before she has a chance to respond.

"It's genius," I say. "Really. The population needs to be controlled, and the best way to do that is by producing a set number of humans each year, maintaining order." I gulp and freeze my eyes to hide what really burns within me. I do my best to push aside the image of all those children being taken from their families. "What these . . . rebels . . . are doing—it's wrong and irresponsible. Kai and I both think so."

"Yes," she says, her eyes brightening. "Overpopulation brings death and disease. Freedom's Batches are the best solution." She shakes her head as though to clear it. "The *only* solution. We cannot risk another Virus outbreak, so the population must remain small and controlled. It's the only way to establish peace." She pauses, and her mouth twists in disgust. "These rebels put all of us in danger. It is selfish and wrong."

Eridian is crazy enough, blinded enough, to believe that Kai and I agree with her sick logic.

I nod, thinking about Sub level Two. I'm sure now, if I had opened that door, I would've seen that woman in the pain of labor, giving birth to what would become a Batch member in the next generation of Freedom's finest citizens. If I walked farther in the room, looked in those stark white tents, I might have seen the other females with bellies as large as Miriama's or the woman killed in the forest.

"I don't understand why they choose to live this way," Eri says. "They try to elude our Techies by not using any kind of electric energy, but it doesn't keep us at bay forever. We'll find them all eventually." She pulls a chair from the shadows and slides it next to mine, sitting with her legs crossed. "They live together, one male and one female, having these children. It is so confining, having to do everything for the helpless creatures."

I think about the countless people who worked together to raise us as children in Freedom, and I can't picture one face. Because there was no specific person, there were numerous people, all doing their Trade work. Even Fosterers, whose job it was to care for small children, alternated daily. They didn't love us or care about us; they just worked to earn points. We didn't have an Arapeta to protect us, to feed us, to teach us. We didn't have a Miriama to take us in her arms and fill our souls with strength with a hug and a whisper of encouragement in our ear. "Mothers," I whisper. "Fathers."

"Terms of imprisonment," she says with a hiss. "Those people do nothing but bind and label these ridiculous ideals of *family*. There's no freedom in it, only grief and unhappiness that drags you down. They are savages with no sense of independence or liberty."

I frown at her. She knows nothing of families. They are love and belonging and sacrifice. If that does not bring happiness and freedom, I don't know what can. Being stripped of the opportunity to choose such a life—that's not happiness. It is despair and oppression. I wonder if Eridian has someone to love. Someone to care about other than herself.

"Can I see Kai now?" I whisper, not really believing she'll agree to it.

"When we get back to Freedom," Eri says, "you'll need to choose your name and Trade in the computer system. Kai will do the same, and after a few days' recovery, we'll send you both to the Remake facility on a special shuttle." She flashes her bright smile at me. "I think you've waited long enough to be Remade, don't you, Nine?"

I smile the best I can. "Eri?" I ask.

"Yes?"

"Who Made me?" Now that there's no secret between us regarding what the Makers actually do, I want to know. "I couldn't have been Made by the Makers in the Core building."

"You were an experiment, Nine."

I know that. And it doesn't answer my question. I bite my lip, not wanting to press her, considering how far I've gotten her to trust me and my intentions.

Eri sighs. "*I* Made you," she says. "I'm one of your Makers."

"What?"

"You weren't an accident, Nine."

I got my red hair from Eridian? The Prime Maker of Freedom One herself? It's impossible. I can't picture her ever subjecting herself to the burden of a pregnancy, the pains of labor. "You're my . . . mother?"

"No. Definitely not." She shakes her head in disgust. "I just made a contribution of my own to the woman who birthed you."

That doesn't make any sense.

"You see, Nine." Eri crosses her legs the other way. "I'm not from Freedom. I escaped from my rebel camp when I was about your age to *find* it. The ideal life. The ability to choose anything I wanted. To be equal. I was taken in and allowed to be Remade, much like we are doing for your Kai. I sacrificed a lot of things— things that were very dear to me—to obtain that freedom."

It explains why a child she Made would inherit her red hair. And maybe before she was Remade, Eri had freckles too. But I'm still confused about what she meant by her *contribution* toward Making me.

"I'm sure you know by now," she says, "that we remove your ability to have offspring during your Remake."

"Why would you do that?" I press my lips together at my outburst. I can't believe I said that out loud. But my heart aches at the thought.

Eri taps her foot, impatient. "There are no unauthorized children born in Freedom, Nine, because we don't want the Virus to return. It's that simple. People who breed without our approval risk our very survival. We're saving people this way."

I nod, my hands sweating. I want this conversation to end. It's disconcerting, wondering what else I may have inherited from this disturbed person in front of me.

"After a person's Remake, we keep the sperm or eggs—store

them, just in case." She pauses, then says gently, "I wasn't always female, Nine."

My jaw drops open. Eridian. She was *male.*

"I used some of my own sperm, since it was the only specimen I knew to have unusual properties. I knew it would produce a nonstandard Batch member. It was easy enough to fertilize a Maker egg and inject it into a rebel surrogate. And it worked perfectly." Eri sits tall and waves her hand in front of me, proud of her little science experiment.

She is my *father.*

My stomach churns, and I think I'm going to be sick. "Surrogate?"

"Yes, of course." She talks slowly as though I were a small child. "We would never put our own citizens through the torture of pregnancy and labor. Not anymore . . ." Her voice trails away before she clears her throat. "We use surrogates—women taken from rebel camps. With eggs and sperm from our Makers, we implant them in surrogate females who serve as incubation vessels. Everything is timed appropriately to produce ten males and ten females every month, like clockwork."

No wonder that woman in the Core building was guarded so well. She really was a prisoner, contributing to the welfare of Freedom in the Prime Maker's twisted and perverse way.

"We give these people a purpose," Eri says. "A way to contribute to the cause of Freedom." She lifts her chin as though she should be rewarded for her kindness. "It's better than burning in the mass fires, don't you think?"

I feel like an invisible hand has wrapped around my throat,

making every breath I inhale a struggle. The smoke, the fires, we saw—those were people burning.

I try not to think about how many people were killed here today. Maybe they refused to follow the Seekers' commands. Or perhaps they were just . . . extras—not needed by the Prime Maker. Either way, this whole thing makes my stomach feel worse.

"I'm glad we had this talk, Nine. It proves the experiment was a success."

I lift my head at that, confused. "What do you mean?"

"Making all Batch members the same, making them equal, only made them want to become different when they were finally Remade. To stand out. To be their own person." She folds her arms with an arrogant smile. "I thought if we Made someone different, someone *other*, someone . . . like me, she'd do whatever she could to become like everyone else. She'd want to belong, want to blend. And considering the amount of trouble we've had from the rebels lately, it's more important than ever to make sure our citizens in Freedom feel like they belong. We don't want them to question things or long for another life—another way."

Eri would have never agreed to give our citizens the choice to live as families. She wants us to feel alone, to want to belong to something. To want to belong to Freedom. Isn't that what I'd always wanted—to belong? To be like everyone else? To be like . . . Theron. My mouth goes dry thinking about how I really was like Eri, willing to do whatever I could to be equal. But then the crash happened. And after all those months on the island, with a family, with Kai, I'm not sure I want to belong anymore. Not to Freedom anyway. I want to belong to Kai. He's all that matters to me.

"And here you are, *my Nine.*" Eri searches her pockets for something. "You're here because you were determined to belong. I knew it from the moment you chose to be male. You questioned who you were and decided to do something about it. Not everyone is that brave."

So if I choose to be *me*—is that brave too?

She withdraws a small glass bottle and shakes it in her hand. "Not everyone believed I could make it happen, but in the end I was right. The experiment worked."

I think of the man in the gray suit glaring at me during my last academic module. I'm sure he was one of several cabinet members betting against me. I wish I could've proven them right from the start. More than anything, I don't want to be like Eridian. I don't care if we share the same genes. It doesn't mean I inherited anything from her beyond my looks. Does it?

"And because of you," she continues with a thrill in her voice, "I'll be able to convince the other Prime Makers to produce test subjects throughout all the Freedom provinces in the world. With access to rebel sperm and eggs, we'll easily have the diversity we need for the experiments."

I realize what Eri has done is insane. There is no freedom in Freedom. I wonder if there ever was.

"I want to see Kai," I say.

"Not yet, my dear," she says, pouring a clear liquid onto a cloth from her pocket. "It's time to sleep. But you'll see him soon enough."

She brings the cloth to my face and covers my mouth and nose. I breathe in the fumes, and everything turns black.

Chapter Twenty-Three

I know that smell. It's the smell of a Healer building. I open my eyes to a white room. I'm lying in a bed, and I'm cold. After reaching for blankets that aren't there, I sit up to find I'm wearing a pair of gray sweats and a white tank. I sigh, slipping my legs over the edge of the bed and walking to a mirror on the far wall. My face is darker than I remember, the result of weeks on the canoe. The bump on the side of my face is gone, and there's no pain in my head. I reach behind my ear and feel the familiar metal nub of a tracker.

My door opens, and my heart starts to beat faster. "Kai?"

"No."

My face drops as a Healer walks in with a portable touch screen. "How are you feeling today?"

Today? "Fine. How long have I been here?"

"Two days," he says. "Any pain?"

I sit on my bed and sigh. "No pain, no dizziness, no numbing, no nothing."

The Healer narrows his eyes at me. "You are free to leave," he says, "but I've been instructed to tell you that in two days at eighteen hundred hours, you are to report to the Core building to choose your Remake and will subsequently be accompanied to your shuttle."

"Thanks." At least I won't be locked away for those two days. Though with a new tracker installed behind my ear, it's almost the same thing.

The Healer walks toward the door.

"Wait," I say, rushing toward him. "Do you know what happened to the boy brought in with me? Kai?"

"He was released this morning and given the same instructions I just gave you."

"Oh."

He rolls his eyes and shuts the door as he leaves.

Sitting back on my bed, I wonder where Kai could be. I'm surprised he isn't here, waiting for me to wake up. I reach for the pair of socks and shoes next to my bed, wondering where I should start looking for him. I slip on the socks, but when I try to get my foot into the left shoe, something inside resists. Confused, I pull out a piece of paper and begin to unfold it when there's a knock on the door.

I spin around, the paper falling to the floor. "Kai?"

The door opens. It's not Kai.

This boy—this man—is taller. His skin is fair and he has finger-length dark brown hair. It's straight, not curly. And his eyes. I know those eyes. They are blue under dark lashes.

250

"Theron?"

"Nine . . ." His voice is a whisper, deep yet familiar.

"Theron!" I run to him and jump into his arms.

He stumbles backward with a laugh, trying to stand straight under my weight.

I wrap my legs around his waist and hold him tight. He isn't real. He can't be. How can he be here, in front of me? I pull back to get a good look at him.

"Theron," I say again with a laugh. I touch his face, his eyes, nose, and lips. I trace the line of facial hair that skims along the length of his jaw. Our hands find each other's hair at the same time, and we laugh together, running our fingers through their lengths.

"Nine." Theron sighs, pulls my face to his and gives me a giant kiss on the lips.

I wrap my arms around his neck. "You're so . . . tall."

"And you're so . . ." He sets me back on my feet and looks down at me, blushing. " . . . female."

We are laughing and touching and smelling and holding. I don't want to let go, afraid if I do he will disappear. We stay silent for a long time, just looking at each other. My cheeks hurt from smiling so much, and my eyes leak happiness.

"I can't believe you're alive," he says.

"Me? How is it *you're* alive, Theron? After the shark—"

He leads me to the bed where we sit down. "I didn't see the shark after you left," he says. "I was so afraid it went after you instead." He runs his hands down my arms and legs, as though making sure I'm still whole. "Nine, you are the most beautiful thing I've ever seen."

I blush, even though he's told me the same thing a thousand times before. I'm sure he's just glad, as I am, that the other survived what we both thought was not survivable.

"I found a broken piece of the shuttle to hold on to," he says. "We were rescued—six survivors in all. They tracked us—" He runs his thumb behind his right ear. "They came a few hours after . . . after I told you to leave."

So it's true. Trackers *do* work outside of Freedom. Mine just stopped working that night in the ocean and continued to corrode during my time on the island. I'm relieved I didn't unwittingly lead Seekers there.

He drops his head and wipes at his face. "I did the wrong thing, Nine, telling you to go. I was so scared, I wasn't thinking, sending you away from the crash site when I knew that's where they'd find us."

"It's okay," I say, lifting his chin. "I'm here. I'm okay."

He looks at me with a crooked smile that makes my heart speed up.

I bite my lip. "I felt terrible about leaving you to that monster. I've thought all this time that if you didn't drown, it would have torn you apart—killed you."

Theron lifts his right pant leg. Just below his knee is the barely noticeable line of a scar. "It bit my foot off," he says.

I gasp and run my finger along the scar.

"I guess I didn't taste very good, since it didn't bother me again," he says with a nervous laugh. "They had to amputate up to my knee during my Remake. My calf, my ankle, my foot—it's all new."

"Can you feel my fingers?" I ask, running them down his leg to his foot.

"Yes, but it's different. I still walk with a limp. I'm not quite used to it, not sure if I'll ever be."

"Theron, I'm so sorry."

"Sorry? You have no reason to be sorry. I'm the one who let you down."

I shake my head. "No, you saved me. Every minute of my life, you saved me."

He cups my face in his right hand. "What happened to you, Nine?"

I take a deep breath. I'm not sure how much I want to tell him about the island. About Kai. Not yet, anyway. "I washed ashore on an island, and the people who lived there found me. They took me in, fed me, made me a part of their fam . . . a part of them." How can I explain to Theron something that means so much to me? I can't even form it into words for myself. "They taught me their way of life, and then they helped me return to Freedom." Technically, it was all the truth.

"I'm never going to let you go again, Nine," he says, pulling me into him. I inhale his familiar scent. It is the smell of comfort. The smell of safety.

"I'm getting Remade in two days," I say. "I'm supposed to report to the Core building then." Of course, I'm not planning on going through with it, am I? I need to find Kai.

"I don't think so," he says. "There's no way I'm going to let you go that quickly now that I've found you again. Maybe we can postpone it, or I can barter my way onto your shuttle and be there while you're being Remade. I'll literally glue myself to you if I have to," he says with a smirk. "I'd run away with you first before letting you leave without me."

His words make me glance at the folded paper on the floor. I slip off the bed to pick it up. Unfolding it, I realize it's the map and set of instructions from Miriama. In different colored ink and with a familiar slanted penmanship scrawled across the bottom of the page are the words:

I can't be with you anymore. Kai.

My knees buckle, and I drop the paper to the floor again. I feel as though I've been stabbed through the heart with a spear. Is he mad because I revealed us in the forest at the prison camp? Because I brought him here, to Freedom? Does he think I did it on purpose?

I don't know how many more extreme emotions I can withstand. After a lifetime of being teased, a plane crash, losing Theron, months on a foreign island, falling in love, escaping the threat of Freedom, witnessing the horrors with the rebel prisoners, the complete joy of finding Theron again—now this? I pick up the paper and crumple it in my hands, stuffing it into my pocket. How dare he.

After all we've been through together, after all our confessions of love and promises of family, he's gone. How could he abandon me like this?

I feel Theron's hands on my shoulders and turn to him, collapsing into his chest.

"Hey, what's wrong?" he asks.

I shake my head against him. "Nothing. I'm fine." I roll back my shoulders and lift my head. "I'm going to be fine."

Theron presses his thumb against my chin. "Do you have anywhere to go right now?"

My chest hitches. I don't even know where I'd go to find Kai, even if he wanted to be found. He could be long gone by now. Out of Freedom, on his way back to Mahawai. All that matters is he's gone, and he doesn't want me. I don't understand.

"No," I say, a painful tightness in my throat. "I don't."

"Good. Stay here, I'm going to check out of work, and we'll spend the rest of the day together, all right?"

Not knowing what other choice I have, I nod and finish putting on my shoes. I give him a smile, determined to enjoy every moment I have with Theron. I'm eager to make up for months of lost time with him.

"On second thought," he says, slipping his hand into mine. "You're coming with me to check out. I'm not gonna let you out of my sight for a long, long time."

Theron takes me to a café on Main Street for a cup of something hot and chocolaty. I'm not used to the sounds of so many people about, and I just sit and watch as they walk by. They laugh and smile and engage in lively conversation, but something's not right. Something I've never noticed before. Their eyes are empty, vacant. They aren't truly happy, no matter how much they pretend to be. Not really. It's like something's missing and they don't know what it is.

They have no thoughts for the bread that needs to be made, the diaper that needs changing, the dishes that need to be washed by hand because they have no dish machine. I can't imagine their minds filled with anything other than how to get their next fix of temporary pleasure. The unnatural colors of the people and their clothing make my eyes tired.

I find myself searching for Kai among the crowd. Maybe he changed his mind. Maybe he's out looking for me right now. Maybe—

"Do you want to go to the cinema?" Theron asks.

I shake my head. "I just want to be with you."

We walk down the street, Theron with a distinct limp in his step. He looks so different now that his shoulders are wider and his chest and back have mounds of muscle. He's a taller, wider, stronger version of Theron, but he is still my Theron. We stop at a clothing store, and I let him dress me in whatever he wants, finally settling on a green dress with a low neckline and a silver buckle on the upper part of my arm.

"I like this color," I say, glad to be rid of the sweats and tank top.

Theron gazes at me. "You look amazing." He pulls me into him for an embrace. "I'm not sure I want to share you with anyone else today."

I freeze at the familiar words. Kai's words. Before I have a chance to react any further, Theron goes to the sales desk and swipes his point card, purchasing two bags full of clothes for me. "Have these delivered to my apartment," he tells the salesman, then turns and takes my hand in his.

We stop at a simulation center and, after paying for half an hour's worth, climb into the same simulation unit. Theron lets me flip through the list of choices on the touch screen in front of us. Violence. Sex. Food. Thrills. I select the term

ENVIRONMENT which brings up another list of choices: tundra, grassland, desert. I smile and choose TROPICAL.

The screen goes black, and the entire unit seems to disappear, leaving us in the dark. Slowly, images appear in front, above, and to the sides of us. A sandy beach. Coconut trees swaying in the breeze. We veer over the landscape like a bird flying through the sky. Green forests, lazy rivers, vibrant flowers. The mountains are dotted with waterfalls, and we zoom in on one, the white churning water at the base of a cliff encompassing the entire screen.

This isn't right. The images are beautiful, but it's a shadow of the real thing. There should be a humidity that hangs on you, forcing you to be lazy and long for a spot in the breezy shade. The waterfall should be sending a misty spray into our faces, the churning water making a noise so loud you feel like the most insignificant creature beside it. The fragrance of plants and flowers should fill your entire being, tingling in your toes and fingers, tickling all of your senses.

And most importantly, where are the people? Miri bouncing a baby on her hip, singing him a lullaby. Ara mending the nets for the next day's catch. Pua and Hemi laughing and swinging in a hammock. And Kai. Where would Kai be? Diving in the reef? Husking coconuts? Kissing the girl he loves under the eaves of the house?

This was a bad idea.

In the scene, we fly to the ocean and into the water, beneath the surface. Fish of every size and color swim around us. I spot a turtle, an octopus, and even an eel peeking out from coral.

We move beyond the reef to deeper blue water and see the large shape of a shark flash its teeth at us.

This was a really bad idea.

Theron stiffens at my side, and I fumble for the exit handle on the wall beside me. "I can't find it," I say in desperation. I press the emergency stop button repeatedly, but nothing happens. Of all the units we end up in a busted one that won't shut off.

Theron grips me with a trembling hand.

"Close your eyes, Theron." He must've obeyed because I feel him relax slightly.

The lights finally come on, and I find the handle, leading us out of the simulation unit.

"I'm sorry," I say, pulling his limping form behind me. "I wasn't thinking."

"It's okay," he says. "You didn't know that would happen." He slides his hand in mine. "I think I'm ready for a buzz now, though."

We enter a nightspot, and I immediately grab a buzz drink for Theron and myself. Theron downs his in a few swallows. After a few sips I feel nauseated, so I give it up. Theron pulls me to the dance floor, but instead of jumping to the heavy beat, I wrap my arms around his waist and choose to listen instead to the beat of his heart. *I'm alive,* the rhythm of his heart says. *I'm alive and strong. I'm here.*

Theron lets me stand there, still, trying to absorb all of him. I close my eyes, chasing away the flashing lights in the building. I begin to lead us in a steady sway to the song of his heartbeat, as though we are the only ones there. His heart begins to speed up, and I smile, imagining my hands in his, him tossing me away and back again in a thrilling twist of movements that make me laugh and shout at the same time. In this dream, I'm afraid I will fall away but I always return, my hands solid in his.

"Kai," I whisper.

"I can't hear you," Theron yells in my ear.

I jerk my eyes open and pull back, looking up at him in surprise.

"What did you say?" he yells, his hand behind his ear.

I reach up and ask, "Can we leave?"

Theron hesitates, looking into my eyes for so long I have to look away.

"Come home with me?" he asks against my ear.

I nod and pull him out of the building. Away from Freedom Central. Away from thoughts of Kai.

Chapter
Twenty-Four

Theron's apartment is small but comfortable. Two stools are pulled up to a counter in his kitchen. A small table and a few chairs sit against the far wall next to a window. His bed takes up most of the room in the center, and a door to my left leads to what I assume is a shower and toilet.

He rushes in front of me, tossing clothes and trash off his bed and kicking them underneath. He scoops up a pile of dirty dishes and carries it to the kitchen sink. "Sorry," he says. "I wasn't planning on company today."

"It's okay," I say, biting back a laugh. "I wasn't planning on running into the ghost of my best friend today." I glance around the room and allow myself to imagine what it would be like to live here. Wasn't that our plan? To have an apartment together in Freedom?

Theron smiles. "Do you want something to eat?"

260

I shake my head. "Actually, I'd really like a shower. Is that okay?"

"Yes, of course." Theron opens the door to the bathroom and grunts as he shifts items around on the floor and counter. "Here you go," he says, leaning against the open door, making room for me to enter. "Do you want me to come in with you?"

My eyes go wide. "No," I say too quickly, cringing at the hurt that flashes across his face. "I mean, thanks, but I'll be okay." I touch the side of his face and smile. I'd forgotten that this was so natural for us, showering together. I'm a little surprised by my instinct to refuse, like it's something I would never consider. It's no doubt a reflection of things I've learned, how I've changed from my time away from him. Away from Freedom. Of course, I didn't consider why it wouldn't be the same for him now.

"Okay," he says, stepping out. "I'll be right here if you need anything."

"Thanks."

The shower is hot and steaming, and the soap from the showerheads smells delicious. I admit to myself this is something I definitely missed from my life in Freedom. It's something I wish I could've shown Kai. I laugh at myself for thinking it. Yes, this would be a selling point for living in Freedom for sure—the hot showers. I shake my head at how silly that sounds. It doesn't matter, though. He's gone.

He. Is. Gone.

I feel light-headed and dizzy, the sensation forcing me to the floor of the tub basin.

Curse you, Kai.

I was ready to give him everything. My love, my life. I kick at the side of the basin. Even the tub makes me think of him, reminding me of the day we started a splash fight with his family. I wonder how long it will take to stop seeing him in everything. To stop missing him every waking moment. Didn't I feel the same way about Theron once? I'm not ready to go through that all over again. I run the shower cycle once more until I'm sure my world has stopped spinning.

When I come out, Theron jumps up from his bed and looks me up and down with a gulp.

"I'm sorry," I say, tugging at the top I wear that falls to my mid-thigh. I found it in the bathroom. It's obviously Theron's and way too big for me. "We didn't think about buying anything for me to sleep in. This looked more comfortable than the dress, and I really didn't want to climb back into those Batcher clothes. I hope you don't mind."

Theron presses his lips together and shakes his head. "You look good in my clothes," he says with a one-sided grin. "Really good."

I place my things in a pile on the floor next to the bed, carefully putting the crumpled map from Miri on the bedside table.

He clears his throat. "I'm going to jump in the shower too. You'll be okay?"

I nod and smile, watching as he closes the door behind him. I wander through his apartment, unable to keep still. Though I told Theron I wasn't hungry, my growling stomach disagrees, so I rifle through his kitchen cabinets, looking for something to eat.

I open the food chiller and laugh. How foreign it feels, to

have access to perishable food kept cold in a simple box. I pull out a couple of eggs and set them on the counter. After putting salt and water on the stove to boil, I fill a bowl with some flour and crack the eggs into the bowl, mixing it together with my hands.

"What are you doing?" Theron's voice makes me jump, and I look up to see him toweling off his hair.

I swallow hard. He isn't wearing a shirt, just a pair of black shorts that sit low on his waist. His body is both familiar and foreign to me. I feel heat rise to my face at the sight of him and wonder if it'd be rude to ask him to put on a shirt.

"Are you *cooking*?" He's genuinely surprised and raises an eyebrow, probably wondering if he should be impressed or make a run for it.

I force myself to look down at the dough in my hands. "Can you believe it?" I ask with a shaky voice. "I actually know how to cook something." Plain pasta noodles aren't exactly gourmet dining, but it's fast and filling.

"Something edible?" He comes to stand next to me in the kitchen and watches as I manipulate the dough.

"Shut it," I say. "Or I won't let you have any."

He snorts. "Is that supposed to be a bad thing?"

"I'm serious." I plop the mess into his hands. "Be nice." I turn on the water at the sink and peel at the sticky flour on my fingers. I nod at the dough in his hands. "Start kneading."

"Start whating?"

I sigh and dry off my hands then take the dough back, showing him what to do. "Push, fold, turn." I knead the dough against the counter, adding flour to the surface so it doesn't stick. "Repeat a hundred times." I grin and hand it back to him, patting the counter to encourage him to try.

"Push, fold, turn," he says, poking at the dough. It barely moves.

"You're going to have to push harder than that." I place my hands over his and press down, so he feels how hard he needs to do it.

"Remind me to never get you angry," he says, bending down to nudge my cheek. I suddenly realize how close we are. It's so familiar, so natural. But it's different, too. I step back and let him finish with the kneading.

I search through drawers for a rolling pin, settling on a large heavy glass instead. When I turn around, I stop breathing. I slide my hand to the base of Theron's neck. There is a decidedly permanent tattoo there. My name, *Nine*, written in curving black letters. He turns around to face me, and I look at him in surprise.

"I had it done as soon as I got back," he says. "Just like you wanted."

I bite my lip to keep it from shaking.

Theron smiles and pulls me close. "I can't believe it's really you." He breathes in deeply. "Mmm. I missed you."

I can almost pretend we've never been apart. Like the shuttle crash and the months on the island were all a dream. Like I've been here this entire time with him instead. I close my eyes and whisper, "You have to roll it out."

He pulls back. "Hmm?"

"The dough," I say, opening my eyes and handing him the large glass. "Roll it out. As thin as you can get it."

"Yes, ma'am," he says, winking at me. He rolls the dough into a giant rectangle, covering the entire surface of the counter. I help him gently fold it onto itself and slice it into thin strips, then drop each one into the boiling water.

"How long does it take?" he asks.

"Two minutes."

"What are we going to do for two whole minutes?"

I meet his gaze. His blue eyes are deeper than they've ever been. They are an ocean I could get lost in forever if I wanted. It's impossible to turn away, and I almost close my eyes.

I'm not who he thinks I am—who he remembers me to be. He sees me as a citizen of Freedom, but I don't think like them anymore. And I can't act like them either. Not after what I've learned on the island with my family. With Kai.

His hand brushes my cheek. He kisses me there, on the side of my face. Then his eyes venture toward my lips, and he kisses me at the corner of my mouth. He pulls away just barely, looking at me. His fingers touch the inside of my wrist, the sensation making me feel . . . uncomfortable.

I step back, shaking my head. I can't do this. I can't—

"Nine . . ." Theron's voice is quiet but rough and makes my breath catch. "I love you, Nine," he says, his voice barely there. His fingers slide along the scar on my upper arm. "I've always loved you."

I watch his fingers and think about how I love him too. Only, I'm not sure if it's the same way he means. I love him like I always have. Is that what he meant?

Hasn't it always been Theron, since I can remember? We were made for each other. Always one, joined. And here like this, together, like we were always meant to be. We can become one in every way, and it will be the most natural thing in the world.

The *thump, thump, thump* of my heart feels like it will explode out of my chest. And I realize this is freedom. Our freedom. If I want it to be.

"Theron." I squeeze my eyes shut and turn away. "I . . . I can't." I can't be with him like this. I can't pretend I never left Freedom. I can't forget what I've learned on the island. I can't forget Kai—no matter how much I want to right now. I just can't.

Theron steps away and reaches to turn off the burner, then leans back against the counter. After gliding his hand through his hair, he nods and looks at me, angling my face back toward his. Softly. Like I'm a fragile piece of glass that could break at any moment. He is way too kind—always ready to take care of me. To say the words that will fill me with comfort when I'm feeling uncertain.

After a minute he asks, "Is it Kai?"

I tense at the name. "How do you—?"

"Kai came to the Healer building this morning. He'd asked around for me by name, and he seemed genuinely shocked when he finally found me." Theron looks at me from beneath his long lashes. "He told me I needed to go to a certain room in the building during my break. He just gave me a room number and left."

Kai had found Theron.

For me.

I glance at the note on the table beside his bed and draw my brows together. So Kai is a jerk with a conscience? Did he

266

find Theron to make himself feel better about abandoning me? It doesn't help as I replay through my mind every moment, every instance I've disappointed Kai. Was this last time just one too many?

Looking at Theron, I see a vulnerability I've never noticed before. It makes me wonder what these months have been like for him, thinking I was gone the same way I thought I'd lost him.

"Because if it's about Kai, I . . ." Theron's voice is tight. He squeezes his eyes shut and takes a deep breath. "I'd be willing to share you. I mean . . . I'd never stop you from . . . if you loved him too, that is." He opens his eyes and gulps. "I would never keep you from what you want." He moves closer. "I won't be selfish. As long as I can have you too."

I don't know how to respond, so I lean my head against his shoulder and instead say, "I missed you so much."

"Don't go." Theron trembles. "You'll stay with me tonight, yes?"

"Yes."

He walks toward his bed and pulls back the covers. Crawling in, he makes room for me on one side.

"In a bit," I say, keeping my distance. "I'm going to stay up a little longer."

"Okay," he says, hesitant.

I give him a reassuring smile and sit in a chair near the window. As I watch him fall asleep, I imagine lying beside him— his body tucked in my side, arms around my waist, embracing me. Something we've done a million times before. But this time would be different. I can't deny the part inside me that says lying in bed with him like that would be wrong—a part that sounds suspiciously like Miriama. I smile, amazed that a parent's words can reach across a wide ocean.

As Theron's breathing falls into his familiar pattern of snore-breathe-whistle, I think of what he said about sharing me with Kai. I sigh, knowing that could never happen, not with Kai, at least. But Kai doesn't want me at all. He has left. Gone. And he practically delivered Theron to me himself. Doesn't that mean something?

It's not like being with Theron would be as it is for others in Freedom. It would be more than just sex—it would mean something. He said he loves me, and I believe him. I would die for Theron; I would sacrifice everything for him. Doesn't that mean I love him too? What was it Pua had said? When a man and a woman decide they love each other very much and want to spend the rest of their lives together . . . and with no one else. I cringe at that last part, thinking of Kai. It feels like the world is pressing in on my heart so tight, I'm in danger of disappearing all together. Is it too much to want to be loved? To let those words Pua once spoke—*promise, love, always*—become a permanent part of me? To want something . . . sacred?

My fingers tug on my hair. It is kind what Theron said about sharing me. Unselfish. Why did it make me feel lesser, then? Is it ridiculous for me to wish he'd want me for himself? To want him to be selfish and possessive and claim me as his own, not willing to share? I feel terrible for desiring that and frown. It's all so confusing.

I wonder if I could stay here with him. Unlike Kai, Theron

wants me. Maybe this place where I've always meant to stay is the place I should choose.

Theron and me.

Me and Theron.

Two perfect pieces in the puzzle that is my life.

Chapter
Twenty-Five

When I wake, it is raining. It's a bad omen—rain in Freedom.

I stand up from the chair I fell asleep in last night, my muscles screaming in response. I walk to the bed and sit on the edge. Theron's back is toward me, and I trace the letters of his tattoo with my finger, remembering the day in Freedom Central when I gave him the temporary ink version. It feels like a lifetime ago.

Theron stirs and I pull back, folding my hands in my lap.

"Good morning," he says, turning over and smiling his infectious smile. "How long have you been up?"

"Not long."

"Are you hungry?" he asks, resting his hand against my bare leg.

I stiffen under his touch, the events of last night rushing back to me. I still haven't figured out how the two of us are meant to fit together.

Theron raises an eyebrow, waiting for my answer about being hungry.

I manage a nod. We never did eat the pasta from last night, and I'm famished.

"Good." He rolls away from me and out of bed. "I'm going to cook you breakfast."

"Tell me who else survived the crash," I say over a plate of eggs and sliced fruit. I push the food around my plate, smiling, thinking about how much Theron would have loved Miri's onions and potatoes.

"Me," Theron says, holding up one finger. He raises additional fingers as he continues. "Caley, Aver, Falan, Edge, and Sora."

Such a small list. I bite my lip, thinking of the other Batch members whose lives were taken from them before they had a chance to really live. Sora survived. I wonder if she knew what happened to the two Batchers she was inseparable from. Cree's body floating in front of me in the water. Bristol . . . killed in the aftermath.

"They all changed," Theron says.

"What do you mean?" We've all changed, haven't we, after experiencing such a tragedy? I can't think how any of us will ever be the same again.

"After we were rescued, we were brought back here, back to Freedom. We spent three days in recovery and being questioned, and they gave us another chance to choose the details of our Remake before putting us on another shuttle. Most changed

271

the usual—hair, eyes, etc." Theron takes a long drink of milk. "But they *all* decided to change genders. Every one of them."

I remember Caley had chosen to become male, but the rest were going to keep their given gender. "Why'd they do that?"

Theron shrugs his shoulders. "I think they wanted to forget. Like maybe by changing they'd become an entirely different person, not who they were before. They could pretend the crash happened to someone *not* them."

"But you didn't change."

"I didn't want to forget who I was," he says, taking my hand in his. "I didn't want to forget you."

I gaze at his broad shoulders, his hair, the stubble growing along his jaw. I'm not sure what changes in Theron are because of the male hormones that naturally surfaced without the blockers or are the traits he chose for his Remake. "What *did* you choose?" I ask. "For your Remake, I mean."

"Besides my name and Trade . . . nothing." His lips twitch. "I think half of me was afraid to get on another shuttle to go to the Remake facility. But really, I didn't want to change because of you." He slides his chair next to mine and leans toward me. "It's silly really, but I thought, how will Nine recognize me, if she sees me in the street or in a crowd? I wanted to be the Theron you remembered."

My eyes follow the curves of his face, examining every familiar line. "You are more than just a handsome face, Theron. You're kind and sure and brave. You can make me laugh until my sides hurt, or tell me I'm so beautiful I can't help but believe it." I smile at his bright blue eyes. "You are love and sacrifice and"—I pause, searching for the right word—"family." He doesn't understand the term, but it means everything to me. *He* means everything. "I'd recognize you anywhere." I bring his nose to mine and inhale, breathing in his essence. Exhale, giving him my own.

I pull back to see his chest, rising and falling. I feel the blood rush to my face and turn away, trying to chase away the sudden onslaught of emotion. "So," I say, changing the subject. "Did you stay here, in Freedom then?"

"No. Even though I decided not to change anything, they still made me go. Made me get Remade, though I don't know why. I figured it was because of my leg, but they also said something about helping my natural hormones mature properly."

I frown, knowing why they made him go. They took away his ability to reproduce, to make babies. My heart sinks. He doesn't even know he once had the potential to procreate. That a freedom was taken from him without him even realizing it.

"Honestly," he says, one side of his mouth rising, "I think they just wanted to tone down my good looks without telling me. Not make the others feel so bad, you know?"

I reward him with a wide smile. "What was it like?"

"Being Remade?"

I nod.

"I don't remember much." He swirls what's left of his milk and takes a drink. "The shuttle landed inside the Remake facility, so I don't even know what it looked like outside, and I've no idea how large the place is. But the parts I did see—it was nothing more than a glorified Healer building. We were ushered to our rooms and after an hour of body scans and needles, I fell asleep and woke a few days later."

"Did it hurt?"

"Not right after the procedure." Theron makes a face. "But having to spend a month inside while the hormones kicked in about drove me crazy. My growing muscles ached more each day, begging to be used. Punching a mattress against the wall isn't the same as hitting the practice bags in our Batch tower. I'm sure the Remakers were glad to be rid of me after our recovery time."

I think of my tender breasts and smile, wondering if I got the better end of the deal.

Theron takes a deep breath. "I'm going to take the day off. But I have to check in with a couple of patients at the Healer building first. Come with me?"

I nod, picking up our dirty dishes and carrying them to the sink.

"Then I thought we'd brave the Core building, see what we can do to postpone this Remake of yours."

I watch him walk through the apartment, head high, shoulders back. Even his limp seems purposeful. He is so sure of everything in his life. No doubts, no fears. I've always wanted to be just like Theron. So certain. So strong. And watching him, here in front of me, after all these months, I realize I am like him.

I know what I need to do, and I know I won't be Remade, because I already have been. My Remake didn't involve a complicated surgery to change my appearance or gender. It was a smoothing, sharpening, cutting away and building—not of my body, but of my spirit. My character, my strengths, my fears and devotion—those are what changed in my Remake.

REMAKE

They would've been impossible to change at the Remake facility, though. It took an island in the middle of a vast ocean to Remake me.

There's only one more thing I need to figure out.

I pull the hood of my jacket over my head before walking into the rain, my hand in Theron's. It's cold out, but not enough to be uncomfortable. He holds an umbrella over us, leading me toward the Healer building.

I won't be going to the Core building today with Theron, nor tomorrow to choose my Remake. Still, I envision the touch screen as we walk through the street and the choices that would've appeared one by one as I make my selections.

Male or female?

I smile. It seems ridiculous to me, now, thinking about what stress that simple question put me through. I am more sure of my gender today than I've ever been. It's what I've been from the start of everything. What I'll be to the very end of it all. What I'll always be.

Female.

One that is brave and strong and determined. If there's one thing I've learned these past months, it's that I don't need to be male to be those things. But a female is more than that. And she's more than just a curvy figure. She's a mother, a daughter, a sister, a wife. She inspires; she loves. And she'll do what's right no matter what. She knows when to quit, and she is not afraid to keep trying.

Hair?

275

I finger the fire red locks under my hood. I don't want to belong. I don't want to blend.

No change.

Skin?

These freckles are a part of me, define me as someone different and not afraid to be different.

No change.

Eyes, lips, nose, legs, breasts?

I hear Pua's voice in my head, telling me everything about us is something to be grateful for. That we should trust the first Maker knew what he was doing in the first place.

No change.

Trade?

I think of Miriama and smile. Even though Kai may never be a part of my life again, I know what I want to be anyway.

Wife. Mother.

Name?

I think of the tattoo on Theron's neck. *Nine* has defined me, it is who I am, who Theron knows me to be. But it's also just a label, one given to me by Freedom, by my Makers, by . . . Eridian.

I may have inherited my physical traits from Eri, but it doesn't mean I *am* her. My spirit is different, unique, individual. Something that cannot be cloned. No matter how much she wants me to be like her, her choices are not my own.

I think of the way Kai described me once, as a wind that creeps and winds and fills your entire being. A peaceful wind that catches you by surprise. This new me, this stronger me, is a surprise to myself as well. One that has encompassed me so fully, I don't think I can ever escape it.

Name?

Ani.

Theron squeezes my hand and says something funny. I look up at him and smile, relishing the brightness in his eyes, the way his lips turn up.

There is one question left. It wouldn't show up on the touch screen in the Core building, but it's just as valid as the others. Maybe even more so. A choice that will define me. One I need to make right now.

Theron?

My feet shuffle to a stop, and I let his fingers slip from mine as he continues forward. I clench my empty hands. They are cold in an instant. I put my hand into my pocket and touch a crumpled paper there.

Theron turns and opens his mouth to say something, then closes it again. He lowers the umbrella, and we are both getting soaked, here in the rain.

"Do you remember that night on the roof of the Batch tower?" I ask. "The night before we left Freedom?"

He steps to me and grasps my shoulders. "I remember."

"You said you'd never leave me," I say. My voice is shaking, and my lips shiver in the cold rain. "You promised."

"I know." His arms tremble. "I know I did. I'm sorry, Nine. I'm so sorry."

I shake my head. That's not what I mean. "You kept your promise. You were with me every day on that island. Every hour."

He pulls me into him, the warmth of my fresh tears sharp against the cold of the rain. "Together and never apart again," he says. "Remember?"

I remember. "I should have promised too, Theron. I'm sorry."

I can feel his sorrow on my skin as he kisses me all over my face. "Oh, Nine." His hands hold my face and I look at him.

For a minute I curse the shuttle that crashed. If we had just made it to the Remake facility, things would be so different. I would be happy to be here, by his side, living with him in Freedom. Even as a male. It would be enough. I wouldn't have this stirring in the pit of my stomach, telling me I need to fight. Telling me *it matters*.

"I have to go," I say.

And he breaks. Because he knows me, because we know each other better than anyone else in the world, he understands what my words mean. His shoulders shake and his eyes fall. "No, no. Please don't."

"I have to." I must do this alone, out of the protective shadow that has sheltered me for so long. I need to leave Theron.

He pulls me to him and sobs into my neck. "I can't lose you again. I can't do it." He shakes his head from side to side, holding me close.

"I'm not the same person anymore," I say, running my fingers through his hair.

"It doesn't change the way I feel about you." His voice is desperate. "I love you, Nine."

"I know. I love you too." But it's not the same. I wipe at my face. I don't know what the point is, here in the pouring rain.

"Take me with you," he begs, his arms pinning me tighter against him. "I don't know where you're going or what you plan to do, but let me come too."

My entire body shakes. It's exactly what I hoped he wouldn't ask—what I refused to ask of him because I knew he'd agree to follow me without hesitation. He even admitted it yesterday at the Healer building; he said he'd run away with me before letting me leave without him. But I'm not even sure I'll still be alive in a few hours, and I can't risk his life. Not for me. Not again.

I shake my head. "You have to let me do this, Theron. You have to let me go."

You have to let me choose.

"No! I won't do it."

I press my lips against his ear. "Theron, *please.*"

His breath catches. "Losing you . . . it's too much. How can I live through that again? I can't."

"Yes. You can," I say. "You're the brave one, remember?"

Theron shakes his head. "No. Not as brave as you, Nine." He strokes my hair, rubbing a few strands between his fingers. "I'm not brave like you."

I pull his mouth to mine, memorizing the feel of his kiss. When our lips part, I feel a piece of me is torn out and left behind with him. A part I know will never be filled again.

I step back, turning away from his crumbling form. I don't want to see the hurt I've caused. Isn't my own hurt enough for me to bear? We are tethered, and I feel a pull toward him, as though no matter where I am in the world, we'll still, somehow, be connected.

I run away through the sloshing streets.

And he lets me go.

Chapter
Twenty-Six

The concert building looms over me like sails of an ancient ship, a symbol of the voyage I'm about to embark on. I walk around the building twice, making sure no one is there. Miri said to wait until night if possible, but here in the heavy rain, no one is out in the open.

On the north side of the building, I find the red metal walking bridge. Water drips from the rails. I count the bridge sections as I walk. One. Two. Three. In the center of the third section is an orange rail with peeling paint, just as Miri described. I lean over the side and look into the water below. It's a far drop, nearly twice as high as Turtle Rock. The rain falls on the water so violently, peaks of white water rise with every hammering drop on its surface. It's going to be cold.

I pull the crumpled paper out of my pocket and read through it one last time, then tear it into tiny pieces, letting them fall into the water below. Taking off my shoes and jacket, I toss them into the water as well. I look around once more before climbing over the rail and standing on the other side. I lean over with my hands gripping the rail behind me. I'm going to have to use the momentum of my fall to help propel me downward in the water, diving down as soon as I break the surface.

After two deep inhalations, I fall. Down down down. When I hit the water it stings so badly from the impact I scream as I sink, losing precious oxygen. I kick downward, my arms pulling me lower and lower. I am desperate to breathe. The space below me is as dark as it has become above me. I won't make it if I turn back now. I push forward with renewed vigor. I *will* do this.

I begin to see a light, but it's not below me, it's far to my right. The current must be stronger in the downpour. I turn to the light, releasing every last bit of air I have. It keeps me from floating up, but it makes me dizzy. I want to breathe in so, so badly.

I finally reach the light and fumble with the trunk, opening it to reveal a pile of small, black rubber devices. It's like the mouth end of a snorkel, but instead of the mouthpiece leading to a tube that sticks above the surface of the water, it ends in a stump with some kind of filter attached. I bite hard on the mouthpiece and inhale sharply, desperate for breath. Water flows into my nose. I plug my burning nostrils with my fingers and breath in again. The air comes, but it's slow and awkward, and I have to force myself to relax a minute before I finally feel like I won't suffocate to death.

REMAKE

I close the trunk and find the round metal door leading into the floor of the ocean. I tug and pull, but it doesn't budge. My hands and feet are numb from the cold water—I can't feel them at all. I'm stronger than I've ever been, so why won't the door move? I pull again and this time it moves slightly, rotating to the left, but then it freezes. I have a thought and grip the handle, rotating the round door instead of trying to pull it straight up. The metal slides against its frame and suddenly pops up, released from the threaded metal on the frame holding it in place.

I can't see anything inside. Nothing but dark and emptiness. I glance at the light around the trunk, wondering if I can carry it down with me. But it's attached to the box, and the trunk won't fit through the hole. I shake my head. I've done hard things before. This is nothing. Nothing like losing Theron. Nothing like losing Kai.

Swimming down into the hole, I pull the metal door into place behind me, remembering Miri's instructions. The door settles into its frame, and all goes black. I stay there, floating in the dark, shivering in the cold water. Miri said the door closing would trigger something, letting them know I am here. I wait and wait. Five minutes. Ten. But I'm still surrounded by water, and I can't feel my limbs anymore.

I begin to breathe faster through my rebreather. I can't get enough air. This is not good. I'm going to die here, in the dark of nowhere, with no one to find my body. Panicking, I reach up, feeling for the round door. It opens easily with my gentle push, and I hesitate. Pulling it back down into its frame, I rotate the door, to the right this time, until I feel it lock into place.

ILIMA TODD

A sound finds its way to my ears under the water. It reminds me of the shuttle dying in the water, the grinding and bending of metal that makes me shiver uncontrollably. After the sound, I feel a tug on my body, like the water surrounding me is being pulled into a drain I cannot see.

After a few minutes, I am crumpled on wet, algae-slick ground, all the water gone. I drop the rebreather and stand as best I can on the feet I can't feel. The smell is musty and the *drip drip drip* of water echoes around me. There's a light far to my right illuminating the dark just enough to reveal I'm in a tunnel. I have to duck my head as I feel along the wall, heading for that light.

When I get there, I see the light is behind a grate, and several rungs are set into the wall. Shaking, I climb the ladder higher and higher, until I come to another round metal door like the one in the ocean floor. My body shakes violently, and I am so exhausted, it takes all of my strength and concentration to rotate the metal door. It doesn't slide as easily as it did underwater. It's too heavy to push up, and I drop my arms, letting them hang with fatigue for a minute before trying again.

But after a few seconds, the door is lifted. I look up to see the face of a man with a full white beard and shaved head. A halo of light surrounds his face, coming from the room he's in. I reach up a hand in relief, expecting him to help pull me up. But instead he points the barrel of a gun in my face.

"Your name?" he asks.

"Nine," I say, my lips still shivering from the cold.

His eyes narrow in suspicion. "Nine is a Batcher name." He pulls the slide back, chambering a round, ready to shoot.

"No," I say in a rush. "The Rise. I'm part of the Rise. I'm Ani."

The man relaxes and pulls me up into a white room with tile floors.

I collapse on the ground, exhausted to my core.

"Welcome to Rise Central," he says with a grin.

I have enough energy to smile back at him.

Evert, the man with the white beard, leads me down a hallway with metal walls. I pull the blanket he offered tightly around me. There are no windows, only flickering torches along the walls. We must be underground. He leads me to a room with shelves lined with medical instruments and bottles of liquids.

"Wait here," Evert says. "I'll go grab the doc."

I sit on a stool in the corner and squeeze out the water that still drips from my shirt.

The door opens again and a woman walks in with hair that almost brushes the ground in a long braid. She holds a tracker gun in her hand. "Hello, Ani. I'm Reyn. I'm here to remove your tracker."

I nod and hold my head up high, ready to do this.

Reyn holds the gun behind my right ear and presses the green button, removing the tracker. I gasp when the pain comes. I hold a piece of gauze at my ear like she instructs while she preps a gel-like solution. Reyn applies the gel behind my ear and bandages it up. My head still throbs, but I smile in relief when I see her toss the tracker device into a container of some kind of acid. It sizzles as it settles in the liquid.

"Here's a dry set of clothes for you," she says, handing me

a pile of folded fabrics. "When you're ready, come on out and Evert will take you to the commons room. I'm sure you're tired and hungry after that whole ordeal, yes?"

I smile gratefully and get dressed when she leaves.

Evert leads me back the way we came, down the torch-lit hallway. We turn toward a set of stairs in the wall that spiral upward. Pushing through a heavy door, we enter a large room filled with people. It reminds me of the eatery in our Batch building. A line of tables filled with food sits on one end. Several people gather at benches nearby, eating and talking.

I'm surprised to see children in the center of the room, playing a game that involves kicking a ball between them. Adults scold, telling them to keep their voices down. I smile. There are families here, then. I look at the other end of the large room where people sit on chairs along a wall, laughing so loud I think someone must have told a joke, and I want desperately to know what it was. I think I'd like something to laugh about today.

My eyes scan the wall, and that's when I see him.

Kai.

I gasp. My heart. Stops. Beating.

He stands against the wall in the corner of the room. One foot is lifted, resting on the wall behind him. He holds a fruit in his hand, peeling away at the skin that surrounds it. He looks . . . tired.

He hasn't seen me yet.

My brows narrow and my eyes pierce him. He left me. I am so angry because *he left me*. I ball my fists and march toward him. I will punch him. Punch him and kick him and slap his face for leaving me alone like that. I don't care who sees me do it.

REMAKE

Kai lifts his head and sees me coming. He drops his fruit and takes a step toward me. And when I see it, I break into a run. All thoughts of hurting him vanish, and I fly into him, knocking him to the ground. I am lying on top of him, holding him so tight, I doubt he can breathe.

It reminds me of the day at the waterfall, when I thought I had killed him. When I thought he had drowned. I didn't care that he had played a joke on me. I was so glad he was alive, I didn't care what he did. I hold him and grip his shoulders hard. I will not let him get away from me again. Never, ever again.

He presses his arms into my back and pulls me to him so fiercely there's no space left between us.

I finally pull away enough to look at his face. I touch the bandage behind his right ear. His eyes are moist with tears. Why is he crying?

"Kai, you are such a jerk. Why are you crying?"

"I was so afraid . . . afraid I'd never see you again." He shakes, squeezing my arms so hard.

I sit up on him, straddling his waist. Anger slips past my resolve, and I slap at his chest. "You left me, you idiot. You left me." I punch him and yell. "I hate you."

He sits up and kisses me so hard I feel like I will burst into flame, right there. I pull back. "No! You don't get to kiss me, you scab. I hate you."

His smile is so wide, so warm despite my outburst. Is he laughing? His eyes burn deep into mine. Full of wanting. Full of love.

I press my mouth hard onto his and pull him close. Crying and laughing, hitting and hugging.

"I love you," he says when his mouth is free. "I love you I love you I love you."

"I don't love you," I say, shaking my head. "I don't love you so, so much."

Kai laughs and kisses the side of my head.

I grab his collar with both of my hands and shake him hard. "Why did you leave?"

His hands touch my face, my hair, my shoulders. His eyes see all of me. "You needed to choose." His voice shakes. "Between Freedom and the Rise—without me as a factor. I needed to know you were choosing for the right reasons and not just because of me. *You* needed to know that."

I throw my arms around him. "I chose the Rise," I say into his neck. "I left Freedom—I left Theron—to choose it."

"I know you did," Kai says. "You are so brave."

Yes. I am.

Acknowledgments

This book. THIS BOOK. Who knew a story I managed to write in a few short weeks would end up being So Much Work? And not just for me. It took a village to raise this baby, and this is the part where I thank everyone involved in bringing it to life.

So great big awkward-hug-thanks go to:

My husband, Daniel, who believed in me even when I didn't. You always said I could do it, and ta-da . . . you were right, of course. You are my hero, my happiness, my best friend. I love you a hundred.

Emma, Parker, Stirling, and Hailey. You are the most well-behaved, patient, smart, kind, and lovable children on the planet. And you are all mine. Which makes me the luckiest mama on the planet.

My dad, who raised me to be a reader, and my mom, who loves him enough to pretend she doesn't notice when he sneaks another bookshelf into the house. I write about the joy of families because of you. And my siblings and in-laws—thank you for reading and loving my stories and telling me I'm the coolest writer ever. You're the best.

M83 for being my writing muse. Your music is behind every word I write. Thanks for being so cool. When are you coming to Utah? No, seriously.

My Plums. Emily Prusso, the day you asked me to lunch changed my life forever, and despite your "ugly kids" and sailor mouth, you will toads be my BFF until those Livermore scientists build a star and beyond. Robin Hall, you're the only person in the world who has read every story I've written and will forever be my first reader—you are the supermom I want to be. Katie Purdie, we've fought, cried, laughed, cheered, and swooned together. You are like a sister to me, and I'm privileged to call you a kindred spirit. You girls are more than my CPs, you're my best friends, my sisters, my heart. There aren't enough heart emoticons in the world to tell you how much I love you. ♥ ♥ ♥

Christy Petrie, Taryn Albright, and Kelley Lynn—you've been with me from the start, and *Remake* wouldn't be where it is without you. No lie. Thank you. And to my readers: Janell, Nicole, Julee, Coral, Michelle, Daisy, and Ashley. Your love kept me going. Also Elana Johnson and everyone in our LDStorymakers Primer group, and Ann Dee Ellis and my WIFYR Boot Camp class. You all helped me rock this manuscript. To my Mom's Night posse and the entire online writing community—thanks for your endless support.

Jennifer Skutelsky, who loved my world and characters

enough to take a chance on this newbie writer and worked to help me whip this baby into shape. And to Katherine Boyle for being a rock-star agent in selling this bad boy and making me feel so blessed to be a part of the Veritas family.

Heidi Taylor and Chris Schoebinger, for believing in me and my writing. Your tireless devotion to Nine and her story means so much. To Lisa Mangum for making my writing look much better than it really is, and to everyone at Shadow Mountain for making my publishing dream come true. I'm so excited to be joining this awesome family.

And to God. Because while I've no idea where most of this story came from, I think you do. I'm forever grateful for the opportunity to do what I love.

And you, the reader. You win twenty trillion cool points for reading my book. Thank you.